Anarquía
An Alternate History of the
Spanish Civil War

ANARQUÍA
An Alternate History of
The Spanish Civil War

by

Brad Linaweaver and
J. Kent Hastings

Sense of Wonder Press
JAMES A. ROCK & COMPANY, PUBLISHERS
ROCKVILLE ■ MARYLAND

Anarquía, An Alternate History of the Spanish Civil War
by Brad Linaweaver and J. Kent Hastings

is an imprint of *JAMES A. ROCK & CO., PUBLISHERS*

Anarquía, An Alternate History of the Spanish Civil War copyright © 2004
by Brad Linaweaver and J. Kent Hastings

Afterword © 2004 by J. Neil Schulman
Afterword © 2004 by Bill Patterson
Afterword © 2004 by W. A. Ritch
Afterword © 2004 by Victor Koman
Afterword © 2004 by Dafydd ab Hugh
Afterword © 2004 by Randall N. Herrst

Address comments and inquiries to: SENSE OF WONDER PRESS
James A. Rock & Company, Publishers
9710 Traville Gateway Drive, #305, Rockville, MD 20850
E-mail:
jrock@rockpublishing.com   lrock@senseofwonderpress.com
Internet URL: www.SenseOfWonderPress.com

Paperbound ISBN: 0-918736-64-1
Hardbound ISBN: 0-918736-63-3
Limited Edition: ISBN: 0-918736-62-5

Printed in the United States of America

First Edition: October 2004

Front cover artwork by Kelly Freas.
Front cover artwork commissioned by James A. Rock & Co., Publishers.

Portions of *Anarquía* originally appeared in the short story, "Days of Wine and Rockets,"
in Nova Science Fiction © 2002 by Brad Linaweaver.

Thanks from the editors to Anita Kulman for her generous assistance with the
Spanish language material. Thanks also to Jack Morgan for his editorial expertise.

Photo credits page 67: G. K. Chesterton, 1935, photo by Howard Coster; and
Ernest Hemingway, 1937, photo by Robert Capa © Robert Capa/Magnum.

CREDITS AND REFERENCES

Much information about the real Spanish Civil War is available on the following Internet web pages. Many of these sites include full color or larger black and white photographs of the real Spanish Civil War along with posters and artwork whose simulacrums appear in the world of *Anarquía*.

http://memory.loc.gov/ammem/today/jul17.html
http://www.spartacus.schoolnet.co.uk/Spanish-Civil-War.htm
http://www.english.uiuc.edu/maps/scw/scw.htm
http://flag.blackened.net/revolt/spaindx.html
http://www.writing.upenn.edu/~afilreis/88/spain-overview.html
http://sunsite.berkeley.edu/Goldman/Exhibition/spanishcivilwar.html
http://www.richeast.org/htwm/SCW/scw.html
http://www.art-for-a-change.com/NoPasaran/spain.html
http://www.sispain.org/english/history/civil.html
http://orpheus.ucsd.edu/speccoll/visfront/
http://orpheus.ucsd.edu/speccoll/collects/southw.html
http://www.users.dircon.co.uk/~warden/scw/scwindex.htm
http://www.weisbord.org/Spain.htm
http://en.wikipedia.org/wiki/Spanish_Civil_War
http://dwardmac.pitzer.edu/Anarchist_Archives/spancivwar/spancivwarhis.html
http://www.guerracivil.org/ (in Spanish)
http://users.erols.com/mwhite28/spain_cw.htm
http://www.geocities.com/CapitolHill/9820/spain15.html
http://www.spunk.org/library/writers/bookchin/sp001642/fifty.html
http://www.nodo50.org/fimpv/carteles.htm (in Spanish)
http://www.ugt.es/ugtpordentro/guerracivil/carteles.htm (in Spanish)
http://globalia.net/huberto/libros/carteles/ (in Spanish)
http://guerraespana.turincon.com/ (in Spanish)
http://www.guerracivil.org/Carteles/Index.htm (in Spanish)
http://perso.wanadoo.es/blanroj/carteles2.html (in Spanish)
http://personales.ya.com/altavoz/enlaces.htm (in Spanish) (many links)
http://www.bne.es/esp/carteles-fra.htm (in Spanish)
http://www.blackcrayon.com

Given the ephemeral nature of the internet, some of the web pages cited above and on the following page, may not exist by the time you read this. Updated links to these and similar web sites will be available at:

http://www.SenseOfWonderPress.com/anarquia_info.htm

or

http://www.RockPublishing.com/anarquia_info.htm

CREDITS AND REFERENCES continued

If the alternate world of *Anarquía* had not come to fruition, some of those peopling its pages might have led lives not unlike those described on these web pages:

http://liftoff.msfc.nasa.gov/Academy/History/vonBraun/vonBraun.html
http://www.time.com/time/time100/builder/profile/mayer.html
http://www.ayn-rand.com/
http://www.csupomona.edu/~rljohnson/Professional/DosPassos.html
http://www.ernest.hemingway.com/
http://www.kirjasto.sci.fi/gorwell.htm
http://www.chesterton.org/

While we have gone to great lengths to assure that the photographs and art work presented in Anarquía have been approved by both those in this realm and that of *Anarquía,* we would appreciate being informed of any items which we have overlooked and which should be specifically acknowledged.

CMG Worldwide, Inc. is the representative for Hedy Lamarr's estate and they operate the official Hedy Lamarr website at

http://www.hedylamarr.com/siteinfo/terms.htm

Some of the images of Wernher von Braun in this book are courtesy of the U. S. Army's Redstone Arsenal Historical Service.

Dedicated to
Emma Goldman

TABLE OF CONTENTS

ACKNOWLEDGMENTS

This book was a long time coming. First we must honor J. Neil Schulman, who was the original godfather of inspiration. He and several other loyal comrades are doing *Afterwords* for this book, but we felt he should be singled out.

Next is the talented and brilliant Ben Pleasants, who enriched *Anarquía* in numerous ways. His knowledge of the Spanish Civil War was an invaluable resource.

Special thanks must also be extended to Vanessa Koman, who provided Brad with a new computer when his old, prehistoric model broke down in the middle of working on both *Battlestar Galactica: Paradis* with Richard Hatch and the *Anarquía* project.

We also wish to thank our parents, uncles and aunts.

We're not done yet! We wish to salute Chris Haslup, who served in the war to liberate Iraq for motives not much different than the volunteers for the Republic in the Spanish Civil War.

A tip of the hat goes to the *Worldly Remains* crowd (Ron Garmon, Jessie Lilley, and Cris Phillips) for inviting Brad to be the token right-winger in their largely left-wing enterprise, thereby keeping him up to date on contemporary radical rhetoric. Toward this end, thanks must also be offered to Lisa Fredsti.

Many a book would have exhausted the names by this point, but we are made of sturdier stuff. We must praise Thomas Cron for his endless support of alternate history. We can't forget Victor Koman, our favorite rocket man. Then there's Bill Ritch, who has the longest record of cheerleading for Linaweaver enterprises. He is matched by the late Samuel Edward Konkin III and his support of projects by radical anarchist, J. Kent Hastings. We can't forget Tracy Tormé, who played a pivotal role in Brad's writing of a previous anti-Stalinist novel, *Sliders: The Novel*. We offer a tip of the hat to the creators of the 1996 film, *Land of Freedom*, the closest the screen has ever come to realizing Orwell's *Homage to Catalonia*.

With one deep breath, we thank Jerry Jewett, Richard Kyle, Martina Pilcerova, David T. Lindsay, Morgan Griffin, Michelle Howard, Caran Wilbanks, Patricia Lucyshyn, James Sutherland, Sue Philips, Mike Everling, Big Lee, Amber Haslup, Ed Kramer, Bill Patterson, Tamara and Chesley V. Morton, Christopher Schaefer, Elayna Little, Jennifer Corbett, Kim Riley, Dafydd ab Hugh, John DeChancie, Buddy Barnett, Dana Fredsti, Steve Tymon, Warren Williams, Brad's ex-wife CCC (Cynthia-Cari Crowder)—and once again, the father of Agorism, Samuel Edward Konkin III. There are almost enough names here to provide extras for a film by the immortal Fred Olen Ray! In Fred's film, *Mom, Can I Keep Her?*, the authors of this novel are chased out of a Chinese restaurant by a gorilla. No kidding!

We just love this field. We are glad that Jim Rock found us for Sense of Wonder Press. And as we build the future from our best experiences of the past, we conclude with an expression of deepest gratitude to the late Virginia Heinlein.

Brad Linaweaver
J. Kent Hastings

EDITOR'S PREFACE

As has been pointed out by others, notably J. Neil Schulman, in the "Afterwords," *Anarquía*'s route to resolution and completion has been almost as torturous and circuitous as that of its subject, the Spanish Civil War. Also, like the war whose alternate history it chronicles, *Anarquía* has had its own set of individual and team "Abraham Lincoln Brigades," that have, at various times, come to its rescue or shored up its battlements.

We would like to take this opportunity to thank all of those who have helped *Anarquía* on its journey from the beginning, and especially those who have helped it along the way while it has been in our hands.

We would, specifically, like to thank cover artist Frank Kelly Freas who persevered in producing our glorious cover art, even after a nasty fall. This accident, which resulted in a painful and persistent hip injury, did not deter Kelly Freas from pursuing his commitment to us and to *Anarquía*.

As publishers and as editors, working on *Anarquía* has been a fascinating experience. We have found, as others have, that *Anarquía* packs so many exciting and unexpected ideas into its pages that working on it creates an infectious commitment to its world. Editing *Anarquía* simultaneously excited our imagination as readers and inspired our creativity as editors and publishers. Consequently, like the friends of *Anarquía* who added the perspectives found in the "Afterwords," the editors were moved to enhance aspects of the novel's presentation. We hope these presentation elements will add to your enjoyment of this unique work.

Both of us have long admired the historical atmospherics created by Jack Finney's use of period photographs in his classic novel, *Time and Again*, and its sense of the reality of that time and place, the sense of "being there." As we edited and fact-checked the *Anarquía* manuscript we were immediately struck by the extremely visual nature of not just Brad's and Kent's, but almost all descriptions of the Spanish Civil War. The time, the place, and the people combined to create a naturally cinematic and artistic visual impact that inspired such disparate word-painters as Ernest Hemingway and George Orwell, painters such as Pablo Picasso, and photographers such as Robert Capa, David Seymour, Gerda Taro and Henri Cartier-Bresson, who died as this book went to press.

As we came across more and more pictures portraying people, events, and machines that inhabit the alternate world of *Anarquía,* we quickly succumbed to the impulse to enlist some of these graphics in order to create a visual context for readers to whom the world of the Spanish Civil War is more ethereal and insubstantial than the most gossamer of will-o'-the-wisps. We thank Jack Finney for the inspiration and we thank Brad Linaweaver and J. Kent Hastings for enthusiastically embracing our addition of these visual trappings to the world of *Anarquía* that they have brought to life so powerfully with words. On the other hand, we want to make clear that any errors in identification or attribution of any of the photos and graphics in *Anarquía* are solely the errors of the editors and publishers.

In like manner, the "Chronology," "Glossary," and "Miscellanea" sections were created by the editors. Any errors in these sections are the sole responsibility of the editors and the publishers.

Finally we would like to say we hope that you, like those who have read various drafts of *Anarquía*, will agree with that master of imagination, Ray Bradbury, that *Anarquía* is "incredible and wonderful." For our part we could not have asked for a book whose authors more creatively employed their sense-of-wonder to dramatically re-invent the reality of the past through the use of wondrous ideas and science. Nor could we ask for a book better suited to be the first original novel published by our *Sense of Wonder Press* imprint. Enjoy!

Jim & Lynne Rock,
Editors and Publishers

The poor man is simply in the wrong job.

—H. L. Mencken, 1932,
in the depths of the Depression

Prologue

In the world we know, Wernher von Braun was a brilliant German rocket theoretician and designer who worked for the Germans before and during World War II and who, after the terrible carnage of that war, became the anchor around which the post-WWII American rocket, military missile, and space program developed.

Before she was known in America as the beautiful actress Hedy Lamarr, she was Hedwig Eva Maria Kiesler, the daughter of an Austrian banker from Vienna. She was a free-spirited teenager, notorious even before her scandalous nude scene in the movie Ecstasy, filmed when she was seventeen. Her mother's affectionate nickname for her was "Princess Hedy."

In 1933, her parents arranged a marriage with an infamous arms manufacturer and designer, the rich and powerful Fritz Mandl. Immensely influential with the Nazi regime, Mandl was close to Adolf Hitler. Frau Mandl was forced to play hostess to a number of powerful Nazi and Fascist visitors. Increasingly disgusted with her marriage and horrified at her husband's politics, she fled her husband, left Europe for Hollywood, became Hedy Lamarr, and, under the guidance of MGM's Louis B. Mayer, enjoyed a successful American film career. During WWII she became a great fund-raiser for the war effort and anti-Nazi causes. Using her estimable brains, she helped develop and jointly held the patent for a scheme for electronic frequency- hopping which broke ground for today's spread-spectrum communications. After the war she became one of the most prominent and well-known screen stars in Hollywood.

But in the world of Anarquía life follows a much different path for the young Wernher von Braun and the even younger Frau Hedwig"Hedy" Mandl.

Hedy's time-line in the world of Anarquía may have begun to diverge from ours during a very special dinner party held at the Vienna home of Fritz Mandl and hosted by his lovely young wife, Hedwig, during the early years of the

1

German Third Reich. No one is privy to the exact details of what went on at that very special dinner party, one which included the most dangerous man in Europe. But we do know that in the world of Anarquía, a handful of significant lives were set on different paths, and thereby was the world forever changed.

We begin the story of Anarquía with the young woman who would later become Hedy Lamarr, on the night that she played the most difficult role of her life.

Adolf Hitler

"Your wife is a perfect hostess, Herr Mandl!"

The speaker made a great production out of his compliment. Taking the hand of the young woman, he placed his dry lips against her smooth skin. There was something about him that disturbed her. As a rule, she was attracted to older men but there was something in the eyes of this one that gave her pause.

Young Frau Hedwig Mandl, née Kiesler, wife of the wealthy and powerful Herr Fritz Mandl, always dreaded her frequent evening tours of duty as hostess to various functionaries of the rising Fascist powers of Europe. These evenings were always distasteful and often boring. Tonight she had every reason to suspect that the line between boring and boorish might well be crossed.

She was accustomed to attempts by men to impress her. But this one did not exhibit the predictable male stance, admiring and eager for her approval. It was as though he were giving her one chance to be impressed by *him*, if she knew what was good for her.

Mandl noticed her appraisal of their guest. He caught her eye and flashed her a slight scowl, a warning for her to behave. Then he beamed with his most artificial smile. "We thank you for your gracious kindness, Herr Hitler."

The most ambitious man in Europe resumed an upright posture. From leader of the National Socialist Party, to Chancellor, to newly minted leader of Germany, there was no telling what role he might next assume.

He smiled. She preferred her husband's scowl.

At moments like this, the perfect hostess liked nothing better than to live up to the nickname her mother gave her as a child, Princess Hedy. A princess had the right—the obligation—to keep men hanging on her every word. Especially when one of the men was a husband she did not love and the other was the first person she'd met out of his usual collection of bores and poseurs who struck her as genuinely sinister.

"Yes, we thank you," she answered slowly, emphasizing the plural. For some time now she realized that Fritz Mandl saw her as a prized possession, much like his armaments at the Hirstenberger Patronen-Fabrick Industries. As such, she was expected to fulfill her function— both in and out of bed.

She could put up with that. She could put up with his insane jealousy that kept her a prisoner in a series of ornate cages. She could even understand the obsession driving her husband to buy up all the black-market copies of her risqué cinematic debut, *Ecstasy*, a foredoomed enterprise at best.

But having to entertain Herr Hitler was going too far. At least his body guards kept a discreet distance. She wasn't certain that they possessed the faculty of speech.

As Mandl's ardor for his young bride had cooled, his ability to read her moods had actually improved. She amused herself with the thought that he probably regretted having told her his *real* opinion of *Mein Kampf*. Hitler had absorbed all the bad elements of the Viennese press and wrote in a polyglot style. He might scream for racial purity but he was, himself, guilty of miscegenation of writing styles.

Although not awed, as were most men, Hitler was naturally fascinated by Hedy. Czechs and Hungarians vied with Germans and Austrians to determine the character of post-war Vienna, the city in which Hitler had starved as a failed artist. But here was Hedy, one of his own (another Austrian), the wife of a toady and, not long ago, the youthful star of a Czech film that gloried in the physical and the purity of nature. To Hitler there was nothing decadent about *Ecstasy*, including Hedy's nude scenes.

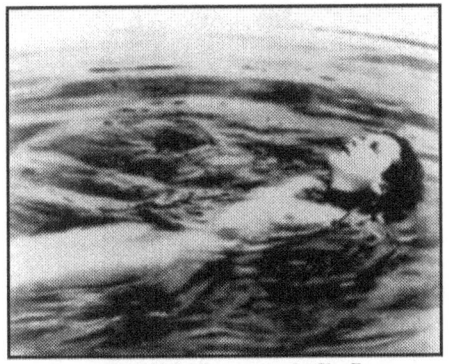

A very young Hedy Lamarr in the film Ecstasy.

As if reading her mind, Hitler took her by the arm and steered her to the nearest couch. "Your husband thinks I came here to discuss business but I really wanted to see you in the flesh!"

Hedy let a smile form. "Don't tell me you wanted to see me with my clothes on."

She studied his face closely. The comment she most often heard from men, eager to impress her, was some variation of the remark she had just made. How would Hitler respond to her attempt to out-flank him?

For the first time, Hitler surprised her. He showed no embarrassment as she might have expected from what she'd heard about his bourgeois tastes. Instead he squeezed her arm and said loudly enough to be heard:

Hedy and Fritz Mandl

"My dear Frau Mandl, I'm enjoying the view of your perfect Aryan profile. Perhaps you would consider posing for Arno Brecker, my favorite sculptor?"

It was a night of surprises and of Hitler's own brand of irony, the kind that just might be sincere and was all the more frightening for it. There was nothing of the jealous husband in Mandl now. "You could be a movie producer yourself!" he chimed in.

"Dr. Goebbels agrees with you," said Hitler. "Who knows? Maybe I'll end up as a producer and turn Europe into a movie location."

The men laughed. Hedy didn't. She tried her own brand of irony. "But I thought you only considered blondes fit for your purposes."

He had a quick response. "We're not that strict. Besides, I'll decide who the blondes are."

Again the men laughed, and again she felt anger dying in her throat. Would this evening never end?

A servant passed a glass of wine to Hedy and a glass of mineral water to her guest. Mandl joined them with his wine and proposed a toast:

"To the torpedoes I will produce for the greatness of the new Germany!" he brayed. He added, a moment later, "And, to the new Europe."

Hitler released her arm but she still felt the pressure where he'd held her. She hated herself for downing her wine in one gulp but she needed it.

Dinner consisted of several courses of refined Hell. She found herself missing the simple crudity of their recent guest, Mussolini. Although a pompous fool, he didn't disturb her the way Hitler did. Perhaps the difference was that Mussolini was just a bad actor and Hitler a very good one.

Hitler reveled in endless monologues, lecturing as though he were a living history book. At the least provocation he'd launch into a vigorous and "knowledgeable" speech concerning the migration of peoples and the fate of nations. She didn't doubt the accuracy of the names and dates he spewed forth but noticed that each bit of information was distorted through the prism of his bizarre racial theories.

Hedy was oddly fascinated but simultaneously repulsed, by his remarks on Spain.

"I love the country," he said. "It is stark. Of course, it can't compare to the beauty of our German mountains and valleys. But it offers a different kind of attraction, something almost elemental, as if from another universe. Spain appears beautiful from a distance but close up it is empty and cruel. One could do things in Spain. One could test theories there."

"And equipment," added Mandl, helpfully.

Hedy concluded that they were both mad.

She concentrated on the special vegetable dish that had been prepared for their guest. Hitler noticed this and changed the topic from Spain back to her.

"I understand that you and your husband sometimes hunt together," he said, before devouring a radish.

"She's a good shot," Mandl bragged.

"You hit where you aim?" he asked, munching on a cucumber.

"Usually," she replied.

Hitler shrugged. "I can't understand this savage impulse to slaughter animals. Where is the challenge in that? How does it improve the world?"

"I only shoot what I'm going to eat," she replied sternly.

Hitler finished his water. "That might be a problem if you were in charge of a war." He laughed alone.

Hedy began to lose her temper and Mandl's warning scowls were ignored. "Earlier you said that you might turn Europe into a movie. I imagine you'd use the new technicolor film stock so that everyone could see the color red for scenes of bloodshed!"

"Not a bad idea," Hitler replied calmly. "Just so long as the red is not the Bolshevik flag."

"Frau Mandl!" thundered her husband. "You have exhausted the subject."

Before she could respond, Hitler interceded. "Please think nothing of it, Fritz. I enjoyed the performance. Be careful you don't lose this darling creature back to the cinema. Especially beware of *Hollywood*

Metropolis, Fritz Lang, UFA films

Jews! They are always attempting to steal our European treasures."

Now she was seeing her own shade of red. "Gentlemen, it's such a burden to be popular. But what could Hollywood offer in terms of melodrama and cheap spectacle that I can't find right here?"

Hitler was unfazed. "You'll have to speak to UFA films about that."

Still she wasn't finished. "I've been dying to ask how many people need fear you?"

Mandl gasped. For a long time Adolf Hitler stared, locking his pale blue eyes to hers, finding in them, perhaps, a reflection of his own perverse proclivity for living on the edge. Then he said the last words he would ever speak to her.

"Frau Mandl, I assure you, no one will be hurt except my enemies."

Nazi "Degenerate" Art Exhibit.

CHAPTER 1

Barcelona, July 1936

The Children

Spain was the closest thing to Hell on Earth.

For the children playing on the outskirts of Barcelona it seemed to be just another care-free summer's day. They knew nothing of anarcho-syndicalism or non-intervention committees. They were blissfully ignorant of Nationalist schemes or Republican principles. They knew nothing of Pablo Picasso or of Barcelona's cultural resistance movement. They never would.

On a tomorrow that they would never see, these children would have their names immortalized by the Republic as part of a Children's Week celebration; they would be lionized in the anti-fascist Sunday comic strip, *Sidrin*, as part of a campaign against Fascism.

But on this still, serene afternoon they were innocent and playful, still only normal children, playing in an abnormal world.

They were only children.

They didn't know a Falangist from the Frankenstein Monster—the ogre in the nightmares of so many little boys and girls in the 1930s. They were too young for politics. But they were not too young to bleed.

They were working-class children. Their parents sweated in the factories in the big city. Some of them had relatives on the farms. They had gone through life without once hearing the notion that they were lower-class. All they knew was that they were Spanish and that they were Catholic.

Their mothers were exhausted and nervous; their fathers absent, or, if present, often drunk and cruel. But the children had never experienced anything else and so they had no idea that they should be unhappy.

There were advantages to this sort of upbringing. They were self-reliant at a much younger age than was the case of children in the middle- or upper-classes. But there was a drawback as well. They weren't very good at following parental advice.

So, when their mothers intoned the mantra of *de que celarse*, a warning to be careful or suspicious lest something bad happen they, especially the boys, tended to shrug off the warnings. Even the girls were not obedient.

The shining metal object they found that day was just the sort of thing their parents had warned them to avoid. But it was attractive, glinting in the late afternoon sunlight of a pleasant summer day. Why, it was just the sort of thing they needed to decorate their "secret" place where no adult could enter!

Eight of the children were present when the object began to tick. Pedro spoke the last words any of them would hear.

"It's not a clock, is it?"

When their parents collected the body parts of their dead children, they were not thinking about politics—with one exception.

Pedro's father saw the severed head of his son and promptly went insane. He was not an important enough man to rate treatment or commitment to an asylum. So he spent his remaining days making speeches on political and theological subjects. He was ecumenical. One day he would make the case for Franco and the Church. The next day he'd expound on the virtues of the Republic. His speeches were almost as long as the real thing.

He wanted to be fair.

Despite propaganda from the Republic, no one ever knew for certain which side provided the bomb that killed their children.

New York City, July 1936

The Pulpmeister

Spain was the closest thing to Hell on Earth.

At least that's how Howard Davidson saw it. Creator of the popular pulp magazine series, *The Inquisitor*, he ground out adventures of the "Turtle" and the "Dove" every month for the Street and Smith publishing company. With a bit of time traveling, his heroes were able to fight the Spanish Inquisition both in period and in the modern era. Their nemesis, the title character, also had a time machine from which he attempted to rewrite history on behalf of a secret society—a society which he ruled with an iron fist.

The Inquisitor stories weren't as popular as *The Shadow*, Street and Smith's top seller. But, then, nothing could compete with a pulp hero

who was popularized on national radio by the mellifluous voice of Orson Welles—not even its competition's truly sadistic *Spider*.

Davidson, however, liked to brag that no series featuring a bad guy did better than his. He was plowing the same ground as Sax Rohmer tilled with "Fu Manchu." Currently Davidson had the top-selling villain pulp. In fact, in this very year of 1936, he was receiving polite letters from prestige publishers of *real* books. The future looked bright.

Davidson's pulp hero series gave him financial and artistic independence beyond that of most of his fellow freelance writers. He was prolific and sometimes even found time to write short stories for another of the Street and Smith's successful ventures. *Astounding*'s venerable editor, F. Orlin Tremaine, liked the way in which the young writer brought sociological concerns to his immodest fictions. On the other hand,

Tremaine couldn't help but notice that Davidson's alien planets bore a striking resemblance to the mountainous regions and great plains of Spain, which suffered from a black and sulfurous rain—mainly on the plain.

As was common in the world of inventive fantasy authorship, Howard had never visited the scenes in which he set his adventures—be they alien planets or exotic Spain. In fact, with one brief exception, Howard had never stepped foot outside of the United States. He had spent most of his life in and around New York City. But he had a hell of a lot of books about Spain and there was no country he wanted to visit more.

For over a year Howard had planned the trip with his girlfriend. At the time it hadn't seemed a problem that she was a Communist. But the war in Spain had finally come between them when she pronounced him incurably bourgeois and therefore incapable of rising above his narrow class interests. She accused him of being a mere tourist, a voyeur and a dilettante, which struck him as a good career summary to use on his resume.

"I hate to lose her," he admitted to his best friend over a beer. "But, she has joined the class struggle at last."

"I know what you mean," agreed John Staples over his scotch and water. "So many on the left are volunteering for the Abraham Lincoln Brigade."

"She's not going to Spain. She's going to *Hollywood!*"

John choked on his drink. He couldn't stop coughing for several seconds and was grateful that they were holding the "wake" for Davidson's lost love in the pulpmeister's apartment instead of in a local tavern. For one thing, they could be a lot franker in private. Sometimes they got into arguments that were too bizarre for the ears of mere bohemians and radicals.

John was a pulp writer, too. His specialty was murder mysteries and his claim to fame included some fine short pieces in *Black Mask*.

"Hollywood?" John finally managed to gasp.

"Well, you know she wants to be an actress. The Party has promised to help her with a movie career and she wants

to work with the radical unions. The ungrateful bitch!"

"But why would she break off with you because you actually want to go to Spain?"

Howard sighed. "She thinks I'll go over there with the wrong attitude, just because I hate Fascists and Anarchists and peasants and priests and Communists."

"You hate everyone, Howard."

"I don't hate bullfighters."

John made himself another drink, having lost so much of his previous one. "How does she feel about bullfighters?"

"Noelle hates them."

They both laughed.

"How was she in the sack?" John asked.

"A good egg. She'd do anything I wanted. You don't find a girl like that every day. She'd screw without talking about marriage. She was a knockout in the looks department. And you could talk politics with her, even a little sports."

"A classy dame," John agreed.

"Yeah, but still a damned Red. The only downside. Well, nothing's perfect. I'll do better in Spain by myself anyway."

John watched his friend finish the last of his beer. He knew that Howard wouldn't pour another. John could knock back three glasses of real hooch to Howard's one timid drink. He was always surprised when encountering a writer who didn't drink heavily.

"Where will you go?"

"The obvious places. Madrid to start. Barcelona for sure. Maybe Guernica. I've saved up enough for this."

John shook his head. "It seems crazy. I mean, unless you're going to fight, why enter a war zone?"

Howard leaned back in his chair, lacing his fingers behind his head. "Well, maybe I will."

"On which side?" his friend wanted to know.

"All kidding aside, you know my sympathies are with the Republic. But I'm going over there as a writer, not as a fighter. Besides, somewhere in that stew of anarcho-syndicalists and Moscow stooges I may find a few Stirnerite individualists. There won't be anything but collectivists on the other side."

John shrugged. "I only read Max Stirner because you talked me into it. I thought that I was selfish until I read *The Ego And His Own*. Only a German philosopher could be that radical. How can there be a social movement made up of people who are so selfish that they don't have allegiance to anyone else? It doesn't make sense."

"I know it sounds strange," Howard admitted. "But they even have a journal I've been subscribing to for years, *Iniciales*. Good thing that I mastered Spanish because of a girlfriend."

"The one before Noelle?"

"Yeah. Rosita. She was a Trotskyite."

Leon Trotsky

"Aren't they all?" John Staples complained to the universe at large. "But when it comes to politics, you have the strangest views of anyone I know. I used to think you were some kind of technocratic Socialist in the H. G. Wells vein. But I couldn't reconcile that with your affection for H. L. Mencken and his last ditch defense of capitalism. Then you met that Ayn Rand woman in person, the author of the weird play where they choose the jury from the audience."

H. L. Mencken

"It's a good play! First appeared in Hollywood. Despite that serious handicap, it made its way here to civilization and actually appeared on Broadway."

"But it's just a gimmick, like a carnival stunt."

Howard shook his head. "You're wrong. It's brilliant. You just don't like it because she believes in passing judgment."

"I suppose so. I think you're taking this trip just so *you* can pass judgment on a civil war! Don't you think you might go with an open mind? This is real life, not one of your stories."

"A moment ago you were suggesting I should fight."

"You know what I mean."

They had reached the awkward moment they usually tried to avoid. But tonight was too serious for diplomacy. John was afraid that his friend might be foolhardy enough to get himself killed.

"Have a drink, Howard," John suggested.

"I've had enough."

"You had one lousy beer. What's the point of getting rid of the Volstead act if this is the best we can do?"

Howard laughed. "You drank the same way during Prohibition."

"We're talking about you. You never had a tipple when it was illegal. Tonight is different. If you want to run off to Spain in search of the Great American novel, you have to drink like Ernest Hemingway."

John pushed the bottle of scotch across the table toward his friend. "Help me kill this old soldier."

Howard grimaced. "You want to talk about my family, don't you?"

"Yeah."

"I don't have to get drunk to talk about them."

"It helps."

"If I drink too much Scotch, I'll be *kilt!*" said Howard, demonstrating that he had definitely spent too much time in the pulps. His friend tactfully let the remark pass without comment.

One shot later, no topic was taboo. John softened him up with a compliment anyway.

"You're a swell writer, Howie. You need to follow the example of Noelle and follow her to Hollywood, if you're so hot for adventure. You can straighten them out in California instead looking for real danger."

"That's the advice I'd expect from my old man," he answered, already a little woozy.

John wouldn't be thrown off that easy. "You're not a crusader, Howard. Not really."

Howard got to his feet. He was a little unsteady from the one drink but he spoke with his usual clarity. He went to the sink and downed a glass of water. Then he got down to cases.

"John, neither of is yellow. We're not crackpots. We don't have a cockeyed scheme to solve the problems of the world. But we *are* more

than just pulp writers. You know what stands between us and legitimate publishers?"

"Let's not go through this again," moaned Staples, already regretting that he'd opened the door to the great debate.

"We're not social register, my friend. There goes one approach to the big publishers. And we're not revolutionaries, fighting the cause of the downtrodden masses. There goes the other approach. Our problem is that we are popular writers with an audience of normal Americans who simply want to be entertained."

"So what's wrong with that?"

Howard smiled. He sat down again and pointed a finger in his friend's face; then he thought better of the gesture and leaned back in his chair.

"The world isn't cooperating." he said. "It's changing so fast that only screwy science-fiction writers have a clue where it's headed. Mere entertainers, such as ourselves, have a better handle on the future than stupid reactionaries and stupid revolutionaries."

John poured himself another drink and took it in one gulp. "So why aren't we stupid, too?" he wanted to know.

"Because we have *imaginations*," said Davidson. "Because we don't have vested interests in the past like the flat-earth Catholics or in the future like the flat-earth Stalinists."

"You left out the Jews," said his friend with a sigh.

"Always a good idea to leave them out, whenever possible."

John Staples was an Episcopalian who occasionally believed that there had been an historical Jesus who rose from the dead. He had been friends with Howard Davidson a very long time and knew of his friend's unusual background with a Jewish father and a Catholic mother. Before Howard was born, his father had repudiated the faith of his ancestors and become a secular socialist. After the Crash of '29, his father became a member of the Communist Party.

The mother remained a Catholic. She convinced herself that her husband's radical politics were in line with Social Justice theories of the Church. She spent most of her free time railing against right-wing Catholics and praying for a revolutionary Pope.

To further confuse issues for the young Howard Davidson, he had an older sister who was the embodiment of a right-wing Catholic and had taken the final vows. She was a Nun who thought the battle for Western Civilization was being fought by Franco, the man her mother despised. Howard also had an uncle, an observant Jew who blamed the rise of Hitler on Christianity, even though Hitler took great pains to distance himself from both the Catholic and Lutheran Churches and was clearly trying to create a brand new religion of his very own.

When Staples learned about his friend's family background, he marveled that Howard had not turned out an alcoholic and a dope fiend. He even gave him credit for not becoming a psychotic murderer.

But he worried that Howard was headed in the wrong direction when his friend launched tirades against Catholics, Jews and Marxists. Why, some of John's best friends were Trotskyites.

"You remember what you said the first time I asked you why you just didn't become a Nazi?" John reminded Howard, smiling.

The other laughed. "Sure. I pointed out that I might not be a Jew according to Jews; but I was a Jew according to Hitler. They wouldn't let me join their club even if I applied."

John opened his cigarette case and lit up. His friend didn't smoke but always extended the courtesy to those who did. As the match flickered out, John ruefully observed, "And then we learned about the book burnings orchestrated by Dr. Goebbels, the poisoned dwarf."

Howard shuddered. "To think an author could do that to other writers. Well, I was figuring out that the Nazis were barbarians by then. If they can do that to books, they'll do it to people. Who knows, one day they may kill as many people as Stalin has been starving to death in Ukraine."

At first, John had refused to believe the reports of the mass killings in the Soviet Union. He trusted the *New York Times* Moscow correspondent, Walter Duranty, who insisted that all such stories were just propaganda. But his fellow pulp writer convinced him that the *Times* had been playing everyone for a sap. Reports from an iconoclastic British journalist, Malcolm Muggeridge, set

Walter Duranty

the record straight for at least two hack writers in New York City.

"I find it hard to believe that Germans could ever be that brutal," said the mystery writer. "Even with an aberration like Hitler in charge, they don't have that Slavic savagery."

"Give them a chance," said the pulpmeister. "Besides, I think they will find their inspiration in how Hitler feels about the Jews."

"So why don't you buy a ticket to Berlin and study the beasts in their lair? That door is still open to travel. You could write the Great American novel about Germany instead of Spain. Except you won't see any bullfights."

They both laughed and their eyes drifted over to a book by Ernest Hemingway. No words need be said about the impact that this single writer had on the "lost generation." Almost every contemporary writer tried to imi-

Jack London

tate his methods. Journalistic sentences invaded narrative prose and took no prisoners. Left-wing politics found an unlikely home with an all-American man, a hunter and a fighter. Of course, Jack London had laid the foundation, sort of the Karl Marx of the new novel. But then, along came Hemingway—he was Lenin and Stalin and all the Bolsheviks rolled up into one vast explosion of testosterone and dialectics and a sock to the jaw!

In common agreement with other pulp writers, the two young men in this small, stuffy apartment on a warm night in New York City decried most of the "big" writers of the "big" books. But they had their favorites and they loved Hemingway. They loved him so much that they really didn't care a fig about his politics.

In contrast, they had both been royally annoyed at George Bernard Shaw's much publicized visit to the USSR in '32 and his endless praises for Stalin. Worst of all, the son of a bitch had referred to Americans as "the most absurd people on Earth" immediately upon returning to England. As far as Davidson and Staples were concerned, Shaw proved there were worse things than being an American pulp writer. Then again, if one of the greatest writers in the world could be such a damned fool, why couldn't just anyone be one of the great writers?

"So you're going to blow all your dough on this trip to Spain so you can become a legitimate writer?" asked John, ready to surrender because it was late and he was tired.

"Yes. But there's more to it than that. I believe that Spain is where the future of mankind will be determined. What happens there will determine if there's another Great War with Germany. It will determine the future of the Soviet Union. All the different philosophies of the Earth are gathering there to be heard and we need to provide the uniquely American viewpoint."

"Gee whiz, Howie! How about all those volunteers with the Abraham Lincoln Brigade?"

"In this case, the Communists don't count. Right now we need the *individualist* viewpoint. Even the damned Anarchists over there are collectivists."

Staples took a good, long look at his friend. "Well, try not to get yourself killed by everyone!"

This time Howard laughed alone. "Maybe I'll unite everyone against *me* and bring peace to the world."

"And what about the plots of the wicked *Inquisitor?*" his friend wanted to know. "And I do mean plots, as in story-lines."

"There's a backlog of material now. And I intend to write one of 'em based on my real experiences over there. Even if I don't get a contract for a novel, the journey will be worth it."

Staples smiled and shook his head. Of all the motivations driving people into that cauldron of despair, he figured that his friend had the most bizarre reasons of any of them.

"Send me letters," Staples suggested.

"I've intended to do that all along. You'll be receiving regular 'Dear John' letters, direct from the front!"

Staples would have thrown his glass at the grinning gargoyle that Howard used for a head, but he didn't want to spill the scotch.

Later, as he headed for the door, completely steady on his feet, Staples said: "You mark my words." He had always been proud that he could hold his liquor.

"And how's that?" Davidson wanted to know.

"Most Americans aren't interested in the war in Spain. They don't care about politics. You should be writing a novel about the Lindbergh baby kidnaping trial. Or, if you must write a novel about war, make sure it's anti-war like that Sherwood play, *Idiot's Delight*. The

Sherwood Anderson Depression is bad enough without worrying Americans about another ridiculous crusade in Europe. We're never going to be fooled again."

"You may be right," Howard said. "I'd feel a lot safer in a world without the Soviet Union and Nazi Germany."

"Have your heroes take a break from fighting the 'Inquisitor' and deal with those two problems, will you?" suggested Staples.

Thus ended Howard's "wake." They said goodnight, one on his way to a late-night assignation with a lady friend and the other back to his typewriter. Lately, Howard Davidson didn't sleep very much.

Morocco, July 1936

The General

Francisco Franco

Spain was the closest thing to Hell on Earth.

"Soon we'll surpass that cesspool of Stalin's," he thought.

General Francisco Franco had decided it was his destiny to change all that and restore a small piece of Heaven for his people . . . if only he could avoid the sin of pride.

He did not think of himself as a vain man. Certainly, he was sure he was not so when compared the other Fascist leaders. Italy's *Il Duce* struck him as comical with his strutting manner and florid outfits. As for Hitler, he thought all the Nazis looked as though they'd just stepped out of a Hollywood movie with extras from a "cast of thousands." In a strange way, he preferred the unassuming dress of the Communist leaders, especially Josef Stalin.

Benito Mussolini

It was one of those supreme ironies of history that he found himself requiring the assistance of one group of revolutionaries against another. To the world at large, Fascism was one big, undifferentiated lump of reactionary fear. Franco knew better. Hitler was as much a revolutionary as Stalin and he intended to turn the world inside out with as much fanaticism as anything that might come out of the Kremlin. Perhaps Hitler was even more extreme than any Bolshevik.

Franco sighed, taking one last look at his reflection in the mirror to reassure himself that he wasn't really vain, but that his uniform was neat and his mustache trimmed. He dreaded the social affair he was about to attend. He had Johannes Bernhardt to thank for this annoyance. Bernhardt was one of the Germans who made his home in Spain. Bernhardt had the ear of the Third Reich and Franco needed to whisper into that ear, delicately but clearly making his point about the desperate nature of his current situation.

Unlike the other Fascist leaders, Franco

wanted only to return the affairs of Spain to "normal." He hadn't even been a particularly aggressive officer in his youth, despite operating in a system where there were far too many officers and not nearly enough opportunities to move up the ladder. He was a cautious man and as a result found himself serving as the voice of moderation between headstrong factions. He didn't even hate the peasants.

For Franco, Fascism was the moderate position, the center of the road between foreign exploitation by international bankers and the extremes of the lunatic left. He didn't bother worrying over the sectarian differences between left-wing socialists, anarchists and communists. He had enough trouble keeping track of all the diverse strands of those in his own movement.

There were times, late at night, right before drifting off to an uneasy sleep that Franco suspected that the Trotskyites and the Stalinists just might be capable of a more reasonable exchange of ideas than some of the nonsense he had to put up with between the Monarchists and the crazier elements of his own Fascist movement. And, if that didn't cause him enough trouble, there was always the Church.

As a good Spanish Catholic, he realized that the political power of the Church was enough to try the patience of the Father, the Son and the Holy Ghost, not to mention a long line of frustrated Popes. For example, there were the members of *Ceda*. They appeared to be authoritarian Catholics until one compared them to *Carlists*, a group so opposed to modernity that they were simply unreliable allies. Franco often daydreamed of sending the *Carlists* back in time to face their supreme Catholic majesties, Ferdinand and Isabella, who would still be too "modern" for those blockheads. At least the King and Queen could do the intelligent thing and use the *Carlist* zealots as new kindling for the royal fires.

Only one event could have ever brought together the diverse elements of Franco's movement—the election of a Popular Front Government composed of radicals sworn to destroy Western Civilization. This current nightmare of 1936 was the end game of the earlier calamities involving the election of a Republican government back in 1931 and the subsequent abdication of the King,

Alphonso XIII

Alfonso XIII. Back in '31, even Franco had not believed things could ever go this wrong. Truly, the world had gone mad.

The war should have been over quickly and the criminal Republican regime replaced with the forces of law and order. Except for one minor detail. The Spanish air force and navy had *declared* for the Republic! It was unthinkable, impossible, a ghastly mess. Now Franco, currently in exile, had no hope of crossing the Straits without help from an outside force. He had to turn to Italy or Germany, or both.

Franco, in 1926, the youngest General in any European Army.

But assistance would not come without a cost. He would have to pay in raw materials that Spain could ill-afford to lose. And then there were the issues of military timing and military pride. Once his forces crossed the Straits, the Germans and Italians would waste no time before they began to wonder, publicly, in ever-louder voices, "When would Franco capture Madrid?" He could hear them already. "After all, how could a ragtag band of left-wing, utopian maniacs stand up to a real military force?"

The *damned* air force and navy, that's how. The traitors! Maybe it would be worth any price to see Germany's Condor legion swoop in and make mincemeat of the Spanish planes.

Franco shook his head in wonder at his own thoughts. It had come to this. He was fantasizing about the destruction of Spanish pilots at the hands of foreign pilots. It would now appear that Fascism was to be an international movement, the same as Communism. A disgrace!

Francisco Franco

Even so, now he must put on a pleasant face and spend the evening with Germans who fantasized making themselves into a new race of gods. Was this any way to save Catholic Spain?

"Princess" Hedy Lamarr

CHAPTER 2

Hollywood Bound

The Great Escape

"Welcome to Hollywood!"

Hedy Lamarr had heard that phrase from numerous publicists, agents and hangers-on. But the words took on a certain weight when they came from the mouth of Louis B. Mayer. He had a special right to say them after the efforts he'd made on her behalf. He wanted her for his stable.

She had first met him in Europe after the *"great escape"* (as she would always think of it). When Hedy turned twenty-one, she decided to leave her husband, but the idea was a long time in coming to fruition.

Her husband, Fritz Mandl, was a great collector of beautiful things and had never lost one before. He couldn't imagine that his wife would leave him just because he was an arms manufacturer doing business with the Nazis. He never imagined that the fact that he was a boorish pig also entered into the equation. But his fawning over Hitler and Mussolini would have been enough. He once joked to her that he used a long spoon when supping with the devil. She asked if it might be the same silver spoon his parents had inserted in him at birth.

In truth, there was a great deal more to Hedy's intended defection than her horror at Mandl's politics. It didn't help his case that he treated her like a prisoner. He was also a barely-sublimated sadist. She tried to be tolerant of that particular idiosyncrasy, little aware that in dealing with his outrages she was developing invaluable skills for a future career in Hollywood. Perhaps most annoying of all, Mandl had no sense of humor about himself.

Increasingly, Fritz Mandl disgusted and bored his young wife. Perhaps the latter trait was his most unforgivable sin in her eyes. Evil and boredom are a most unappetizing combination and Hedy had partaken of her fill.

She approached the problem with her usual flair. First, she hired an attractive young maid who was exactly her size. Then she ordered an extra uniform to use as a disguise in her escape. Hedy further prepared by initiating a pleasing "dalliance" with the newly-hired young maid, during which Hedy persuaded her to access the "tippling" supplies of an older maid, the one who had been designated by Fritz as Hedy's "guard." Hedy then had access to the young maid's spare uniform; and pleasing access to the young maid herself (the better to pleasure them both and to give Hedy a taste of freedom and satisfaction, both of which had been sorely lacking in her life for some time). Hedy had always been very democratic about allowing both sexes to worship at her throne and it was a relief to find pleasure again with someone who, though aggressive and inventive, was nothing like the pig that her husband had turned out to be.

The day of the "great escape" finally arrived and the plot quickened. The old maid, a battle-axe who had been given express instructions to watch the young mistress of the house at all times, was drugged as planned. The young accomplice was given somewhat more than a peck on the cheek for old remembrance's sake. Fritz Mandl, supplied by Hedy with his own dose of temporary Lethe, was deep in the arms of Morpheus when Hedy gave him the slip.

And when Hedy, disguised as a maid, finally left the Mandl mansion that had been her prison, she never looked back.

Fritz Mandl did not take these events well. He hired several men to locate and return his wayward bride. However, he made a characteristic mistake. He underestimated her. She knew the streets of Vienna far better than any hired tracker.

Now, she had to travel alone. She quickly made her way to the train station and boarded it just as it was leaving the station, as planned. Her marriage would be annulled. She had truly burned her gilded bridges, and cages, behind her. As she prepared to board the train, the young Hedy felt the exuberant thrill of new freedom and unlimited possibilities. These were feelings she recognized from the time before her marriage to Mandl and they were feelings she vowed she'd retain and rejoice in for the rest of her life.

Hedy ran madly through driving rain to catch her train to freedom, tearing her maid's uniform as she jumped from the platform just as the train began to move. She was with ticket, but otherwise was *sans* money, almost *sans* clothes, and definitely *sans* regrets.

As the train pulled from the station Hedy caught her breath and glanced around the car. It was filled with older travelers, studiously ignoring the disheveled young woman in the equally disheveled maid's outfit. Hedy was glad for the respite from attention and looked about with the bright eyes of an intelligent young woman who has just been given or, rather, has just taken a new lease on life's possibilities.

Perhaps that aura of happiness and the possibilities she sensed for the future affected her first impression of the handsome young man she saw, sitting in animated conversation with a friend, a man who turned out to be an expatriate German by the name of Wernher von Braun.

As she approached the empty seat across from the handsome young man and his friend, her interest was piqued. This man, she observed, was a *rara avis;* an apparently masculine specimen who didn't seem remotely interested in her, even in her soaking wet (and now) abbreviated French maid's costume.

"Very unusual," she thought. She further mused that, as a distressed young lady who was forced to leave on short notice with few clothes and even less money, perhaps she should concentrate on locating someone who showed an interest in *her* rather than on someone whom *she* found interesting.

She truly was a damsel in distress and no matter how attractive the strong, aloof type might be, what she needed now was more along the lines of "knight in shining armor."

But she was not *feeling* particularly distressed, and she *was* a damsel who had read a lot of books. On this occasion of exploring new friendships, as it turned out, what she sensed would matter more than her appearance or even her appetites. She had learned more things while living with her husband than merely various ways of submitting to his will.

As she sat down across the aisle from the oblivious pair of men she leaned her head back and relaxed as the train pulled from the station. Across

Wernher von Braun

Konrad Zuse

the aisle Wernher von Braun was discoursing with his friend on two of his favorite subject areas: rocket propulsion and travel in space. As the two men talked Hedy became interested in their conversation and, being who and what she was, she turned and looked across the aisle, caught von Braun's attention, and said, conversationally, "But rockets, not fins, would steer the ship in space. Because there's no atmosphere, only reaction mass can change the direction."

Von Braun and his friend gaped at her as if she had just steered in from outer space herself. And thirty minutes later the three left for the dining car together. The men's first surprise had been that anyone on the train, let alone a young woman, understood anything about rockets.

Their surprise and interest deepened when they belatedly noticed that this particular young woman looked as though she'd just stepped off a French postcard. Wernher and his friend were obsessed with rocket science, but they *were* men and they were still breathing.

The dinner invitation was not long coming. Hedy was flattered that they had finally noticed her as a woman but she let it be known that what struck her most about Wernher and friend was that they had first been impressed by her knowledge and ideas. It was a pleasant, unaccustomed, and unexpected feeling of belonging that she experi-

A French Postcard

enced, chatting with men whom she found "sehr gemütlich" on her first day of freedom from the "Mandl Prison."

Shortly after their initial discussion, Wernher's friend, Konrad, recognized her. Wernher von Braun was one of the few young men in all of Europe who hadn't seen *Ecstasy. His* favorite film heroine was Gerda Maurus, star of the late 1929 film, *Die Frau im Mond,* about a trip to the Moon. Hedy forgave him and went on to describe her life with, and escape from, Fritz Mandl and the information she had learned, sometimes literally, at, under, and over his knee, during their strange marriage. How could she have been Madame Fritz "Weapons Man" Mandl and not become intrigued by weapons of the future—and how to counteract them? Especially when trapped in a marriage consisting of overwhelming boredom and complete access to books and factories full of information about rockets, shell trajectories and weapons research. "It was inevitable," she shrugged, with uncharacteristic modesty.

Hedy admitted that, while she was listening to their conversation, she wondered if it might not be wiser to keep her mouth shut. But, she confided, she couldn't tolerate the idea that having just *gained* her freedom that she would then fail to speak her mind and share the knowledge she had garnered during the ordeal of her marriage. "Why make the break and gain your freedom if you don't *use* your freedom?" she asked.

Hedy also noted that, while it was bad enough being a woman when it came to serious discussions, her beauty was actually a handicap.

She recounted the events of the evening she had spent with Herr Hitler and how that occasion had resulted in a fierce determination to spend as much time as she could, while imprisoned in the Mandl household, learning about the new weapons and the principles behind them that Mandl was developing. She was sure that she had learned a lot and she believed that someday her knowledge might be useful.

At least researching her husband's businesses had helped to keep her mind occupied while she waited for an opportunity to escape.

She told the new men in her life everything. Several bottles of champagne kept them all in a jolly mood although no alcohol was needed to loosen her tongue. In fact, between her acting career and her hostess stints during her marriage, it was no wonder that she held her liquor better than they did!

When her two new friends offered to help her with money and introductions to friends, she assumed that they would expect the usual "quid pro quo," which, in fact, she was not loathe to grant her congenial benefactors. But they were gentlemen and did not press their advantage. Flattered and already attracted to the tall man with his dreams of tall rockets, she made the first move toward Wernher von Braun herself.

He won her heart completely when he told her that he'd left Germany when he was eighteen and now considered himself a "citizen of the world." She thought that his story of how he became estranged from the Fatherland would make a fine movie. At the time of this conversation, she was stroking his cheek while sharing his sleeping compartment. The gentle swaying of the train made everything seem right so she kissed him. Whereupon, he promptly fell sound asleep. As she left the compartment to have a smoke in the corridor, she smiled to herself as she heard him muttering in his sleep about various mixtures for rocket fuel. One of the formulas seemed to be named Hedy.

He was the most unusual man she'd ever met. In the next twenty-four hours she came to know him more intimately as they discussed everything under the sun. She was rather accustomed to the ways of older men. Von Braun was the first man she'd met who was near her own age and yet still possessed the air of authority that attracted her to older men. But he was low key about his masculinity and in no way a bully. Up to this point in life, she always had to be the teacher with men her own age. But despite his lack of experience, he finally took charge the next time they were alone in his compartment. Upon reflection, she decided it was like being made love to by a physician. He approached her body as though it were a problem to be solved.

As they lay in each other's arms, their hearts slowed down and their minds sped up. Making love had removed a barrier between them. Suddenly they were discussing the ideas, feelings, and concepts that really mattered to them. They were beyond rockets. They were beyond wine. It was time to truly discover each other.

"Sex is a disruptive factor," she said, lighting a cigarette.

Von Braun chuckled. "You're the only woman who would say something like that."

She passed him the cigarette and said, "You've never met a woman like me."

"I'm not as experienced as you are, " he said. "I imagine that you've been doing this sort of thing for some time."

She playfully punched him in the arm while flashing a white smile. "So your analytical brain is always working!" she said.

"How old were you when you had your first experience?" he asked suddenly.

"I was nine. A female servant in her thirties crept into my bed one night and played with me. It was a new kind of play."

"Nine!" he said in a low whisper. "And what about the male of the species?"

She paused thoughtfully for a moment. "Well, I suppose the *first* was when a man exposed himself to me, except there was no touching."

Von Braun shook his head and took a drag on the cigarette. This girl was remarkable.

"Boys came shortly after," she continued. "One of my girlfriends got an older boy in my room and encouraged him to seduce me."

"What was she doing all this time?" asked von Braun.

"She watched," said Hedy with a shrug.

Von Braun took that as his cue to study her face again. Her fine features entranced him. He held her chin and examined her face as if it were a rare treasure.

"You're a voyeur, too," she said, removing his hand so she could kiss his palm.

"You make me think of new worlds to conquer," he replied.

She touched his cheek. "I won't forget you, Wernher. When other men talk that way, they mean to make money or take over countries. You literally want new worlds!"

"New worlds like your heavenly body," he said. They kissed a long time.

They parted company with a promise to write. This encounter had evolved into something more serious than she had, at first, realized. She had a feeling she would see him again.

To Hedy, those events on the day of her "great escape" would always seem fresh and young, as if they had happened only yesterday.

Hedy in Hollywood

Hedy and Louis

As her thoughts abruptly returned to the present, she accepted Mayer's invitation to take a seat in his opulent MGM office. With all the details of that remarkable day suddenly flooding back, she felt as if she had gone through the motions of a movie script, although not the kind of thriller MGM would ever make. It felt more like a picture from UFA films, or maybe Warner Brothers.

Since her escape, Louis B. Mayer had become the new father figure in her life. He was much nicer than Mandl. He was both a movie producer and an older man who promised her the stars and the moon. It now crossed her mind that Wernher von Braun might be more likely to deliver on a promise like that—literally.

This new, older man was very important and she realized from the start what he could do for her. So she decided that she

Louis B. Mayer, MGM Studios

would never make love to this one. They had a genuine liking and respect for each other, and besides, it would be bad for business. It wasn't
even necessary. They had other passions to bind them.

To Mayer, she was still Hedwig Eva Maria Kiesler, the Viennese
starlet who had already managed to create two scandals in her short
career. The most recent was running out on her famous husband; however the first scandal was the one he really enjoyed discussing.

But first things first! He started to work on her name the moment
she expressed interest in coming to Hollywood. Her childhood nickname of "Princess Hedy" was all he needed to cobble together a new
name that he promised would be up in lights if she followed his advice;
and wouldn't be down in the gutter if she continued listening to him
after she made a mark in America.

The game continued between them for a while. She even sailed to
New York City on the same boat with her would-be mentor. He repeat-
edly told her that he respected her more than most actresses. One day it
dawned on both of them that he actually meant it.

So now the game was spent and she sat in the powerful producer's
office in the heart of Hollywood. It was 1936 and she was under contract. But for some mad reason she found herself thinking about her
brief flirtation with the German rocket man instead of about her career.
She wondered if she'd ever find another man as intelligent as von Braun.
She daydreamed that they might get back together and have an actual
romance instead of one brief sexual encounter (and several weighty,
intellectual conversations). She recalled their last conversation when they
agreed that the true "revolution" required an ability to judge the individual without concern for race or class.

She was rudely jerked back to reality by Mayer who was discussing
an issue of more pressing concern to him and, therefore, to the Studio.

"Your ass!" he blared. "You've got a great ass but Americans are
different than Europeans when it comes to that sort of thing."

"What do you mean?" she asked, dazed by the abrupt change of her

L. B. Mayer

train of thought and from the intense audacity of one
of Tinsel Town's greatest moguls.

"The wives over here are the problem. You can get
away with bare-ass scenes in Europe but American motion pictures are for the whole family, especially here
at MGM."

He lit a cigar. She smiled, idly considering the
amazement she would have experienced if he'd asked

her first if she minded his smoking. At least he was gentleman enough to offer her a cigarette, which she gratefully accepted. Most men would have used lighting her cigarette as an opportunity for some physical contact, but not Mayer. He was all business with her. She liked that.

"Of course, there is a *gray* area," he admitted. "We can loan you out to other studios to build you up. In fact, that's our usual policy. By the time you make your first MGM picture you'll be even bigger. Now, if you

Hedy Lamarr

did some partial nudity for another studio that wouldn't cause us any trouble here."

He smiled benevolently.

She smiled back and let it grow until her pearly white teeth had his full attention. "You needn't worry about that, Mr. Mayer," and she continued to smile obediently.

"Good, Miss Kiesler. Now I hope that's enough formality between us for a while. Your English is coming along fine but you still need to work on the accent. We don't want you losing it completely, you understand, but it still needs to be toned down. There's always room for foreign allure in the MGM stable."

She simply couldn't resist the impulse to neigh. She did it so well that Mayer stared, his cigar drooping slightly from the corner of his mouth.

"I didn't know you did animal impressions," he said.

"I like horses," she deadpanned and then sighed. She could learn every language on Earth and still not be able to fully communicate with an American banking institution that smoked cigars and talked about her ass.

Suddenly Mayer surprised her by raising the tone of the conversation. "Do you remember the first political question I ever asked you?"

That was easy. To the best of her recollection he had only asked her one political question ever. "Yes. You wanted to know if I was a Communist or had any sympathies in that direction."

"Do you remember why?" he asked.

She would never forget. The moment he found out that she had personally challenged Adolf Hitler, he quite reasonably assumed that she was an anti-Nazi. She, quite reasonably, assumed that an American Jew would approve.

She was mostly right. But she received her first lesson in American

ANARQUÍA

IMMEDIATE EPIC

The Final Statement of The Plan

BY

UPTON SINCLAIR

The book, "I, Governor of California, And How I Ended Poverty," was written in August, 1933, and has been for a year the best selling book in the history of the State.

But meantime the crisis has deepened, and California draws every day nearer to bankruptcy.

Plans for bond issues, which seemed practicable a year ago, are seen in September of 1934 to involve too great delay.

The EPIC Plan has been revised in the light of a full year's criticism. We have learned from our friends how to improve the Plan, and from our enemies how to present it more effectively.

This is the final statement of the Plan, and supersedes all other statements.

PRICE 15 CENTS

END POVERTY LEAGUE 1501 SOUTH GRAND AVE. LOS ANGELES, CALIFORNIA

politics—and business—that day he put her on the spot. Mayer pointed out that there were two kinds of anti-Fascists: Communists, and everyone else. He was fine with Hedy if she belonged to the second category.

"I remember our conversation," she answered.

"We have a Communist problem in California," he said. "They are infiltrating the unions. Then there's EPIC, a left-wing movement which stands for End Poverty in California. They aren't all Communists but they are pink enough to be a problem."

"Pink? I don't understand," she admitted.

He nodded. "That's OK. Just keep working on your English. The point is that now everyone's getting all worked-up about Spain. American Communists are running over there to help the Republic. We have plenty in California who are going. Sometimes I think that warm climates grow Reds. Maybe anywhere with olives has a lot of Reds there. Hey, that's good. Olives have red centers, get it?"

"Russia is cold," she replied.

Mayer scratched his head. "You are a smart woman, Hedy."

"Smart enough to work out a good contract with you, Louis. Without a manager."

"I know, my girl. No need to brag. That's not becoming."

Hedy tapped Mayer's desk with her forefinger. "It's your own fault that you offered me a six-month contract at $125 a week. That gave me some idea of your tendencies with new actresses."

"But that was when I first met you in Europe," he countered. "I was offering to bring you to Hollywood and make you a star! Bob Ritchie, your agent at the time, thought it was a great idea."

"Men! I never forgot that Bob was an American first in those negotiations. He actually thought it reasonable that you expected me to pay my own way to the states!"

Mayer mumbled to himself and then actually harrumphed. "You can't blame a man for going after a bargain in the marketplace."

Hedy showed the producer her pearly whites which usually brought out a jello-like quality in men. "Louis, you can't blame me for knowing my future value based on what I had already accomplished in Europe. You wouldn't have met my price if you didn't think I was worth it. I wasn't *insulted* by your low offer. I was *amazed* at what you were trying to get away with."

Mayer nodded. "The truth is that I've dealt with a lot of business women but damned few who look the way you do."

"Thanks for the compliment, Louis. How many women are invited to discuss politics with you?"

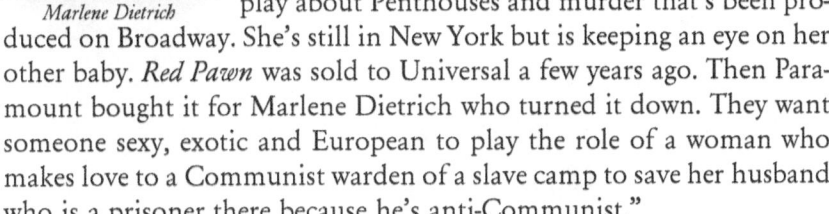
Marlene Dietrich

"I brought up politics because I'm thinking of loaning you out on your first American film. It's going to be a bit controversial."

"What is it?"

"It's called *Red Pawn*. An anti-Communist woman wrote it. She's from Russia so she brings some first-hand knowledge to the property. We first noticed her when she sold MGM the rights to a play about Penthouses and murder that's been pro-duced on Broadway. She's still in New York but is keeping an eye on her other baby. *Red Pawn* was sold to Universal a few years ago. Then Paramount bought it for Marlene Dietrich who turned it down. They want someone sexy, exotic and European to play the role of a woman who makes love to a Communist warden of a slave camp to save her husband who is a prisoner there because he's anti-Communist."

"That might be my lucky part," she said. "You know I'm a democratic liberal. I hate Communism and Nazism equally."

"Spoken like a good American!" Mayer beamed. "After that we may lend you out to another studio for one more project, *Algiers*. They are trying to sell it as a vehicle for Charles Boyer. A few of these lesser films will build you up and then you'll be ready for something big right here at MGM."

Charles Boyer

She gave the low, throaty chuckle that Mayer adored. "So long as I keep my ass in line, right?" she said.

He came around the table and took her by the elbow, helping her up. "That's my girl. You know, I love you for telling off Adolf."

"Why don't you make an anti-Nazi picture?" she asked in all seriousness.

He grunted. "You should know the answer to that. For the same reason no other Jewish producer will. We won't be taken seriously because we're Jews. Right now only a Gentile can get away with it. And then, there's the financial consideration. Germany's a big market for all our pictures and what can you do when Berlin hosts the Olympic Games?"

Hedy bit her lower lip. "Yes, what can you do?"

"Cheer up," he said. "The time may come! If I ever make one, I'll be sure and put you in it."

As he walked her to the door of his office he let his hand slip down to her rear. He gave her a strong, firm pat. She smiled. It was the least sexual experience she'd ever had. Just business.

The Hollywood producer had criticized that part of her anatomy and now he was apologizing to it. No hard feelings. Both Mayer and Hedy expected to make a lot of money from every part of her anatomy.

Hedy in Hollywood

Hedy Makes a Picture and Meets Frank

Months later, Hedy Lamarr was on a Paramount sound stage, marveling at the detailed set for a Siberian prison camp. She'd been invited to see it by the director. She didn't hold it against him that he had the first name of her ex-husband.

She wore one of her most conspicuously "normal" outfits for the occasion. Of late, she found herself putting more thought into buying clothes to dress down than when she put on the Ritz for the glamour look.

A blue cotton skirt was coordinated with a light jacket, both set off by a shell blouse with an attractive white ruffle to the neck. Just before getting dressed she debated over whether to wear the white or blue pumps and settled on the white.

It was Sunday afternoon and the only other actress on the lot was dressed in a tight, black leotard. She was taking a break from exercises.

The two women silently examined each other and then exchanged smiles. Where did the idea ever get started that it was a man's world, anyway? When it came to tooth and claw competition, the male of the species was a piker.

As Hedy poured herself a cup of coffee, she overheard the director and the cinematographer chatting about her. "So what if she doesn't have the best set of tits you've ever seen?" the director challenged the other man. "It's still a nice rack but what she's really got is the most gorgeous face I've ever seen."

"You gotta point," the other man admitted.

"Her forehead is the highest I've ever seen on a girl where it's still attractive. Her chin is a masterpiece. The cheekbones and eyebrows are so perfect it almost hurts to think about them."

"Don't forget her lips."

She smiled as she sipped her coffee. With every passing day it became more evident that Hollywood was her kind of town.

Suddenly she sensed that she was being watched. She quickly turned and saw a tall, lanky figure leaning in the doorway. Her first

Gary Cooper

impression was that it was Gary Cooper but then she recognized differences in the face. The man could be Cooper's brother, though.

She waited for him to say or do something. He didn't. That was not a normal male reaction, especially not with her! For several long moments they remained still, eyes locked. Finally, she could no longer abide the insolence of the man and said, "Who the hell are you?"

"Someone spying on you, the same way you've been spying on our director."

"*Our* director? Are you in this picture?"

He nodded. "The name's Frank," he said, extending a long, lean hand. There was something magnetic about him. She couldn't believe it but she found herself walking over to him. In the back of her head a little voice was nagging: *that's not in the script, darling—he's supposed to come to you!*

She liked the feel of his hand. "You must be the actor they sent from New York to play the husband."

"Yes, hardly worth the expense when you consider the cost of bringing me in."

She laughed and the spell was broken. At least she felt her normal self again. "It's true we only see you a few times in the story but they are crucial scenes. And we kiss."

"How about a rehearsal?"

As a rule she liked forceful men. She allowed Frank to start something. If she liked it she might help him finish it. He used his hands as well as his tongue. The kissing was all right but the hands were better. He had an easy grace about him and held her with a firm confidence that made her whole body tingle.

They came up for air and looked at each other again. They stared as they had before but this time it was friendlier. The man's gray eyes seemed to pierce through her blue ones into the very center of her brain. The manner in which he looked at her implied that he could possess her as easily as he held her gaze.

She realized that she wouldn't break off first. Not this time. She felt excitement at her own stubbornness.

When she first heard that an actor was being sent from New York, and that he wasn't a big name, she couldn't fathom why. There was an abundance of local, starving talent right here in Hollywood, at Paramount's fingertips.

Now she understood. This man was unusually arrogant. He projected a supreme confidence that was genuinely unusual. His wide mouth was almost unattractive when he smiled but the eyes became more in-

Bela Lugosi as Count Dracula

tense. The overall impression was one of detached amusement at whatever life might throw his way.

He took Hedy Lamarr as his due. He broke off the staring contest so that he could resume the kiss. But he didn't go straight to her mouth. She felt her pulse quicken as he nibbled at the base of her neck. She wouldn't have been surprised if he he'd sunk his teeth in, like Lugosi in *Dracula*, but the next moment his mouth again fed on hers.

Some women felt weak at times like this but Hedy always had the opposite reaction. There was no conflict between her mind and her body. She was always in absolute control.

And this man from New York was a good lover. They had reached the threshold when she would have to make the decision.

"Do you want to make love?" she asked.

"Yes," he said it like a command.

Her eyes darted around and determined that no one was in sight. If the director and cinematographer had chanced upon them they were, evidently, gentlemen and were nowhere to be seen.

"Follow me," she said, taking him by the hand even though she could have pulled him along another way.

"Your dressing room?" he asked, as she took him up the steps.

"I think it's supposed to be mine but they haven't put a name on it yet."

"We'll make it yours tonight," he said as he closed the door behind them.

Inside the narrow room, illuminated by a light so bright that it hurt her eyes, they got down to business. There was no kindness in his smile, only a sense of command. He reveled in holding the upper hand even as his long fingers began to caress her nipples through the thin material of her blouse. His wide, white grin sent shivers up and down her spine. She wanted to reassert control but he wouldn't let her.

"Let's have some drinks," she breathed.

"All right. There's always time for a drink."

She broke away and opened a drawer where a bottle of bourbon had been left at her request. It was always a good idea for a new place to be prepared before she arrived. But there were no glasses. She held up the bottle and he grabbed it out of her hand.

He drank from the bottle first and then passed it to her. She took the neck of the bottle between her firm, strong lips and swallowed more than he did.

"I like professional women," he said.

She adored him for that. She was immune to normal flattery of the "you're so gorgeous" variety. But she was always ready to be appreciated for what she could really do.

She did not expect him to take her free hand in both of his and to lower his warm lips to her tremulous flesh. That move seconded her opinions about this man, one way or the other. She was not about to give him the satisfaction of yanking her hand away. It was difficult to be only inches from his lean, strong body and feel the firmness of his demanding touch.

"Is this professional behavior?" she heard herself ask, an inch away from sighing.

"Consider this a bribe," he said.

Whatever special pull had gotten him this job on the film, Hedy was more than happy to expand her horizons with this New York actor.

Later she would learn that he was the husband of the author—a woman who was still busily engaged on the other Coast pursuing efforts on Broadway as well as dabbling in Republican politics. American Republican politics, that is.

Hedy wouldn't be all that disappointed when she found out that he was married. She'd be more annoyed by the fact that he had started his career as an extra in films and had met his future wife when she was in Hollywood.

Which meant that he really wasn't a New York actor, after all!

CHAPTER 3

The Vatican

The Padre and the Cardinal

The Spanish priest was nervous. He had never received a summons to Rome by someone as important as Cardinal Celi. The last time he entered St. Peter's was for his ordination. That seemed a long time ago but his memories had never faded. Today they came back with such force that he realized that Vatican City was what he dreamed of when he longed for Heaven.

Walking down the corridors of a thousand-year-old building produced in him an eerie sense of alienation. Only the living plants tended by the monks provided a link to contemporary reality. The vegetation was green and alive and probably younger than he.

He was ushered into the richly furnished and deeply silent office of a prince of the church. The Cardinal, in his sixties, projected a zestful vigor that the priest had lost in his thirties. Although only forty-five, Father Palma would strike an observer as the older man.

As the Spanish priest leaned forward and kissed the ring on the hand of the Italian Cardinal, he thought he heard a curious tinkling of bells. There was no breeze and upon raising his head he didn't notice any bells in the room. Not one for portents and omens, he didn't give the moment another thought. The last thing he expected to find in

Rome was evidence of the supernatural.

Cardinal Celi didn't waste time. "I have a job for you in a little-known division of the Office of Propaganda."

"Your eminence requires that I take up a career in politics?" asked Palma. Outside of the Church, not many people knew that Propaganda had first been developed to serve the Church instead of the State.

"We are all embroiled in worldly politics now," said Celi with a sigh. "You grew up in America before your parents returned to Toledo. I spent many years in England. We have, therefore, much in common. I have read extensively in British literature and its journalism. You are similarly acquainted with American works. We must arrange teams of readers and analysts to understand *all* of our opponents if the Church is to survive the coming dark days."

"I don't understand," the younger man admitted.

"What remains hidden from you?"

Palma fidgeted in his chair. "I mean to say that it's obvious why the Church is studying the ideology of the Nazis and the Bolsheviks. Hitler and Stalin present radically different threats; but what is the concern over English-speaking writers and journalists?"

Celi smiled and poured his priest a glass of fine, red wine. He joined him in a toast to the Pope. Then he settled comfortably into his large chair and tried to educate the man from Spain.

"You know who Disraeli was?"

"A British Prime Minister of the last Century?"

"A Jew who became one of England's greatest prime ministers. He was once asked to identify his religion. He answered that all wise men have the same religion. His questioner persisted and Disraeli answered that wise men never tell."

"Was he a convert?" asked the priest.

Cardinal Celi shook his head and sighed. This was going to take longer than he expected but the Spaniard had shown keen insight in some of his writings. Considering that many priests in Spain were virtual illiterates, this man's talents were not to be wasted. He was naive and merely required enlightenment—but never illumination.

Benjamin Disraeli

"Let me try another approach," said the Cardinal. "Take a good look at me. Do I remind you of anyone?"

The question took Palma by surprise. But then he thought long and hard. "Why, yes, now that you mention it. You could almost be a twin of the American Founding Father, Benjamin Franklin. You'd simply need to grow the hair on the sides of your head longer and add bifocals. You have the face and the great dome of a bald head."

Benjamin Franklin

Celi nodded. "You are observant. Sometimes I wear an eighteenth century costume for very private parties. You mentioned bifocals. Did you know that Franklin invented them? He also invented the lightning rod, for which various members of the American clergy criticized him for interfering in God's domain. He also discovered the Gulf stream. Somehow he had time for these scientific milestones while helping lead the American Revolution, achieving diplomatic miracles at the French court, revolutionizing journalism and composing the *Autobiography*. He also invented the glass harmonica."

The priest had no idea where all this was leading but he nodded vigorously and volunteered, "The man was clearly a genius."

"Yes, a true genius, unlike many of our political 'geniuses' strutting the Earth today! Every dictator is a genius to hear him tell it. Of course there are real geniuses in the world right now but they are primarily scientists and engineers. They have no gifts in statecraft. Everything is so specialized these days," he sighed.

Celi let silence settle over them like the dust covering the rare tomes that filled the Cardinal's book shelves. The more the older man spoke, the more confused his priest became.

"I'll get to the point," said Celi. "Franklin was a Mason, a dedicated enemy of the Church. Hell is large and contains multitudes."

This statement truly shocked the priest. He was used to this kind of talk in the Spanish villages. It seemed crude and out of place here.

The Cardinal read his priest as if thumbing through the pages of one of his books. "Where do you think Disraeli ended up after he died?"

Palma opened his mouth but no words came out. He cleared his throat and tried again. "Well,

Benjamin Disraeli

when many Spanish Jews converted to the Church at the time of the Inquisition, they were called New Christians. It was widely understood that many of the conversions were only to avoid burning at the stake. The Jews continued to practice their rites in private but every now and then they'd be caught and punished."

Celi frowned. "Punished? Don't you mean corrected, shown the light of right reason? Well, never mind."

"I suppose Disraeli was that kind of convert," the priest offered, helpfully.

Celi pursed his lips. "What difference would it make if an English Jew was sincere or not in converting to the Church of England? It's the *wrong* church and they are all going to Hell anyway!"

Father Palma had trouble breathing; the room had suddenly become uncomfortably close and stuffy. "I'm confused," he muttered.

Cardinal Celi reached into his desk and produced several books and magazines and newspapers, all in English. The priest's eyes scanned the titles and caught the names of George Orwell and G. K. Chesterton. But what really seized his attention was the garish cover of an American pulp magazine.

Against a flaming yellow background a nearly naked woman with an impossibly small waist struggled with a lean, yet muscular figure in blood red robes with a pointed hood through which glowed hate-filled eyes. In the background a silver object, constructed of metal triangles, and shooting out blue lightning bolts, hovered ominously over a mound of human skulls.

"What in Heaven's name is that?" asked Father Palma.

"Not Heaven, actually, but the other firm," said Cardinal Celi, frowning. "This will be part of your American reading, the latest installment of *The Inquisitor*. The author recently arrived in Spain. All sorts of people are visiting your lovely country nowadays."

"But what is it?"

"An inferior version of the scientific romances developed by Wells and Verne. It's the American assembly line at work, as though Henry Ford had gone into publishing."

Palma gingerly lifted the magazine between thumb and forefinger as if it might be carrying germs. "Why do we care about pornography?"

H. G. Wells

"Because we care about influencing the minds of people. If nothing else, we care about millions of American Catholics."

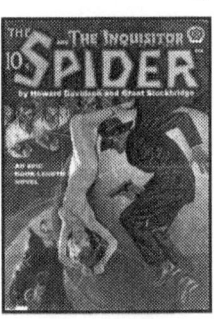

"They've never had effective censorship of periodicals," lamented Palma.

"Don't be a fool," snapped the Cardinal, patience at an end. "*Forget* the cover. *Forget* the sensationalism. The problem with this magazine is the intellectual content which is *never* censored in America."

"Intellectual?" echoed Palma, dismayed.

The Cardinal flipped to a certain page and read.

"During the Spanish Inquisition, a female heretic was burned at the stake even though she was pregnant."

Palma grimaced. "That would be atrocity propaganda if you had a pamphlet there instead of a fairy tale."

The Cardinal's brow wrinkled but the already yellowing page of cheap newsprint remained perfectly smooth. "The statement I just read is actually true. The source is even cited: one Cecil Roth, a Reader in Jewish Studies at Oxford University. He is doing a study that is sure to be a great advance on that old Protestant standby, Foxe's *Book of Martyrs*.

"The point is that the general public would never read an academic study on Spain's dark days. But they will learn about this unfortunate event in what they read for escapism."

The Cardinal finished his wine before continuing. "I should have

said Spain's *previous* dark days. But the public is always willing to learn its history as well as theology from popular entertainment. Why do you think the Nazis are so obsessed with their motion pictures?"

Father Palma followed the example set by the prince of the church and finished his wine as well. Emboldened, he blurted out: "I'm having trouble seeing what all these things have to do with each other; I mean Franklin and Disraeli and naked women on magazine covers."

"Elementary," answered his instructor.

"Back when the Church wielded real power, its primary concern was where its flock would spend eternity. To the modern mind, there is something peculiar about Catholics killing an expectant mother; but the Spanish authorities no doubt thought they were going to save her soul from eternal torment. They no doubt had a theory about her unborn child that does not exactly comport with modern thinking on the subject. Even we who serve the Church have forgotten the older way of thinking!

"Now that the world is about to be ripped to shreds again, the past is just as real as all the impossible futures promised by anarchists and communists and capitalists and democrats. They all deny Original Sin. Even Catholics have forgotten how to be Catholics. We have a chance to set things right. Maybe we'll begin in Spain."

"But how?" Father Palma really wanted to know.

The Cardinal waved the science fiction magazine under his priest's nose. "If you had this time machine and you could go back to meet Benjamin Franklin, would you try to convert him to the true faith?"

"I suppose so."

"A waste of time! Franklin wouldn't listen. Once a Mason, always a Mason. But you might try to persuade him to keep his more skeptical opinions to himself. Perhaps you could find a way to blackmail him. A role model is found in Disraeli whose rule for the good life was to talk politics endlessly in public, but never religion!

"You see, we should never concern ourselves over saving the soul of a genius. Far more important is to salvage the souls of fifty Spanish peasants or fifty English workingmen. That's where we have a significant point of agreement with the Communists; but only on that single point. We are here for the mass of mankind! The only justification for a brilliant mind is if it voluntarily surrenders itself to the good of the Common Man. Poor old Galileo could never grasp that basic point."

"And what about Hitler?"

"Spiritually, he serves our oldest enemy. He is both more compli-

cated and simpler than the Communists. Actually, the most dangerous Nazi is Alfred Rosenberg. That's why we put his *Myth of the Twentieth Century* on the Index of Banned Books. If the Reich conquers Europe, they will try to replace us with a Nordic Church."

The Spanish priest couldn't understand how the world had become so complex and so bizarre. His voice was

Adolf Hitler   small as he barely whispered, "Franco wants to save the

Francisco Franco

real Church and the traditional way of life."

"Of course he does. He's *our* Fascist. The General is more than an adventurer like Mussolini. He will have to work with the revolutionary Hitler but he must be cautious. For one thing, Hitler doesn't want a total victory for Franco. He wants the cauldron to keep bubbling while he draws up his plans and keeps his eyes on the Mediterranean."

Father Palma felt as though he had just enrolled in a doctoral program at a quaint little university on the shores of the River Styx. "So what is the threat represented by America and England?"

"The threat of individualism, of course. The dead end of Protestantism. We can only pray that one day they will see their error and rejoin us in the true communion. Maybe they will even apologize to the Virgin for all their calumnies over the centuries."

Father Palma now felt that his head was about to burst. It wasn't a physical ache so much as an agony of the soul. "Will I return to Spain?" he asked hopefully.

"Eventually. But you have work to do here first. Now I have a question for you. How far do you think your little war will spread?"

Palma's body sagged as he answered. "I fear that it is the beginning of another Great War that will engulf the world."

The Cardinal stood and put his hand on the priest's shoulder. "Well, look at the bright side. We may have more converts than ever! Peacetime can be dangerous for the soul."

Now Father Palma really felt sick. Again he had trouble breathing. He prayed to get outside into the fresh air.

The Cardinal sensed that his man couldn't take much more and declared their first session to be at an end. He wrapped it up.

"Later I'll explain the special problem we have with Eric Blair—that's the real name of George Orwell—and there's an even more severe difficulty with our fellow Catholic, Gilbert Keith Chesterton. That fat rogue is a most unpredictable journalist."

Palma had never read Orwell but he enjoyed many of Chesterton's detective stories. "What's the problem with Chesterton?" he couldn't resist asking.

G. K. Chesterton

"He almost died this year."

"Yes?"

"Well, he recovered. A new medical treatment. Now we find out that he refuses to support Franco. A real disappointment after the fine work he did on behalf of Mussolini back in 1930! And, it gets worse. He is working on a new book in which he displays a certain degree of sympathy for the anarchists."

Father Palma couldn't believe what exploded out of his own mouth: "Bloody hell!"

"I couldn't have said it better myself," the Cardinal assured him.

Cardinal Celi sat for a long time after he'd finally permitted the priest to exit his chambers. Was it only his imagination or had the room become perceptively warmer in the last hour?

For a moment he thought he heard the tinkling of bells.

In the Kremlin

The Secretary

Josef Stalin

There were other great religious buildings in the world besides those in Vatican City. Deep in the bowels of one such edifice sat a man smoking a pipe. Although there was much splendor to be found in the vast structure, Joseph Stalin lived in a small, sparsely furnished apartment.

He had once studied for the priesthood. Later, however, he discovered a new calling that he now pursued ferociously, to the dismay of many and the fanatical acclaim of others. His thoughts now turned to the day, in 1931, that he met George Bernard Shaw on the English writer's widely heralded goodwill visit. Ironically, the world famous-heretic had expressed concern over the planned destruction of the Church of the Savior. The church was an ugly eyesore looming over the far more important building in which this man now sat in glorious solitude. He ordered it demolished in 1933.

Church of Christ the Savior

Nothing could be allowed to compete with the architectural perfection of the Kremlin. Stalin would never permit it.

It had been easy, however, for the Soviet leader to deal with the elderly playwright. Stalin empha- sized the care that the Union of Soviet Socialist Republics had taken in preserving the older and more historically im- portant churches as museum pieces. That was enough to

The Kremlin

persuade Shaw that he was dealing with a civilized man in a civilized post-revolutionary society.

It was curious that he should dwell on such a trivial matter today, of all days. Perhaps his current attention to events in Western Europe accounted for his wandering thoughts. He was about to make a decision concerning a far more important—and even more antiquated—institu- tion that loomed on the western horizon. He had decided, therefore, to keep his own company and smoke his pipe until he resolved what to do about Spain.

Of course he didn't need to be alone in order to enjoy his long stretches of contemplative silence. He often wouldn't speak a word at a meeting of the Politboro. At least not until the end. By then his com- rades would have spewed forth oceans of words as Marxist intellectuals are wont to do. On those occasions at which Stalin would finally deign to speak, every ear in the room struggled to hear. Sometimes he would deliberately lower his voice and make them all lean forward in order to pick up every nuance.

When they did that, he imagined they were all stretching out their necks to provide the General Secretary of the Communist Party with a more tempting tar- get. In his present mood, the map of Spain on his desk was reminding him of necks wait- ing to be cut. On the map, the country seemed like a grotesque head sticking out into the ocean. The neck was France.

He looked over his desk. An unopened bottle of vodka and an untouched supply of Black Sea caviar might have tempted him some other time. But not when he had de- cided to smoke and think. In addition to his

Josef Stalin, 1935

memory of its pleasant salty taste, the caviar provided an additional pleasant association. It came from the one place in his empire where he felt really relaxed, especially when vacationing on the Black Sea with his young wife, Nadezhda, and their friends. The diminishing circle of their friends . . .

He ran his hand across the map of Spain. What to do about this one? There were almost too many considerations, even for him. He accidentally knocked a letter to the floor from an eminent Russian scientist. Retrieving it, he shook his head in wonder at the nonsense that was always crossing his desk. But at least this man was harmless and still useful in his daily work.

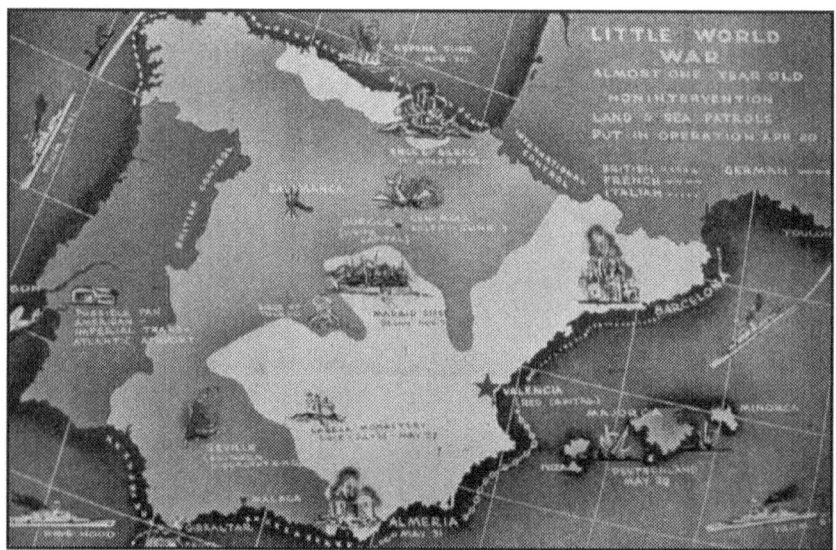

Stalin didn't often admire audacity but he wasn't opposed to it as a matter of principle. This professor began by acclaiming Stalin as the builder of true socialism and therefore of the future. He had certain types of heroes in mind. The man was obsessed with the aviator Charles Lindbergh as an American version of Lenin's idea of the man of the future. He named some German flyers on which he bestowed the same honor. Finally, he also had the good sense to include some Russians.

But, the crux of the letter concerned a 1929 meeting between Lindbergh and the rocket expert, Robert Goddard. This poor professor was convinced that the first country to master rockets would conquer the world. Therefore, he worried about Germany's artillery and arms limitations as she was currently bound under the Treaty of Versailles. The professor feared that Germany would use *rocket research* as a dodge

Robert Goddard and Charles Lindberg

around these constraints. He worried, further, that this rocket research might lead to some dangerous German military advantages.

Stalin almost tossed the letter in the trash and then thought better of it. He filed it in his desk. The professor was a typical intellectual. Instead of assuming that Germans would simply ignore the rules about heavy guns and shells, the poor man fantasized they'd launch an impractical rocket program worthy of a boy's serial adventure.

The leader of the Communist world had more important things to do. He had to get back to the problem of the Spanish War.

Again he fixated on France, the neck attached to the Spanish mess. He didn't want a problem with France because he didn't want a problem with the League of Nations. He wondered why France didn't support the Republic over the Fascists, simply for her own self-interest. He blamed the British for confusing the issue and for not just leaving bad enough alone. The two Capitalist democracies had set up Nonintervention Committees. How very typical of them! Lenin would not have been surprised.

Vladimir Lenin

Stalin had his own choices to make. Under no circumstances could the Soviet Union enter this war officially. That was the first consideration. The second consideration was a far more serious matter and it cut to the very core of what Stalin was building and what his ultimate enemy, Trotsky, sought to undermine.

His pipe had gone out. As he refilled it, he let his eyes drift over to the single book on an otherwise empty shelf, *The Foundations of Leninism*. The writing involved in the creation of that book had not come easily for him. His greatest pride was that Trotsky found fault with the prose.

His other great pride concerning the book lay in the fact that average workers eagerly read the book and often admitted it was the first time that they had really understood Lenin. Officially, Stalin embraced Trotsky's other criticism: that there were no original ideas in Stalin's contribution to the Marxist oeuvre. By the time his enemy realized his mistake it was too late.

Even as a boy, Stalin realized that if he became a priest he would never contribute anything original to Theology. A belief system was only useful if the masses believed. The secret to power was to find what most people believed and operate accordingly. Jesus had served as a

Karl Marx

guide to that secret for a long time, but now his day was done. Marx and Lenin now replaced Him.

But there was still room for originality, even a necessity, if one wished to climb to the top of any power pyramid. Here the great Trotsky with the floating abstractions in his head, sailed right over the reality of what Stalin was doing, and failed to recognize the seed planted in Stalin's clumsy book.

The Communist Party boss became adept at quoting Lenin out of context and patiently began constructing the case that true socialism could be achieved in the USSR regardless of what happened in the rest of the world. Trotsky was right, of course, when he insisted that Lenin always intended Communism to be strictly an international movement—hence the importance of the Comintern.

Leon Trotsky

But Trotsky found himself on the wrong side of the practical issue, as usual. As for the Comintern, Stalin learned that national interests could be served through an international organization. This was simply a matter of reality. The capitalists weren't going to just roll over and die, while the Fascists were as ruthless as the Party itself.

And one day these two forces might come together against the Soviet Union. Stalin could not allow that to happen, even if it meant that occasionally he had to form an alliance with one enemy against the other. He thought the best idea the Party hacks ever generated was arguing that Fascism was the final stage of Capitalism. That was a good one!

Whatever happened in the years to come, Stalin would save the Russian people no matter how many millions of them he had to kill.

But now he must solve the Spanish problem, threatening, as it did, to stand in the way of building the future. The second consideration—after the importance of the Soviet Union not entering the war—was that Moscow should not be seen as an "exporter" of revolutions. Especially not now when the world was moving in the dangerous direction of another full-scale European war.

But, there was yet a third consideration, the problem of public image. The leader of the Communist Party couldn't be seen to stand idly by and do *nothing* when a revolution was erupting in Spain. Every idealistic fool was flocking to the banner of the Republic. Because it was a

civil war, the intellectual class lied to itself that no national interests interfered with the purity of revolutionary ideals.

The incredible fools.

Lenin's famous question, "What is to be done?" weighed on Stalin's mind. For all the times he was glad that his mentor was no longer around to block the progress of his protégé, Stalin would have been perfectly happy for the bearded ghost to appear before him now and offer some sage advice.

Concluding his musings, Stalin quickly produced the outlines of a workable plan. A few more puffs on his old pipe and the initial tactical decisions were made. He would work through Vladimir Antonov-Ovseyenko, an old Red Guard soldier who would make good use of his time as Consul-General in Barcelona. The man was a natural-born infiltrator and he would have his work cut out for him in that cesspool of anarchists, Trotskyites, and other counter-revolutionaries. He would never be taken in by the lies of the deviationist, factionalist POUM, whose so-called Marxist leaders had dubbed him *Stalinist Thermidorians*, the poison dictator. Vladimir could also help with the problems in Catalonia, a place swarming with infantile leftist vermin.

No one to the left of the Party could be countenanced. It was just that simple.

He blew smoke at the map and envisioned the clouds of his vengeance descending on the countryside. Franco was the least of his problems but he'd have to fight him somehow. The solution was the Comintern. All aid must go through the international organizations.

The Comintern members would send in their own volunteers and they, in turn, would form organizations to receive the aid. They could also infiltrate other organizations that would receive aid in the same manner. The charming sadists in the NKVD would keep tabs on everyone. Best of all, a chain of export-import firms would be set up throughout Europe to keep everything flowing. That trick always worked well for the British.

Stalin put down his pipe. He had the plan. Now he could enjoy some of that caviar and vodka. As he opened the bottle, the final touch of his plan fell into place.

Ideally, not one piece of equipment should reach the Republic until they guaranteed payment. No Anglo-American banker could run a harder bargain. It would take some really strange twists and turns for him to extend credit, although he supposed that anything was possible.

He knew that the Republic had a gold reserve of five-hundred million dollars. They could send it by train to Odessa. There was nothing the world's premiere Marxist-Leninist leader liked better than payment in hard currency.

With a roar of satisfaction he opened the Vodka and drank straight from the bottle, like a good Russian peasant. With his other hand he made a fist and struck dead center at the heart of Spain laid out before him.

CHAPTER 4

The Geniuses

Young Rocket Man at Play

"Those boys will be the death of us," said Mom.

"That's the trouble with genius," said Dad.

The boys in question were Konrad Zuse and Wernher von Braun. Konrad was their son. They had basically adopted Wernher. It helped that the Zuses ran a foster home. But no one was fooling anyone about the bond of friendship that had grown between the two boys. Konrad didn't make friends easily and Wernher was even worse. The boys would have become best friends under any circumstances that brought them together.

The Zuses were middle class. They never expected to receive into their care a young man from their social betters. But, so far, the life of Wernher von Braun was worthy of Wagnerian Opera, and it was only the beginning.

Von Braun was a classic example of a Prussian aristocrat: quiet, distant, and undemonstrative. He couldn't help it. Getting him to tell his story had been a labor of love for the Zuses, and finally he relented and the tale was told.

His tragedy began in 1922 when, at the age of ten, he conducted a precocious experiment involving his little red wagon. Inspired by a co-

Wernher von Braun

medic French silent film depicting a trip to the Moon, Wernher made his first serious effort in the field of rocket propulsion. He tied six skyrockets to his little red wagon. They were Chinese handmade rockets and von Braun announced, "I'm learning Chinese!"

The experiment was not exactly a success. He launched the wagon into the center of Berlin where it exploded. The event might have remained a comedy except that a woman was killed.

Von Braun's family was important. But so was the family of the deceased. She had been a high-society matron. There was nothing von Braun's father could do to keep his son out of Juvenile Hall.

As a result of this calamity, von Braun's mother became seriously ill. She never fully recovered and his father always blamed him. Sadly, the day the doors of the prison for adolescents slammed shut on their son, the family gave up all hope for young Wernher. They had wanted him to be a great German musician. Now he was just another German victim, lost in the ruins of a shattered Empire.

His pre-adolescent aristocratic style didn't win him any friends in Juvenile Hall. The thugs who beat him up were usually Communists or members of a fledgling political party called the National Socialists Workers Party. He hated them both. Eventually he learned that he could usually save himself by playing them off against each other.

Given his size and strength, Wernher almost always won any fair fight. That's why the Communists and Nazis ganged up on him. From this experience he concluded that both groups were made up primarily of cowardly bullies.

The Zuse family had no disagreements with Konrad's outspoken friend about the followers in these political movements. The father merely pointed out that it was a mistake to conclude that the *leaders* of these movements were also cowards and could, therefore be dismissed as inconsequential. It was more accurate, he claimed, to view them as dangerous psychopaths who had discovered the road to power through the mob.

The Zuses had been having adult conversations with their son for years and sometimes forgot how unusual that was. The new lad fit right into this pattern and it was only a matter of time before von Braun was virtually adopted by the family.

There was, in fact, no better place for young Wernher to end up. He lived in an open house for intellectuals and engineers and scientists. Von Braun had found a new home. He never spoke of his mother's death and the final estrangement from his real father.

But it wasn't enough that the young von Braun had his dream of interplanetary travel. Young Zuse had a dream as well and one just as fantastic. He was obsessed with building the world's first thinking machine. His favorite play was *R.U.R., Rossum's Universal Robots*. The Czech author, Karel Capek, had coined the term *"robot"* to describe a race of artificially-created thinking machines

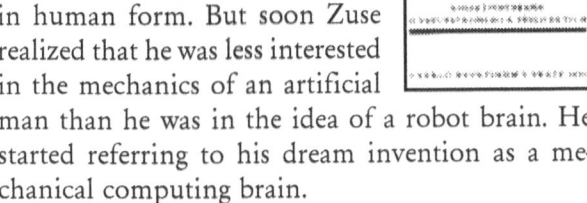

in human form. But soon Zuse realized that he was less interested in the mechanics of an artificial

Robot's Rebellion

man than he was in the idea of a robot brain. He started referring to his dream invention as a mechanical computing brain.

The next logical step was for the two teenagers to imagine Zuse's computer brain *inside* von Braun's super rocket. Together they would explore the solar system, genuine partners in an enterprise where each depended on the other.

"Do you think they're crazy?" asked Mom.

"Who cares?" answered Dad. "I never thought I'd see Konrad cooperate with another fellow being. I thought he was both too brilliant and too selfish. I never realized that all he needed was someone else just like him."

Sometimes, when the night was warm, the boys would go outside together and look at the stars. In any other household in Germany, they might have been looked at askance. There might have been mutterings that there was something odd about those two.

But not here. They were safe here. Any attractive young girl would have been welcome to join them in their gazing at the stars and the Moon. They'd accept her quickly enough . . . so long as she could do the math.

"Why do you want to leave the Earth?" asked Konrad on one of those evenings. They'd stopped looking through his telescope and now lay together on the grass.

"Religious people always say they want to go to Heaven after they die," von Braun answered, "but I know they're lying. Have you ever really listened to them?"

"No."

"Well, I have. Their idea of Heaven is the same boring life they've experienced all their lives."

"That's just being bourgeois."

Von Braun hooted. "You're wrong. All classes are the same when it comes to this. They are all of the Earth and if they can't be on it, they want to be in it. I'm not like other people. I want to explore the Universe. I want to enter the Heavens, not as a spirit but as a living man."

Konrad let out a low whistle. "I believe you. The stupid blockheads would probably be afraid of you when they should be more afraid of me. You just want to leave them behind."

"What do you want to do?"

Konrad Zuse tapped his chin with his right forefinger and then made a proclamation. "Replace them, of course."

Von Braun sighed. "Isn't that too much like the people we hate? The Reds and the brownshirts, I mean."

"Not at all. Bolsheviks just want everyone to be factory workers and soldiers. Nazis want everyone to be militaristic street brawlers and peasants. I want to replace everyone."

"With robots?"

"With superior minds. But we'll never get there through natural means."

"What about eugenics?"

"Racial nonsense or class nonsense. It can't possibly work because they're breeding the same human stock no matter what they do."

"And your solution?"

"Build better brains artificially and then create hybrid human-robots. Then everyone will speak the same logical language. We'll pull down the Tower of Babel!"

The two young men didn't talk for a while. A soft breeze stirred their hair. The stars shown down like the billion eyes of curious angels. Finally, von Braun put in his two marks worth.

"You're crazy, you know."

"Of course! The same as you."

"No, I'm crazy in a different way."

"So you wouldn't care to join me in creating the New Man?"

"That's not my department," said Wernher von Braun.

"Well, it's just idle speculation. In any case, of the two of us, you are the more dangerous."

Von Braun propped himself on an elbow for a better view of his best friend. "What do you mean?" he asked.

Zuse sat up and looked his pal in the eye. "What I want to build is a lot harder than what you will build. Rockets will be quite advanced long before I get the kind of robot brain I'm really after."

"So why does that make *me* dangerous?"

Zuse looked up to the sky but not to see the stars. He was just exasperated. "Wernher, where will you aim your rockets?"

The long Prussian arm pointed straight up. "I aim at the stars."

"That's what I figure. But others will see a more immediate use for your dream. You are building one of the greatest weapons the world has ever known."

"I am?"

"You are."

"I never thought of that."

Zuse laughed. "After your time in Juvenile Hall? Remember how you got there? You turned a child's wagon into a flying bomb. That should give you some clue."

"Are you saying what I'm doing is wrong?"

Konrad Zuse laughed again. "Certainly not. But sometimes I think the most naïve people in the world are aristocrats. I have something you lack, Wernher. It's called common sense. You'll just have to make the most of life with the gifts you have and then hope for the best."

Von Braun stood up and looked at the sky. "I suppose I'll be attacked by religious leaders."

"A badge of honor," said Zuse. "The priests will say you're immoral and the rabbis will say you're unethical. And you know what they'll do when the next war comes? They'll thank their idiot God for the weapons you'll put in their hands and forget that you had anything to do with it."

Von Braun wrinkled his brow in thought. "I'm not the cynic that you are."

"You're an idealist, the disease of the upper classes. That's why we'll make a good team. You aim at the stars and I'll keep your feet on Earth. We'll be a great team in the next war."

"What makes you so certain there will be another?"

"The Treaty of Versailles guarantees it."

"You'll fight for the Fatherland?"

"Maybe not," said Zuse, which surprised them both.

"You wouldn't go over to the allies?" von Braun challenged him.

"Certainly not."

Von Braun laughed. "So maybe we're two pacifists. We can sit the next one out."

Zuse jumped to his feet and began dancing around his friend. This was the most unusual behavior von Braun had seen since Juvenile Hall.

"Wernher, don't you get it? We'll simply choose our own war. Maybe we'll declare ourselves a country and make war on the rest of the world."

"And why are we doing this?"

"To build the future. Think about it. Every political moron wants to construct a new world, right? But when he's finished, it's just the same old world with new people on top and the old establishment dead or in exile. What's new about that? Who cares who is rich or poor? Who cares who is master or slave? It's the same old shit."

"I've never thought about it that way," von Braun admitted.

"When you and I talk about a new world, we actually mean it!"

The two stood silent in the night. Zuse had surprised himself with his own words. Von Braun had never thought about such things before.

They were two teenage boys beginning a conversation that would last them the rest of their lives. They were old before their time, literate, analytical, a bit mad. There were no "adult" conversations going on at that moment as important as theirs.

Wernher von Braun had decided that the most dangerous revolutionary is one who acts with almost perfect indifference to his own fate when he seeks, not power, but the truth. The quest for knowledge bound the two boys to one another.

"We'll just have to find the right cause one of these days," said Zuse finally. "Then we'll tie your red wagon to it and you can count down to blast-off!"

"What if there's a God?" von Braun asked suddenly. He had received Catholic instruction as a child.

"The odds are against it but I hope there is one," answered his comrade.

"Why?"

The young man who would build the world's first computer was very clear: "I'll admit my faith. If there are gods or goddesses, I believe they only care about humans who are like themselves."

Sometime During the War
The Farmer

Once upon a time there was a man named Orgaz. He had no politics. He had a little bit of religion. He had one wife and two sons. Most of all he had work.

From a very young age his father had instilled in him the essence of pride. He never thought about it. He could not tell anyone the meaning of duty. But in his soul was the basic hierarchy of values that General Franco always talked about: family, Church, country.

Orgaz worked the fields. His skin was naturally brown but a whole life spent in the sun had darkened him until he almost seemed part of the dark, rich soil himself. He was like the land. The land is neither heroic nor cowardly. It persists.

If supporting his wife and children was brave, then he was a hero.

If volunteering to fight for causes is the mark of courage, then he was a coward.

He was in the wrong place at the wrong time. He was in the wrong job. The revolutionaries came to him and said he had a duty to the people and his own class. He didn't know what they were talking about. He was told about the Republic. It was the first he'd ever heard of it.

They warned him that he must develop a revolutionary spirit or things might go badly for his family, who knew even less than he did about such things. He was still very confused but he said he would try to learn. It would have helped immeasurably had he known how to read.

The Nationalists came later. They delivered almost the same speech, except that they said he had a duty to his country. They used the same words as the revolutionaries except they didn't care about classes. The important thing was the he was Spanish. Almost as an afterthought, they reminded him that he had duties to the Church. He explained in his faltering way that he'd already paid the tithe and hoped that he and his family were safe from eternal damnation, at least for a while.

His wife asked him if he could explain what all the people were telling him. They had gone years without many words exchanged between them and now suddenly they were besieged with strangers who talked and talked.

"They want me to do things," he said.

"What things?"

"Many things. Different things. I'm not sure," he admitted.

The land was simple and he respected it. If, sometimes, it did not feed him and his family, it never lectured him. The land wasn't Fascist or Anarchist or Communist or Socialist. The soil had no opinions except one. If you worked it and the weather was good and the rains came at the right times in the right amounts, you would have food. If not, not.

The men who came to Orgaz confused him and gave him headaches. Sometimes he wished they'd go expound their theories to his cow. The cow was a good a listener and understood just about as much.

One night he dreamed that one of the "talking" men came and said these words to him:

"Orgaz, I am here to speak for the land. You are not expected to do anything but farm. If you have a good crop, you don't have to do anything with it you don't want to. After all, your fellow Spaniards leave you alone when you have nothing but dirt. They don't come and try to take away your dirt. They don't ask you to put it in sacks and give it to different strangers who make a claim upon you. So from now on the same rule applies to your crop. If you want to sell it or trade it or give it away, it's yours. There is no government any longer. There is no landlord. There are no soldiers or committees of land reform. There is no one to collectivize the farms."

"Where did everyone go?" he imagined himself asking in the dream.

"God took them all away."

"Why?"

"Because God doesn't like them anymore."

He woke up in a cold sweat. He was afraid he might have sinned in his dream so he got on his knees and said several Hail Mary's. His wife wondered if he was all right but he told her to go back to sleep.

For several days no one bothered him and he felt a deep contentment. Perhaps all of the strong men and their fierce words had moved on and they had forgotten Orgaz. There was no deeper bliss for a man of the soil than to be ignored.

But he was not so fortunate. They came, finally, and arrested him. At first he wasn't sure who was taking him but then they told him. Franco's men were arresting him as a terrorist. They put him in the back of a truck.

One soldier told Orgaz he was an Anarchist. Another soldier corrected the first and said that he was a Communist. As he tried to find out which he was so he could apologize to all concerned, one of the officers told the men to shut up. The crime of Orgaz was that he was arrested and that was all anyone needed to know.

In a strange way, Orgaz almost felt relieved. The officer was easier to understand. It was like the simplicity of the land instead of the confusion of politics.

They drove a good distance and then picked up another man. He screamed, "Death to Fascist pigs!" No one bothered to reveal the man's political affiliation so Orgaz assumed that he already knew what he was and didn't need any assistance.

An hour later they picked up a third person, a bedraggled old woman. She spit at the officers and said nothing. She made Orgaz think of an old witch. Then they drove another hour.

As the sun was coming up they reached their final destination. It was precisely nowhere. Orgaz had expected some sort of building at least. He assumed that they were taking him to prison.

For one sad, fleeting moment he hoped that perhaps they'd been brought to this place to do some farming. The soldiers didn't look very well fed.

The three prisoners were taken out of the back of the truck and told to line up. They didn't do it very well. The soldiers formed an even more ragged line and started fiddling with their rifles.

With a sinking feeling Orgaz realized there wouldn't be any farming. "What about my family?" he blurted out.

The officer in charge answered, "Don't worry. They're not on the list."

Although Orgaz had meant to ask who would take care of them, he elected to leave well enough alone. If his wife and children were not to be shot he'd take what solace he could from that.

The Spanish word for misfortune is *desventura*. It carries a deeper meaning than the English equivalent. For Orgaz, the full import of his situation came to him a moment later when he saw one of the officers approach the other. He was brandishing his list and muttering so swiftly that it was difficult to make out the words.

The commanding officer swore. Orgaz could make that out, and then he heard the last words of the conversation.

"How could this farmer be the *wrong* man?" asked the officer in charge.

"It's a mix-up. The name is similar to one of the POUM members."

The burden of command weighed heavily at that moment. "We came all this distance to shoot three. Only three!"

"I'm sorry, sir. What do we do?"

Orgaz could have told them, if they had bothered to ask his opinion. It was a lot like farming. You could only abide so much wasted effort. Sometimes you brought in a miserably small crop and called it a day.

They allowed the three a moment to pray. Only Orgaz availed himself of the opportunity. The other two prisoners didn't seem very religious.

Right before the bullets crashed into his skull, Orgaz felt sorry for the officer who was put on the spot like that. Neither of them was having a good day.

Dear John #1

POSTCARD FROM HOWARD DAVIDSON

Dear John,

Sorry that I haven't had much time for letters. I promise to rectify that soon. The weather was terrible this winter but now it's starting to change for the better. I think the spring is going to be pretty nice in '37.

You can see from the card that I'm in Guernica, a gorgeous old Basque town. I'll be moving on to Madrid next week. I'll wrap this up for now with an old Protestant verse about this alien planet I'm visiting:

> *Of all the nations in the Universe,*
> *There's none sure can compare*
> *With Spain for bloody sentences*
> *As I'll to you declare.*

CHAPTER 5

Madrid, Spring 1937

The Literati

Dead soldiers lying like so many broken dolls in a pile. A human intestine dangling from the jaws of a hungry dog. A wailing woman, consumed with grief, embracing the body of her lover in a field of corpses.

These were the images the writer had jotted down in his notebook. But they were the furthest things from his mind when it was time for him to make a public statement. After all, he was expected to be a thinker as well as a reporter and an artist.

"I like Communists when they're soldiers, but when they're priests, I hate them," said Ernest Hemingway.

The highest paid war correspondent in the world knew how to play a room. He had just finished singing a Spanish folk song, while accompanying himself on the guitar. The other writers making up his court at the Hotel Florida hung on his every word. They were all staying in the same section of Madrid. It was a point of honor with them that no one showed visible signs of panic whenever Nationalist bombs exploded nearby. Hemingway was among them, the embodiment of heroic manliness in an intellectual's trade. The other writers didn't want to show any yellow around him.

As for himself, part of his courage was to tweak the nose of Marxist

Ernest Hemingway

orthodoxy while at the same time ingratiating himself with the Comintern. If he played his cards right, he would have access to Soviet-trained generals the other journalists would only see from afar. It always helped that he was a celebrity. The only party discipline that appealed to him was staying just sober enough to make love at the end of an evening's song and dance.

Dos warned him that he might end up writing for *Pravda* if he didn't watch his step. John Dos Passos was "Dos," his companion on this journey. He'd think of him as a comrade except that, of late, Dos was so critical of the Soviets that Hemingway feared he might slip from being an independent man of the left and turn into a dreaded reactionary.

John Dos Passos

The world was in a mess.

Hemingway promised himself that his time in Spain as a journalist would be as important as his experiences in the Great War that led to his most successful novel (to date), *A Farewell to Arms*. It helped immeasurably that this current conflict transcended the usual patriotic hot air. This was the first war for progressives and radicals since Lenin came to power in 1917. But in many quarters the Bolshevik victory had been falsely perceived as just a Civil War among Russians. Jack Reed had done his best to correct that mistake in his *Ten Days that Shook the World*. The first Communist society was a challenge to the entire world.

John Reed

Now the Civil War in Spain was potentially even more important! People from all over the world were volunteering for the Republican cause. What writer worth his salt would pass up the opportunity to be part of a revolution for the rights of man? This was especially true for a red-blooded all American writer like Hemingway who, through some inexplicable misfortune, had not been present at the revolutionary founding of his own country. Spain provided the opportunity to correct that oversight by the Almighty.

The only problem on this glorious day in 1937 was that Madrid had misplaced the Café Fornos, one of his favorite hang-outs from the past. In its place now stood a dull office building. This was carrying revolutionary change too far.

He had noted the absence of the café a few weeks ago when he first arrived in Madrid. Today he felt its loss with a special intensity. He had promised Dos Passos a drink on those special premises. He didn't want to feel like a fool on the first day of April. Then again, he hadn't seen much of Dos lately and the café might not have made a difference. Dos had become obsessed with finding a missing friend, not an easy or perhaps even a wise thing to do in the middle of a war.

There was one way Madrid could make it up to both of them. The city was in the process of expanding its position as the current capital of the Republic. Maybe if it became the capital of a "new world" revolution, even eclipsing Moscow, the great American novelist could forgive it for tearing down the Café Fornos.

Of course, the actual government had already been moved to an area of theoretical safety in Valencia. That happened back in November. He had begun posting dispatches on March 22nd. At least the Republic was showing some strategic sense. Perhaps it had a chance, after all.

Also in Madrid's favor was the fact that the wine supply was holding out. Hemingway had already emptied a wineskin before making his public appearance. Now he was working on the same full-bodied red wine, but with the aid of a glass.

A hand shot up from the crowd of writers. If Hemingway recognized the man, he would effectively transform a casual meeting of writers and reporters into his own personal press conference. He didn't hesitate.

"Yes?" he asked.

"Do you have any copies with you of *Death in the Afternoon?*" the man inquired with a thick French accent.

Hemingway shook his head but was secretly pleased that his book on bullfighting remained a popular favorite. He couldn't set

foot in Spain without hearing about his book on bulls. Two minor controversies dogged his tracks as a result. He had criticized the Second Republic, founded in '31 after King Alfonso fled the country, for trying to restrict the proud tradition of the Matadors. The other quarrel was purely personal, a result of Max Eastman taking the

Max Eastman side of little old ladies against a manly art while pretend-

Max Perkins

ing to be the better man. Hemingway hated hypocrisy.

At least, he hated certain kinds of hypocrisy.

"Actually, I'm here to write a *new* book!" he said to a smattering of applause. "But that's not as important as offering honest reporting about this noble cause. What is the worth of any book when compared to the authorship of a new world!"

Having neatly conflated the role of the journalist with that of advocacy, he received another, more energetic round of applause. He pushed his wire-rimmed glasses back on his nose and smiled at the tavern keeper. "How about a round of drinks on my publisher?" he asked with his characteristic grin, often compared to Teddy Roosevelt's. "Old Maxie won't mind."

And the truth of it was that Hemingway could get away with a lot from his editor, old Maxwell Perkins when he delivered the goods.

He got no argument from his fellow wordsmiths. But he received something else, just as the motley crew of thirsty writers bellied up to the bar. He turned to see who was tapping him on the shoulder and saw a shorter man with a large head and neatly trimmed goatee smiling up at him. The man was holding up a copy of *Death in the Afternoon*.

"I brought my own," he said and Hemingway instantly recognized a fellow American.

"A good break for you," he said. "As I told the Frenchman, I'm fresh out."

"The book has been with me all over Spain. I was in Guernica last month. Not much is happening there. Anyway, I was wondering if I could have your autograph?"

Hemingway snorted in the manner of one of his prized bulls. "You're my first successful request for an autograph on this trip. OK. What's your name?"

"Howard Davidson."

As Hemingway filled most of the title page with his signature, he asked, "What paper are you with?"

"Actually, I'm a fiction writer," Howard told him.

"Have I seen some of your stuff?" asked Hemingway, returning the book.

"Depends on whether you read the pulps," said Howard, producing a rolled-up copy of the November 1935 issue of *The Inquisitor*. Hemingway

Gertrude Stein

laughed as he glanced at the title of that issue's installment, "The Crimson Citadel."

"May I give you that one?" asked Howard hopefully.

"Tell you what," replied the world-famous novelist, "just send me a number of these through my New York publisher. Maybe I'll pass one on to Gertrude Stein." He tried to curb a malicious smile but the pulpmeister caught a glimpse.

Crestfallen, Howard tried to put his best face on the brush-off. "It will be easy for me to deliver copies," he said. "I live in the city."

As Hemingway passed the magazine back to its author a large, pudgy hand intercepted the object of lost desires.

G. K. Chesterton, 1935

"Mind if *I* take a look at that?" asked a baritone voice.

Both men turned to see a very large and very fat man wearing old-fashioned spectacles and puffing on the remains of a thoroughly vile little cigar.

"I don't believe it," said Davidson.

"I thought you were dead," said Hemingway.

"The reports of my death were not exaggerated," answered Gilbert Keith Chesterton. "They were merely premature. I was saved by a doctor whom I once thought a quack. In my simple credulity, I must pronounce the affair a miracle."

The two Americans stared in astonishment, watching the famous English writer peruse the decidedly purple narrative of an American pulp magazine. The man's mere physical appearance in this place seemed a miracle all by itself. The fat man didn't seem the type to rough it, at least not at this stage in his life.

Hemingway on the Front, 1937

Hemingway never ducked when he heard the whizzing of bullets. He knew the odds as well as an experienced officer. He had become jaded about exploding shells. But he could dread the adverse traveling conditions of the younger men who came to volunteer for the Loyalist cause. Hiking in the barren countryside; sleeping in dirty train cars among sick, filthy and coughing men; unable to dry off when soaked by freezing rain—these were the true horrors of war! Death by bullet or bomb paled into insignificance against the terror of disease.

Yet here was G. K. Chesterton, a vision from the Edwardian Age, looking none the worse for wear. A few of the other writers began drifting over, intrigued by the spectacle of something new under the sun.

"Do you mind if I hold onto this?" Chesterton asked Howard, brandishing the copy of *The Inquisitor.*

"Not at all," gasped Howard. "I've always loved your novel *The Man Who was Thursday.*"

"Yes, it may be my most popular piece among those outside the faith," he said.

"I'm partial to *The Man Who Knew Too Much,*" said Hemingway.

"I would have thought you wouldn't care for my paradoxes," smiled Chesterton.

"I don't mind those as much as I do your overuse of metaphors," answered Hemingway. "Once a year I allow myself a simile!"

"You should allow yourself more of them," said Chesterton. "I liked your description of the soldier in the Great War who seems pregnant because of the weaponry he carries under his raincoat as protection from the downpour."

"Thanks," said Hemingway in clipped tones. "But it's not as if men fight wars in order to give us grist for our literary mills."

"A nice bit of imagery," said Chesterton with a smile.

Hemingway reminded himself that it was April Fools Day. He couldn't have picked a more auspicious date for this unlikely encounter. He prided himself on being a direct man with clear purposes. Life was about the moment of truth. It didn't matter how many or how few of those moments crossed your path. When you faced such a moment, you didn't turn your back on it.

In many ways, he saw Chesterton as the enemy of the human race. He put the British writer in the same camp as his mother. They both subscribed to ancient superstitions as a guide to living. The differences between them were incidental. Chesterton was a member of the Roman Catholic minority in England, while his mother discontented herself as a bible-thumping prude, a unique strain of intolerant American Protestants. They were both believers. The time had come for the world to grow up.

Mussolini

And so, Hemingway fired off the first salvo. "That was a nice piece you wrote about Mussolini some years back."

"No better than what you wrote on his behalf," replied Chesterton.

Damn! Chesterton's material on the founder of Italian Fascism had been more widely discussed than Hemingway's brief observations to the effect that the *Duce* wasn't all that bad. This was truly a day of surprises. Hemingway found it difficult to dis-

Martha Gellhorn

like a man who read him as thoroughly as Chesterton seemed to have done, and without publishing a single bad review.

H. L. Mencken

Already he liked Chesterton better than H. L. Mencken who never gave his books a decent break.

Suddenly there was flash of light. It wasn't a bomb going off. Neither was it an angelic visitation coming to the aid of the rotund Papist. Blinking his eyes back into focus he saw the grinning face of his mistress, Martha Gellhorn. She was holding his own camera that he'd been using to take pictures of the war. She'd caught the two literary titans together.

Hemingway noticed that Davidson was preening himself, stroking his goatee in a perversely suggestive manner. Well, it would be a simple enough operation to crop out the science-fiction writer later.

Marty threw Hemingway a kiss and mouthed, "I love you, Hem." Then she exited with a flourish.

"You are a famous man," said Chesterton as he puffed on the last of his cigar.

"What really counts is how we use our fame," said Hemingway and then dealt with this moment of truth. "Do you support Franco?"

"No," said Chesterton.

"Hooray!" said Davidson. "We're all good guys here."

Hemingway stared in amazement at his fellow Yank. Was this guy for real? But Chesterton put a fine point on it by patting Davidson on the shoulder. "Yes, it is all about heroes and scoundrels, isn't it?"

Davidson bit his lip as he remembered the copy of his magazine under Chesterton's elbow. "I'm afraid that you'll find that my work is a little bit anti-Catholic," he said sheepishly.

"Don't worry about it," answered his newfound friend. "It's not as easy to be anti-Catholic as you think. Sometimes it requires a career in the Church."

A reporter from the *Times of London* chose this moment to interject.

"Do you support all the revolutionary elements of the Republic?"

At first, Hemingway almost answered, so accustomed was he to being the center of attention. But he knocked back his drink and let Chesterton respond to the question clearly intended for him:

"The Republic is untidy like any democracy. You might as well ask if I support everyone in Parliament! Although if you narrow your question to the House of Lords, I can reply with a resounding *nay!*"

A woman with a pinched face got into the act. She was the only one in the room wearing a beret and a red scarf, mimicking the dress codes of POUM; but, it was general knowledge that she was only a writer from a small left-wing paper in Greece. Hemingway hated the sound of her voice. She reminded him of a librarian who would never let him check out books from the adult section back when he was a kid.

"Aren't you a notorious defender of Privilege and the Church?" she spat out at Chesterton.

"It is because I defend the Church that I must attack privilege," he responded mildly.

"But the Church and the Fascists are one!" she shrieked. "The POUM recently executed a priest for informing on villagers who admitted they were against Franco. They told him this in confession! How can you defend that?"

"I can't and won't defend that," answered Chesterton amiably.

"They shot him!" she replied angrily.

"A priest who violates the sanctity of the confession has more to worry about than a few bullets ending his life."

She cackled. "I thought you believed in the sanctity of life."

"I believe in the sanctity of the *soul*. A short, brave life is better than a cowardly long one."

She wandered off, mumbling to herself.

"You are not a normal Catholic," Davidson suddenly blurted out.

Chesterton smiled. "I'm sure you mean that as a compliment."

Hemingway grunted. These two were the most unlikely creatures he'd encountered on this trip. He must bring this matter to a close. Most importantly, he must get the spotlight back on himself.

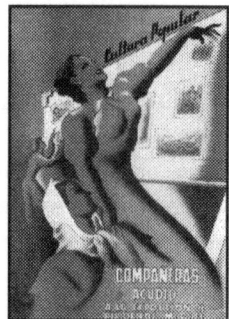

G. K. Chesterton

"Mr. Chesterton," he said in a slow and ponderous voice. Right away he had the crowd with him again. Formality was not the norm with him.

"Yes, Mr. Hemingway?"

"Why are you here?"

"For the same reason, I imagine, as yourself. To observe and write but also to lend aid to the Republican cause."

Hemingway shook his head. "Are you crazy? Catholics are not wanted here. The Roman Church is part of the problem. They are part of the landlord class that starves the peasants and workers."

"I come from a country where the Roman Church is not the landlord," he said.

Howard Davidson couldn't help blurting out, "I know the answer!"

There were few things more irritating to Hemingway than someone actually answering a rhetorical question. Especially when that someone was a pulp writer.

"The Distributist movement," Davidson went on, encouraged by a nod from Chesterton. "They advocate redistribution of the *land* instead of monetary wealth. They have a lot in common with Jeffersonians."

"Exactly," said Chesterton. "The poor people of Spain have been told for a long time that they don't own the land. How does collectivization of the land change anything? Isn't that another form of rent, at least in practice?"

"The people will decide for themselves," said Hemingway grimly. "They don't need any advice from you!"

"Do they need advice from Moscow?" asked Chesterton.

A voice from the back of the room interrupted. "You don't know me. I'm not famous. I'm not a writer. I'm just a man."

A thin, disheveled figure shuffled over to where the well-dressed, well-fed men stood. He went straight to Hemingway and said, "Don't worry about Moscow. They don't want land reform. They oppose collectivization of the farms."

Hemingway and Chesterton exchanged looks of surprise but neither responded to this statement. Therefore, it fell to Davidson to challenge the man.

"How do you know this?"

The man scratched his head and shrugged. "I know. I'm an anarcho-syndicalist. I wanted to fight but I have a damaged leg. I have friends and they talk—not as much as you gentlemen, but they do talk."

Hemingway laughed at that.

"Spain is simply a testing ground for Stalin and Hitler," the man continued. "This Spanish conflict is just a dry-run—a practice ground for the *real* war still to come. That's all it is. The world is going to be destroyed if we don't destroy all the governments first."

With that, the ragged figure turned and left.

"So, Chesterton," said Hemingway, "does that sound like a fellow who just wants to own his own land?"

Chesterton flicked the ashes off his vest, all that remained of his cigar. He sighed. "No, but I'm talking about the peasants. They don't have any fine theories. They have only the land, when they're left to it."

Hemingway had this bull by the horns and he wasn't about to let go. "Are the Distributists going to fight?" he asked.

"Yes indeed. They are working with a radical American group that has its own financing and is forming alliances with men like the one who just shared his wisdom with us."

A young woman joined Chesterton. She had a thick Cockney accent. "We are combining our forces with Durruti," she said. "Gilbert is not staying with us long but he felt that he had to make this trip at least once."

Hemingway was stunned. "Buenaventura Durruti?" he echoed. Some of his contacts in the Comintern had described this anarchist leader as violent and irresponsible. For a time he was thought to have died right here in Madrid during the gloomy month of November '36, but the reports of his death turned out to be a ruse. When the man resurfaced, he was a bigger hero than ever— but not to Hemingway, who disliked all anarchists.

Buenaventura Durruti

"He despises the Church," Hemingway confided, but his listeners evinced no surprise. "You must be performing miracles right out of the Bible if you expect to ally yourself with him."

Franklin D. Roosevelt

"We are not a religious group," Chesterton corrected Hemingway. "Our two groups have Christians of different denominations as well as religious Jews and even a few atheists. But there are no Communists, Nazis, or Fascists."

"What is this other group called?" asked Hemingway.

"Our American colleagues call themselves Agorists," said Chesterton.

"Yes, and unlike we poor Distributists, the Agorists have a lot of money," said the Cockney girl.

"I've heard of them," Davidson added his two cents. "They even have an Institute. The leader is a Canadian eccentric named Konkin. FDR and the New Dealers have been trying to get him through the IRS. The Feds assume he must be one of the richest men in America but nothing ever sticks. He only appears in public occasionally to dine at the finest restaurants. Then he disappears again."

"I won't ask how he is financing your brigade," said Hemingway.

"Gold," Chesterton volunteered. "Much of this war is being financed by gold on both  sides."

Hemingway let that sink in. Whether building a new world or preserving an old one, there was no getting away from the curse of Midas. He had many friends who had hidden away gold coins and family heirlooms when Roosevelt had tried to collect all the gold in '33. He didn't doubt that many Germans did the same thing when Hitler tried to pull the same stunt that year.

He was getting a headache and the day had barely begun. Maybe he could have taken Davidson or Chesterton alone, but the combination was too much. He needed to wrap up this visit to their bizarre intellectual realm, a cerebral anomaly far stranger than anything he had expected to find in Spain. This war was bringing crank theorists and odd zealots out of the woodwork and creating impromptu intellectual collaborations of which even he had not dreamt.

He concluded with a simple inquiry. "It's been a pleasure meeting you," he said to Chesterton, extending his hand. "Do you still love France as much as you did in the old days?"

"Yes, and I know how much you love Paris," he replied. "You're a rare American in that regard."

"I am?"

"I'll prove it to you with a question for our young friend. Howard, what do you think of France?"

"I hate it, of course."

"Why?"

Howard didn't even have to think about it. "The country's full of Frenchmen!"

"The Crimson Citadel"

Excerpt from Part III

Somewhere in the Pacific Ocean, shrouded in fog and malice, was the island of the most infamous villain the world has ever known. On this outcropping of volcanic rock he had constructed a fortress from which to exert his final, baleful influence over the Earth.

The year was 30,000 A.D.—and the Inquisitor awaited the arrival of the only two beings in all of space and time who could thwart his machinations. As the air began to crackle with blue electricity, he rose from his throne to welcome the Turtle and the Dove to his arcane domain.

His face was a sardonic mask, dark eyes glaring over high cheekbones. His lips twisted into a sneer as the Time Traveling Machine materialized. The Turtle exited first. Of the dynamic twosome, the Turtle was always the swiftest.

"It ends here," said the Turtle, brandishing his pulse gun. The Dove was close behind with his long bow and quiver of atomic arrows.

"Don't be premature," sneered their nemesis. "You wouldn't destroy all hope for the human race without first making a confession, would you?"

"I've got a confession for you right here," the Turtle ejaculated.

"Well, then, what about Mary?" cackled the perfidious purveyor of the night-side of the soul.

"Mary! You fiend!" shrilled the Dove. "She's safely deceased in the eons of the past."

"That's what you think," gloated the cone-headed menace, his voice muffled by the heavy material of his hood. "Behold!"

Two shambling monsters of vaguely human aspect carried a struggling, naked, voluptuous, perspiring young maiden to the top of a stone dais that the alert time travelers noticed at that moment. A tentacled monstrosity pulsed hugely at the apex of the weather-worn steps.

"All of humanity's genetic structure lies dormant within that monster," said the Inquisitor. "The sacred gift of life is about to be passed on to your virginal fiancée, Turtle! Nothing can stop this event unless you would abort the future of the species with your pathetic, flaccid weapons!"

"But why?" the Dove wanted to know.

"You know why," hissed their foe. "The wars that began in the 20th Century ended with a complete holocaust of mankind. Only a *new* humanity, bred for docility and obedience, can survive. That is the true meaning of the 'meek inheriting the Earth.' Unless, of course, you would leave the world to this race of monsters you see about you."

"They seem docile and obedient enough to take orders from you," said the Turtle through clenched teeth. "Why do you need the return of real humanity?"

The Inquisitor laughed. "You fools," he gurgled through his hood. "These monsters have no *souls*. I must have humans again so that I can save them. Now you will witness the glorious rebirth before I send your mortal frames into the cleansing fires of yonder volcano!"

"Oh, yeah?" said the Turtle. "What if I deal with your octopus right now?"

"No," screamed the Inquisitor. "Don't shoot at the jeweled eye of the monster. You'll blow us all to atoms!"

Hollywood, Spring 1937

Hedy's Career Advances

Hedy Lamarr was bored.

Her career was going well. That wasn't the problem. *Red Pawn* had wrapped and showed every sign of being a success. She'd had a nice fling with Frank, the second male lead. That was pretty much over now, although he didn't know it.

Mayer kept throwing his considerable weight around on her behalf and succeeded in having *Algiers* moved up on its schedule. The star, Charles Boyer, was all in favor of an earlier shooting date because he

Ilona Massey

couldn't wait to work with the beautiful Austrian actress. She liked him and wondered what might develop.

In her brief time in Hollywood, she was impressed at what Mayer could do for her; especially considering that her first two films were not even at his studio!

Everything was going well in Hollywood and she had no cause to complain. She'd become friends with another European beauty invading America, Ilona Massey. The press agents were trying to build up a rivalry between them. Massey was the voluptuous blonde and Lamarr the smoldering brunette.

The whole thing was pretty ridiculous. When they were together they didn't even talk about the men they dated or the ins and outs of the business. Mainly they talked politics, which meant they worried about Hitler.

Hedy's boredom flowed from a deep frustration that her life had become frivolous in a world on the verge of blowing up. She hadn't left Mandl solely to have a better personal life. She didn't escape his clutches just so that she could be an actress again.

She wanted to *fight* Mandl. She wanted to fight everything that he, and Hitler, and the Nazis stood for. Making movies was all well and good, and could even serve the cause—when, and if, Hollywood producers had some guts.

But meanwhile, she wanted to do more. And she had only one hope that she might be able to do something important.

The young German rocket scientist she met on the train when she made her dash for liberty had not forgotten her. He wrote regularly. When his first letter appeared in a bag of fan mail, she grabbed it out of the hands of the publicist and made it clear that the writer was an old friend with whom she wished to communicate directly.

She and Wernher had kept up a regular correspondence ever since. It

soon became apparent that he was harder to keep track of than was she. Hedy had no problem making certain that his letters got through directly to her bungalow. Every time he wrote, however, the postmark showed that he had moved. Each of her letters had to search him out in a different part of Europe, once even across the Channel, in England.

Then, at his instigation, they started playing a game. They worked out their own private code. She was pleased, not only that he considered her intelligent enough to keep up with him but that he was right!

They talked about only one subject in their coded letters: rockets, and communications having to do with rockets. Hedy would sit at her desk, a glass of wine by her side, and draw diagrams. Ilona Massey came over during one of those sessions and asked what she was doing.

"Preparing for a science fiction picture," Hedy said with a smile.

There was one comment that Wernher von Braun included with his first missive that Hedy did share with the other actress.

"He didn't know if his letter would reach me so he wrote this in block letters, in English, on the back of the envelope: I AIM AT THE STARS!"

Condor Legion Service Medal for duty in Spanish Civil War.

Breast Badge of the German Kondor Legion (Panzer Section)

CHAPTER 6

Guernica, April 1937

Condor Legion

Ernst thought it was the most beautiful day he had seen in a long time. The sky was a perfect blue. Not a cloud was to be seen, which was just fine with General Wolfram von Richtofen, the man giving the orders to the Condor Legion. Ernst, for his part, preferred the clear weather to the muddy political thinking of his commander who kept referring to the Basque people as Reds. Ernst knew better than that.

The general was not po-  litically sophisticated but it hardly mattered. He had a good military mind and Ernst was one of his pilots. On this beautiful afternoon of April 26th, 1937, the Basque town of Guernica would go into history books as the first community to experience the full fury of an attack from the air.

Down on the ground it was market day. Ernst knew that the Basques weren't Reds. They were actually capitalists. But they were on the wrong side. Today that would be a very unprofitable place to be. The men bringing their sheep and cattle to market failed to appreciate the significance of recent events when Republican troops from Marquina fell back to the little town of Guernica, a good six miles behind the lines.

Today would forever change the idea of "the lines" in modern warfare. One of the instruments of this hard lesson was to be the Heinkel 51 fighter piloted by Ernst. He waited his turn as the attack began at 4:30 p.m., led by a Heinkel 111 bomber, the pride of the Condor Legion's special squadron.

Condor Legion Heinkel He 51 – the last of the biplane fighters.

A church bell was ringing as the heavy plane arrived dead center over the town and released its payload of death. As Ernst came into the fray with the rest of the full squadron he flew low enough to see what was happening on the ground in detail. People were scurrying in every direction, attempting to help those injured from the first load of bombs.

The Condor Legion laid down a barrage for an invasion that might come, or might not. That was up to the Nationalist army. For the Germans, in truth, the rain of bombs was the beginning and end of the operational objective: a demonstration of German might. There was much more happening here than an aerial display by one of Franco's allies. The Third Reich was sending a message to the world. It was a message of terror.

As for Ernst, he wasn't completely comfortable with his mission but he carried out his duty. It was best not to think too much about strafing civilians fleeing into the fields surrounding the town. They didn't have much choice when their pathetic shelters collapsed and they were forced back into the open air choking from the dust and

Wolfram von Richthofen

debris. Ernst told himself that he didn't have a choice either about scorching the earth.

The Heinkel He 51 being prepped for battle.

At times like this he thought about his parents who had been driven to madness and suicide during the harsh and bitter times preceding the rise of Hitler. The world didn't care what happened to Germany back in the times of the "Great Inflation" when it took a wheelbarrow of money to buy a loaf of bread. The people of Europe and Great Britain and America had shown little concern over the failure of President Woodrow Wilson to keep his promise to Germany, a failure which ultimately broke the American leader in body and soul and guaranteed the horrors brought on by the terms of the Versailles Treaty. France and England danced on the German corpse and foolishly assumed that would be the end of it.

Adolf Hitler rose up and declared that nothing was finished. He promised oceans of revenge, tidal waves of vengeance and a veritable whirlpool of retribution. Young men like Ernst raised their right arms and said, "We are with you! Give us an army and we'll march; give us a navy and we'll sail; give us an air force and we'll fly. Those who get in our way will soon learn to regret it!"

Spain was simply in the way. Communists and anarchists were responsible for the chaos in Spain just as their German counterparts had been responsible for worsening Germany's condition until only Hitler and National Socialism could save the day. Now General Franco wanted to save Spain, but his Fascism was too little and too late.

Hitler had decided to use Guernica to send a message to the world. The times were ripe for revolutionary change but it had to be the right revolution. It had to be his!

Thinking about the larger picture always helped on a mission. Ideology made Ernst feel better as he shot down children and watched them fall twitching in his sights. Ideology was not a

Hugo Sperrle

luxury. It was a necessity when you had to kill people.

Behind him came the next wave of the attack, the heavy Junkers 52. They would carpet bomb the town over a period of hours, utilizing techniques that were perfected by the Legion in earlier attacks on Republican positions in Oviedo. The world had never witnessed destruction on this scale. The night before, Ernst and a colleague amused themselves by imagining how Goebbels, the always-inventive propaganda minister, would present this technological military breakthrough to the world.

One thing was certain: the nation with the most advanced science and technology would eventually dictate terms to the whole planet. The Nazis had every intention that they should play this role.

Suddenly a top-secret message came in on the Heinkel's equally top-secret teleprinter. It was the strangest message that Ernst had ever received. The stalwart lads in the decoding department had intercepted a radio message that, once translated, still didn't make any sense. The decoded enemy message stated that they would fight the Condor Legion with *Matadors*. Short of a bullfight in the air, the message had to be slang or code that eluded the experts.

"Watch out for anything unusual," the message concluded. Ernst grinned at the comical bureaucratic propensity for stating the obvious. Apparently there would never be a revolution in the history of the world that would manage to eliminate the absurdities of military bureaucratic routines.

Frankly, it was the same brand of bureaucratic dullness and caution that Ernst figured would keep the Nationalist army on the ground from following up and taking the devastated town below. But, he reminded himself once again, that was almost inci-

Recruitment Poster for Spanish Civil War.

dental to the real point of the exercise.

The only military objective that the Condor Legion might not achieve would be the destruc-

Captured Heinkel He 111, medium bomber, first used in Condor Legion.

tion of the Rentaria Bridge. They weren't really equipped for it, although it would be a nice bonus for the old man. But everyone on the mission understood that the primary objective was the terror bombing.

As for Richtofen's conviction that they were killing Reds, the old man was probably too much of a reactionary to appreciate the irony of this attack on one of the few pockets of capitalism left in war-torn Spain. However, the radicals of the National Socialist movement certainly understood the broader implications of Hitler's movement. Ultimately the Nazis must stand against the two monstrosities that had been created by world Jewry for the purpose of permanently weakening the Aryan race: Capitalism and Communism.

Ernst appreciated this radical viewpoint more than some of his friends in the Condor Legion. Not every pilot was equally enlightened on political matters and they didn't have to be. Nazism was a big tent and could accommodate a wide diversity of viewpoints so long as all members subscribed to the fundamentals of race, blood and soil.

When it came to strategy, well, that was best left to a genius like Hitler. He knew how to play his enemies against each other. Small minds would accuse him of hypocrisy and inconsistency. Stupid leaders of the SA had made that mistake and paid for it with their lives. The one thing

Ernst counted on was that everything Hitler did was ultimately for the good of the Aryan race. Hitler's Germany would surely show the way to the future.

So if it became necessary to kill a Basque woman with a spray of bullets, that is what Ernst did.

As he circled back for another strafing run, Ernst saw something odd. He didn't immediately connect it with the warning he'd heard over the radio only a few short minutes before. His mistake was easy to understand. Flashing lights on the ground could be explained in many ways: a trick of the light, the sun glinting off metal canisters or even reflections on a body of water.

But these lights didn't stop or resolve themselves into a familiar pattern. They produced an explosion of rainbow colors swirling around on the ground with sparks spilling out at the edges. There was something almost hypnotic about this repetitious pattern. It was definitely not something a pilot should become fixated upon. He was about to take his own advice and shift his concentration to other, more critical aspects of his mission, when the strange light show lifted off the ground and headed in his direction.

"What the hell is that?" the voice of one of the other pilots crackled in his ear over the radio.

"I don't know, but we better report it," he answered back.

"It's headed for you, Ernst!"

"I know. I see it. I'm taking evasive action."

Even as Ernst pulled back on the steering column to bring his nose up preparing an attempt outrun his pursuer, the bizarre light show, whatever it was, accelerated. A glance at his altimeter gave him the bad news. He was still too close to the ground to bail out. His fate was tied to his plane now because the sparkling light show coming at him through the air was not going to allow him the time he needed to reach a safe altitude.

Well, if he couldn't outrun his pursuer, he could try to get out of its

Heinkel He 111 medium bomber, crash landing.

way. The plane groaned as Ernst radically changed its pitch. The yoke of a Heinkel 51 was very sensitive and it didn't much care for what the pilot was trying to do with it. He ignored its protestations and banked to the left and said a prayer.

This Heinkel He 111 has been permanently retired from battle.

Maybe the gods were listening but, if so, they answered with a dark Nordic sense of humor. The swirling thing just missed him but exploded anyway and badly damaged the plane. Despite his maneuvers he'd have to make a crash landing. He hadn't gained altitude, he'd lost it. Bailing out was not an option.

Ernst's ears were ringing as he worked to halt his screeching descent. Pulling back on the throttle to slow down, he reduced power and watched the nose drop to a few inches above the horizon. He tried to turn his head to see how much damage had been done to the rear of the plane but his neck felt as if a jolt of electricity had been passed through it and held him rigid. As he tried to lift his hand to touch his neck, his arm hurt more the higher he lifted it and he felt a stabbing pain in his side.

Well, this was no time to worry about how badly hurt he was. All that mattered was the plane. More than ever, he and it were bound together, now by the wounds that had been inflicted, in common, on them both. A little voice in the back of his head started nagging him. There was something else important. Something that he was forgetting. Reluctantly he glanced at the Field Teleprinter in his cockpit, a critical piece of secret technology that must not fall into enemy hands.

But speaking of hands, his were full right now. Taking any time to destroy the top-secret equipment (the existence of which Germany had successfully kept to itself since its invention in 1929) might guarantee his death. If he could survive the landing, then his first duty must be to destroy the device. It shouldn't be difficult. The teleprinter consisted of only two moving parts, a rotating drum and a typewriter. Certainly he could smash these beyond usefulness before the enemy grabbed them and gained a means of intercepting German communications.

Wehrmacht: "We Fight in Spain."

He swore bitterly at the bad luck which had caused part of his cockpit to be severely damaged, with jagged pieces of metal sticking out in all sorts of places while the delicate communications device remained in pristine condition.

Even his control panel was damaged so he'd have to make this landing by pure dead reckoning. He looked for any stretch of ground that could accommodate him as he flew to earth. He'd made one emergency landing before and recalled his frustration at being unable to make a pass over the ground before committing himself. There was no choice then and no choice now. Thank God he could still lower the wheels.

He brought the plane in slowly and stalled out at the last second, gently pulling back on the yoke as the wheels touched down. It would have been an excellent pinpoint landing if the craft hadn't been so damaged, but the plane tipped over and skidded to a crunching halt that knocked the breath out of him.

Ernst always liked to keep promises that he made to himself, especially ones that concerned his duty. Despite new injuries, or damage to his body that only now became apparent, he tried to reach for a wrench with which to smash the communications device. His right arm was severely injured. He worried that he might have suffered permanent damage to his "Sieg Heiling" arm.

But, he didn't need to worry about that. Before he could complete his task, his cockpit was ripped open and half a dozen hands reached in and pulled him, rudely, from the wreckage. At the edge of his vision he saw gloved hands go to work on retrieving the Field Teleprinter.

He expected to be in the center of Basque opposition but, as he looked around, he saw a group who appeared to be of an entirely different origin. Ernst was aware that the black and red handkerchiefs tied around the necks of these men identified them as anarchists. He wondered what *they*

Anarchists (FAI and CNT) join forces.

Anarchist women from the Durruti column.

were doing in this fight. He could see a large truck with a canvas covering on a short rise from where he had crashed. The vehicle obviously belonged to his captors.

"We are members of the Durruti column," said a large bearded man, in perfect German. The others in the group were all clean-shaven. They wore large belts that held all manner of ordnance. Some of the men were walking collections of hand grenades. Others had canisters he did not recognize.

"Thanks for the gift," said a man with gloves. He was the one who removed the Teleprinter from the plane. He spoke in Spanish.

"It was unintentional," answered the pilot. His Spanish was good but he had an accent. He also was finding it hard to breathe.

"How does it feel to murder women and children?" asked a woman in their ranks. For some reason he was surprised at how attractive she was with flashing blue-green eyes and dirty blonde hair.

"I do my duty, the same as you," he said.

They thought that was funny. "We are the last people who care about that," said the bearded man in Spanish. "Do you agree with your German philosopher Kant that you have a duty to yourself?"

"I don't understand," said Ernst.

"You are dying," said the other. "We have no intention of saving you. But we will let nature take its course."

Ernst looked down at the spreading stain of red under his right armpit. Funny that it didn't hurt more. He only felt exhausted and dizzy. But now that he stopped to think about it, the dizziness was growing worse and he felt as if he were drifting.

"Do you know anything about the device that brought down my plane?" he asked but the attention of his hosts was elsewhere.

"One of our German pilot's com-

BUENAVENTURA DURRUTI

Soldiers of the Durruti Column, Aragon, August 1936

rades have spotted his wreckage and is coming to investigate," said the man with the beard.

"Let's give him a proper welcome," said the woman.

They had propped Ernst against the side of his plane, his position provided him an unobstructed view of what they were doing. Again, the bearded one spoke to him in German: "We don't have enough of our toys to stop what the Condor Legion is doing today. But we were ready for a test and we got wind of your little outing. While you shock the world, we are shocking you! The world will know about *this* soon enough!"

This was the device they pulled out from the back of the truck. The sight of it was like a tonic to Ernst. He could focus again, if only for a few minutes. He couldn't believe what he saw.

There were two small rockets on a circular platform. Wires snaked down from the tubes to this metal disk. Ernst could also see some kind of radio receiver attached to the disk on which sat a device with what appeared to be movie film running through it. A man came over to the device. He had a backpack with metal objects sticking out from the top that Ernst didn't recognize. He also carried some kind of control device that glowed as he activated it.

"What is it?" Ernst asked, feeling something warm and salty beginning to seep into his mouth.

"Why, it's the Horns of the Bull," answered the woman with a smile. She didn't seem angry with him any longer. He assumed that if he'd fallen into the hands of the Basque women they would have torn him to shreds.

"My God," he said. "You're the Matadors! And those aerial torpedoes are the horns of your bull."

Anarchist soldiers assembled during the Spanish Civil War, all members of the Durruti Column.

It was one thing to die in the service of the Father-land. It was quite another to hallucinate in the last minutes before death. Yet this impossible device had to be real. It had ended his career, hadn't it?

The rockets be-gan to spin against each other. Film began to race through the radio re-ceiver and the light show began. Us-ing the control de-vice like some kind of magic wand, the anar-chist Matador guided the en-tire assembly up into the air. The rockets ro-tated against each other, held together by the wires to the platform. It was a kind of sur-real, airborne gyro-scope that threw off smoke and sparks and made a whistling-howling sound unlike anything Ernst had ever heard—or would ever hear again.

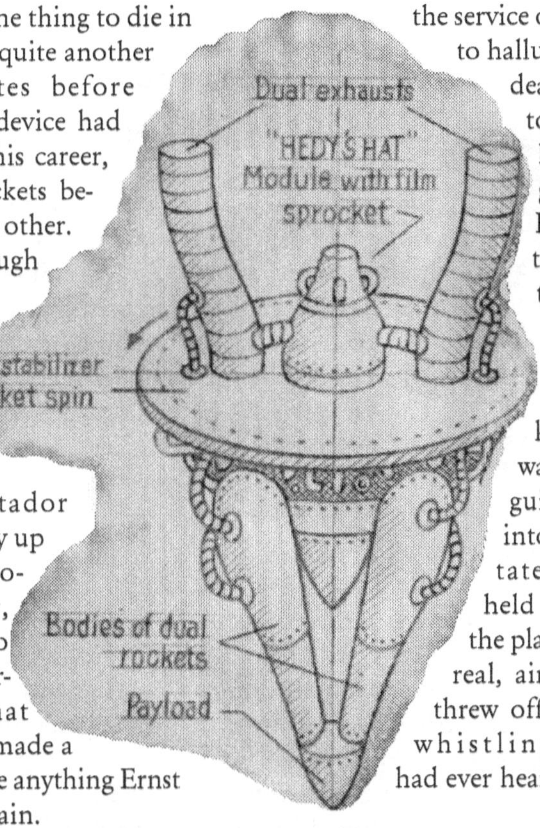

Dual exhausts

"HEDY'S HAT" Module with film sprocket

Gyro stabilizer & rocket spin

Bodies of dual rockets

Payload

As he watched the device headed for another unlucky plane of the Condor Legion, his last thought was to wonder how a bunch of Spanish anarchists ended up with something more advanced than any weapon of the Third Reich.

How was that possible?

Guernica, Pablo Picasso, 1937

Germany, the Early 1930s

Wernher and Konrad

When he turned eighteen years old, Wernher von Braun was worried about the draft. The Nazis were a few years away from taking real power; but as the new decade of the 1930s dawned, the warning signs were up. A more militaristic Fatherland was inevitable, with or without Herr Hitler.

Both Zuse and von Braun drew the same conclusion the day the Stock Market crashed in '29, and New York City took on some of the characteristics of Berlin, with its own dose of chaos and suicides. If the city of prosperity could fail, then anything was possible.

Anything that was bad!

"This means another Great War," said von Braun.

"No, it means the first planetary war," countered Zuse, "a true world war that will realize another prediction of H. G. Wells."

"I won't stay here," said von Braun. "Let Germany and my real father go to hell together. At least my poor mother isn't here to see her worst nightmares come true."

Zuse sighed. He didn't like it when his friend became too emotional. They had a special friendship born of the mind. It wouldn't do for either of them to become overly sentimental. That was one aspect of the German character neither could abide. This disdain for sentimentality was also one of the few views they shared with the brown shirts and the Reds.

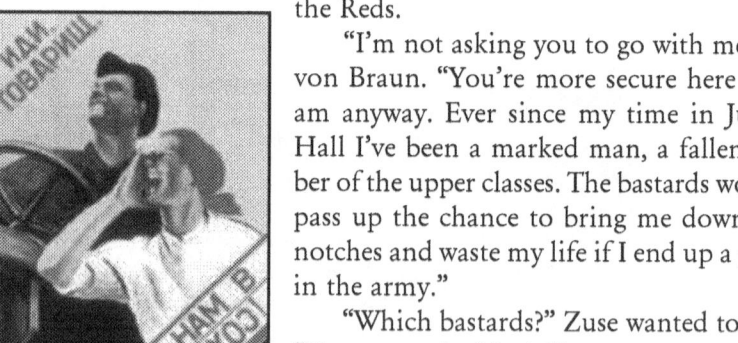

"I'm not asking you to go with me," said von Braun. "You're more secure here than I am anyway. Ever since my time in Juvenile Hall I've been a marked man, a fallen member of the upper classes. The bastards wouldn't pass up the chance to bring me down a few notches and waste my life if I end up a private in the army."

"Which bastards?" Zuse wanted to know. "You mean the Nazis?"

"I mean any of them. Nazis, Communists,

honest members of the Centre Party. It makes no difference, Konrad. I'm fallen. The workers would grind me underfoot just as readily as the bosses and the aristocrats. They could all line up and purchase tickets for my humiliation."

Zuse put his hand on his best friend's shoulder. "I'd say that you were paranoid if I didn't know better. So, other than helping me build a technocratic utopia of scientists and engineers, you have no other politics?"

Von Braun grinned. "The closest I can find is the anarchist position. But most of them are collectivists, the same as everyone else I hate. I'm not sure they would appreciate my unique gifts. But I'll say this for them. The anarcho-syndicalists are the only communal types who don't turn my stomach!"

Max Stirner

Zuse grimaced. "You're forgetting the Max Stirner types. Did you ever read *The Ego and His Own* that I lent you?"

"Of course I did. But his version of individualism is so extreme that you don't get enough cooperation and division of labor to build the world we want! We're stuck again."

"I know what you mean," Zuse sighed. "Our politics are best summed up as simply the future. We must be the most extreme individualists to achieve this, but we also need vast resources and precisely-tuned organization to realize our goals."

They were having their conference in the playroom attached to the larger house. It was a Saturday and the rest of the extended Zuse family, and their fortunate charges, were off having a day of official fun and games. This left the boys free to arrange a makeshift office, as they usually did when the opportunity presented itself. They spread out their diagrams and notebooks over the billiard tables.

Today would have its fair share of surprises. "For the first time in my life, I'm wrong about something!" announced Zuse, snapping his fingers. "We don't need a State. We need people able to organize, but that isn't necessarily a State."

"Organize enough people and you have a State," said von Braun, morosely.

Zuse shook his head. "You've been so busy worrying about your rockets and fuel mixtures that you haven't been paying attention to the intellectual salons my parents keep arranging for us. Do you remember Richard von Mises?"

Ludwig von Mises

"Oh, sure," said von Braun, fondly recalling another member of their select fraternity. "The man is a good mathematician. He's one of the few you've introduced me to who has an inkling of what we're trying to accomplish."

Zuse grabbed a virgin notebook and soiled its pristine pages with furious scribbles that most people couldn't decipher to save their lives but posed no mystery to his friend. Then he solemnly intoned, "You and I are going to become students of this man's brother, Ludwig von Mises, who is currently developing the most radical and logical theory of unregulated Capitalism you've ever seen."

"Isn't Capitalism pretty much bankrupt, no pun intended?" asked von Braun.

"It will come back bigger and better than ever, but next time the important people will be technocrats like us."

Von Braun made an expression as if he'd just taken a mouthful of sour lemons. "Konrad, isn't that what the socialists and communists also say? Aren't they also interested in putting the technocrats in the driver's seat?"

"Of course, but that would inevitably lead to the planetary war we've feared, Wernher. Because socialism is a fantasy. It can't work."

"What about Fascism?"

"Depends on what you mean. Most of it is really just jackbooted socialism with a willingness to make a deal with capitalists who don't want a free market."

"And what does that get us?"

"More war, of course."

Von Braun sat down and put his head in his hands. "We are in accord. The world depression guarantees the greatest war of all time no matter what policies are adopted by the governments here, there, anywhere."

"Wait a minute," shouted Zuse, wearing a demented smile that gave Wernher the creeps. Sometimes he wondered about his friend.

"I may have made another mistake," said Zuse. "How unusual."

"We should notify the press at once," said von Braun.

"My dear rocket man, we have forgotten to ask what *kind* of war the world
will have, and what *kind* of peace. We may
be able to make a difference, after all.
Maybe we can avert total planetary disaster by determining, or at least supporting, the right kind of war."

"What in blazes are you talking
about?"

Zuse had a ready answer. "The world's
States will fight a war that might very well
destroy civilization if they are not
stopped. The only people in the world
crazy enough to make war *against all* the

States are anarchists but they come in two distinct varieties. The anarchist "commune" types and the extreme "individualist," free-market types
stand in complete opposition to each other, but all of them share a common aversion to the State. Right? No one has ever tried to forge a serious
alliance between them before. As the majority of humans prepare to became slaves to various dictatorships because of economic woes, a growing
minority will be ready to do anything to secure their freedom. These are the
sort of people who can respect radically different life-style choices, including economic choices. No one else takes liberty that seriously."

Von Braun shook his head. "We're having another of our beer hall
bull sessions, minus the beer. The people who want freedom don't have
the resources we need."

Zuse jumped up from his chair and spun around as if he'd just
joined the ballet. "That's all changed. They can build what they need.
They can homestead it as well."

"You mean steal?"

"Of course. The governments of the world
will now be stealing more than ever before, mark
my words. What that means is that *everything* is
up for grabs. We are going to form our own
little syndicate, just the two of us. You can travel
around Europe looking for the right kinds of
allies and backers. I'll foot the bill. There are many
ways that we can maintain contact but when necessary we can meet at that summer resort area
where my parents took us last year."

"Peenemünde?"

"Yes, you remember the name. Good."

Von Braun laughed. "We are only angry young men. Where are you going to get the money for all this?"

Zuse tapped the side of his nose and winked. "One genius should never ask another genius that question. Don't worry about it. Concern yourself with this instead."

Zuse passed his friend the notebook. As von Braun squinted his eyes and started reading. He received the free bonus of a running commentary.

"I've written down phone numbers and addresses. The whole von Mises family is worth cultivating. You might want to look up Margit in Austria. She's an actress. Personally, I think the most beautiful actresses are Austrian, and maybe a few Italians.

"Then there's an old associate of my family's, Gustave. He'll provide you an introduction to Emma Goldman in Paris. You haven't read her works yet but you must. She was too much of a libertarian even for America. They sent her to Russia and she was the first radical to see through the lies of the great Lenin himself so you can imagine her perspective on Stalin. She is probably the most individualist anarchist who is comfortable working with communes and employing collective strategies. She'll introduce you to other radicals who broke with Stalin, another breeding ground for anarchists."

Emma Goldman

Vladimir Lenin

Von Braun emitted a low whistle. "Konrad, in all the time I've known you I had no idea you were this immersed in the specifics of radical politics. I thought you were more, you know, theoretical."

Josef Stalin

Konrad paced the room and didn't speak for a long moment. Then he turned to face von Braun with an expression his friend had never seen before. It was a mask of solemnity.

"I study the human mind," he said. "It is easier to master conventional modes of thought than radical ones. You know what *radical* means? It means the root, that which is fundamental. The most difficult mode of thought is to follow a premise to its *root*, to its logical conclusion.

Most people are afraid to define their terms because that would bring
them a step closer to having to initiate a logical chain of thought. Most
people would rather die than do that."

"I agree."

"Our task is to find all the best alienated minds in the world. Not
the conventional best; and not those who are alienated but who fail to
reach our intellectual standard. Once we find our kind of people, we
can do more with your rockets and my thinking machines than even we
can imagine."

"Such as?"

"For starters we prevent the coming world war."

"How?"

"I've already told you. By fighting a war of our own!"

The "Tom Mann" Centuria. English-speaking volunteers in Barcelona, summer 1936, before the International Brigades were formed as distinct fighting units..

CHAPTER 7

Madrid, Spring 1937

Howard and Hemingway

The loud knocking woke up Howard Davidson with a start. "Hey, pal, get out here!" came the rumbling voice of Ernest Hemingway. "Big news!"

Bleary eyed, Davidson stumbled to the door. He was pleasantly surprised that the world famous novelist considered him worthy of disturbing, especially after the way he'd passed up a copy of *The Inquisitor*. Maybe he was rising in Hemingway's estimation. One could always hope.

People were milling around in the hallway. A woman's voice called from downstairs saying she was making drinks for everyone.

"That's Marty," said Hemingway. "She makes great drinks, especially under fire. What are you doing asleep in the early evening?"

The change of subject caught Davidson by surprise. "I don't think I slept last night at all. I remember drinking and before I knew it I was having breakfast and . . ."

"Took a nap, huh?" Hemingway interrupted. "You can't sleep in Spain. Too much going on. I woke you up, because your town's been attacked by German planes."

"My town?" Davidson echoed as they went downstairs.

"Yeah, Guernica. The Nazis hit it with everything they've got. You should've stayed there. Think of what you missed!"

As Martha Gellhorn shoved a drink in Davidson's hand, he reminded himself of the common gossip that she and Hemingway were having an affair. "Hope you like that," she said with a smile.

Davidson swallowed something he didn't recognize. He certainly didn't want to let on to these members of the literary elite that he wasn't much of a drinker. His friends in New York would be amazed to see how well he was holding his liquor. Staples would never believe it! The secret was to nurse each drink as long as possible and drink plenty of water in between drinks. So far he'd found the water of Spain agreeable, unlike the bad experience he'd had on his one visit to Mexico.

"That's my own special rum concoction," Martha said. "It's not as good as the drinks Josie makes." She turned to Hemingway as he put an arm around her. "Speaking of Josie, has Dos found Robles yet?" she asked.

"No," came a new voice from the doorway. Davidson couldn't believe his good fortune. Now he was going to meet John Dos Passos! Thoughts of Guernica were temporarily eclipsed by the more important issue of whether or not he should ask Dos Passos for an autograph.

Hemingway introduced Dos to the new people. Howard Davidson had his big moment but all he could think to do was compliment Dos Passos on his book, *Three Soldiers*. Dos was barely paying attention,

John Dos Passos

anyway. He had other things on his mind. Howard figured out that Josie was the girlfriend of a man Dos Passos was trying to locate.

Suddenly Dos Passos looked Howard straight in the eye. "I'm glad you liked *Three Soldiers*. José Robles translated it into Spanish for me. He's my best friend in Spain and he's gone missing."

"The fortunes of war," said Hemingway blandly. "I'm sure he'll turn up."

"Yes," said Dos Passos. "But alive or dead?"

"With the Fascist beasts on the loose, who can say?" said Hemingway.

"You know what I mean." Dos Passos sounded grim. "I'm worried about Stalinists in this case."

Hemingway passed one of Martha's drinks to the other big-name writer.

"Sometimes you forget the nature of war, Dos."

Dos Passos accepted the offer and continued. "And you forget all the unpleasant evidence that Stalin is no better than Hitler and Mussolini when it comes to crimes against humanity!"

Dos Passos swallowed his drink in one gulp and stared at Hemingway. No one was going to out-macho Hemingway without a fight so he gulped down his drink even faster. All this furious imbibing inspired Howard to take another cautious sip of his rum.

"Life isn't always pleasant," said Hemingway. "We can't expect revolutionary times to accommodate our American black-and-white morality."

Dos Passos waved away another proffered drink from Martha. "Life has been pleasant for us, Ernest. That's why it's all the more important that we don't disregard the suffering of others. The truth is more important than ideology."

A drunken old man in the back of the bar shouted out, "What does this have to do with Guernica?"

"Nothing," said Dos Passos, tipping his hat. "We'll talk about this later." He left the room.

"So, Howard," said Hemingway, grabbing him in a bear hug, "we'll have to hold the fort for American writers tonight."

"Aren't there any Brits left? Where's Chesterton?" he inquired, noting the absence of the British celebrity.

"Off somewhere lending undeserved prestige to the lazy anarchists," said Hemingway. "Who cares? You're the man of the hour tonight."

"I am?"

"Sure. You're the only science fiction writer here, aren't you? It's Herbert's hard luck that he isn't here."

"Wells?"

"Yes. Since we don't have the benefit of his august presence and talent for marathon thinking, we'll have to settle for you."

Howard put down his drink. Now that he realized he was on the spot, he wanted to be at his best. "What are you talking about?" he asked.

Hemingway smiled. The pulp writer was finally standing up for himself. About time.

H. G. Wells

"Reports are coming in about some kind of new, secret weapon that was used against the Condor Legion. Apparently a few planes were actually brought down by this mysterious thingamajig. Sounds like some kind of Buck Rogers death ray. And now get this: no one is taking credit for it! The defenders of the town don't know a thing about it."

"What does it have to do with me?" asked Howard.

"It's right up your alley, super hero stuff. Isn't that the sort of thing your characters might pull off? The Crab and the Vulture, or whatever."

"The Turtle and the Dove," Howard corrected him.

Hemingway scratched his cheek. "I have plenty of contacts and so far no one knows anything. But it's a fine thing that happened. The Nazis needed a thorough pasting."

No one in the Hotel Florida disagreed and so everyone had another round of drinks. Howard Davidson resumed nursing his original drink and wondered what the hell was happening to the world.

"You know, I'm reminded of a verse from Hillaire Belloc," said Hemingway. "I probably wouldn't have thought of him if his old pal Chesterton hadn't shown up here the other day."

"Belloc is an anti-Semite!" muttered his girlfriend.

"We all know he's French," countered Hemingway. "Even Goebbels complains that the French are better anti-Semites than

Hillaire Belloc   the Germans. Anyway, Belloc got off

a great verse after General Kitchener wiped out thousands of crazy dervishes at Omdurman. He wrote:

Whatever happens, we have got
the Maxim gun, and they have not!

Joseph Goebbels

"Isn't that fine? It goes beyond anybody's politics. The better gun wins the day. That's why these rumors of a secret weapon count for something. We must doff our caps to those who imagine the future!"

Howard no longer cared if Hemingway intended to make fun of him. He enjoyed the comparison with Wells even if Hemingway had meant it sarcastically. He was happy that he was here at all, and in this rarified company.

But he was sorry he hadn't asked for an autograph from Dos Passos. He was less sorry that he had missed the carnage that would forever be associated with Guernica.

For the next few days he would try to learn what had actually happened there. What if a secret weapon had actually been used against the Condor Legion? If he could find out first, he could file a news report like one of the big boys.

Wouldn't that be something?

Barcelona, May 1937
Eric Blair

From the roof of an old cinema he could see the stars. There weren't many out tonight. The sky was empty. That's the way he felt. For the first time since coming to Spain he doubted his reasons for being here.

The only way to allay the emptiness welling up inside was to gaze back down upon the huddled structures

Eric Blair
(George Orwell)

of Barcelona. At least there was more illumination in the streets than in the sky. The sporadic fires seemed to be consuming the hopes of the revolution.

There was so much gunfire that it sounded like rainfall.

The popping and the

cracking sounds made him think of the musical cacophony of a fireworks display, except this special music meant burned skin and the death of people instead of a celebration of joy.

On this night in May, 1937, worker killed worker in the streets of Barcelona. Eric Blair, the man the world knew as George Orwell, wished that he was back on the Aragon front. That had been the reason he came to Spain, to fight the Fascists. Now he found himself caught in the middle of a fight between the Republican government on one hand and the CNT Anarchists on the other. As a member of the POUM, he couldn't be more in the middle because that was precisely where the independent Marxist militias found themselves.

As far as Orwell was concerned, everyone in Barcelona was precisely where Stalin wanted them to be. The future was grim. How different from a mere six months ago, in December '36, when he had first come to this Barcelona with a letter of introduction from the Independent Labour Party. Right off the bat he was asked if he happened to be a Stalinist and he answered with a firm *nyet*.

He had the choice of joining the independent Marxist POUM or the anarchist CNT. He chose the former. From what he had learned since, his sympathies for the Anarchists grew every day. In a way this was to be expected. For years he had jokingly referred to himself as a "Tory anarchist."

But he wasn't about to turn against the POUM. He had fought with them and seen their mettle. He respected them, even more so now that they were in real trouble. Tonight in a fine old Spanish city it was clear that everyone who wasn't under Stalin's thumb was the target of the new government policies.

So the man the world knew as George Orwell kept his post atop the old cinema building. He could see all points of access to the Executive Building of the POUM directly across the street. He had a special reason to protect that location. His wife, Eileen, was there. Whatever happened he would do his duty and protect what was his and hers.

How different it had seemed when he arrived in Spain by boat and took passage to Barcelona aboard a rickety old train. He still remembered the faces of the peasants who stopped work in the fields to salute the train carrying foreigners who had volunteered for the Republican cause. That

train ride in December of 1936 was his first taste of just how international the war had become.

. . . Rubbing elbows with Germans and Frenchmen and Czechs put him in an expansive, cosmopolitan mood. The only prejudice he ran up against was from other Englishmen who were put off by his Etonian accent. But upon discovering the identity of their countryman, they overcame their proletarian bias. He was a hero to all of them. He had earned their respect over the years and now raised the ante by volunteering to fight the Fascists instead of just writing another book.

One hardened, older man with callused hands told him that he'd originally disliked Orwell when he read what the great man of the independent left had to say about the hygiene of the working classes. Orwell had written that they had a distinct odor about them because they didn't bathe frequently. This man had held a grudge against the stuck-up intellectual who made that observation—until one day when he got over a particularly bad head cold and had his first strong whiff of the special smell.

"You 'ave a bad 'abit," the man told him aboard the train. "You tell the truth."

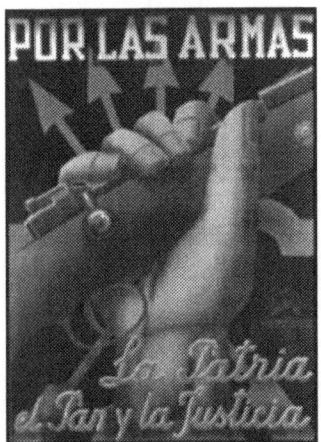

When he reached Barcelona and saw the ragtag condition of the volunteer militias, Orwell was true to form. He informed the first person of authority that he came across that he, Eric Blair, had some military training. In no time at all he was instructing men in the Lenin Barracks.

In short order he was made an officer and sent to the Aragon front in January. He was part of a centuria, its mission to defend a hill in Alcubierre. As a cabo, a corporal in command of twelve men, he was confident that he'd be in the thick of the action in no time.

Durruiti Column, Aragon, 1936

He only required a few weeks in the Aragon to learn about the peculiar nature of this conflict. On one hand, the war was truly a cataclysmic event. He had seen that evidenced in the workmen's clothes worn by everyone in Barcelona. He heard it in the casual nature of the forms of address now used by everyone; and this in a society that had recently been one of the most stratified in Europe. These men and women knew what they were fighting for.

Whatever kind of corporate imperialism had corrupted Italy and however strange and inhuman the National Socialism of Hitler's Germany, the Fascism of Franco was very specific to Spain. He sought to restore the old feudal order. The Republic said in one collective voice: "Never again!"

But all these high abstractions came down to earth on the front. Here it was a civil war again. On the Aragon front, Orwell saw how Spaniards fought Spaniards. They had a casual quality that didn't so much outrage as surprise his very English soul, forged when he'd served as an Imperial policeman in India. In Spain, there was a sort of respect between soldiers that was the polar opposite of how the symbols of privilege and power were being trashed.

He'd seen true proletarian hatred in the destruction of churches in Barcelona. Workmen treated the demolition of the buildings and the religious images as a methodical job. The past must be eradicated!

None of that zealotry was here on the front. His comrades saw the Fascist soldiers as misguided members of their own class. They'd be just as happy to convert them as to kill them.

There were times when Orwell worried that his men deliberately missed hitting the enemy and that the Fascist soldiers might be returning the favor. But he was as ready to learn as to instruct. That had always been his approach to any new experience.

It was cold in the winter—the worst cold he'd ever felt in his life. Maybe the soldiers on both sides were waiting for the Spring to thaw them out. Then they'd smell the roses and eat cherries.

They'd smile at the birds flying overhead. They'd re-member their wives and girlfriends and how sweet life could be.

Then they'd be ready to resume killing.

And somewhere, some fat, sleek philosopher of the left and some fatter, sleeker theologian of the right would prattle on about "just war" theory. How he hated that! How he wished he could get them in his sights just once. But he could never have the revolution he really wanted because it would never discriminate in the way he trusted only himself to do.

That freezing winter on the Aragon front, he re-ceived one intellectual surprise that brought into focus

Josef Stalin

the reasons why one had to be very careful when selecting one's targets in a revolution. It was during the collecting of firewood that Orwell met Alex Lucyshyn, a Ukrainian.

They quite naturally hit it off when the subject was Stalin. Coming from his background, the young man had personal insights into the boss of all the Russias that supported Orwell's views. But then came the surprise.

"I suppose you should know that I'm a Catholic," he said.

"Really?"

"It's just that I've read enough of your work to know that you don't think much of the Church. That didn't keep me from loving Down and Out in Paris and London."

"One of my most ecumenical works. But when you say that you're a Catho-lic, do you mean that's how you grew up or do you still count yourself among the faithful?"

"Both. But at least there's no question of my loyalty to the Republican cause. I'd shoot the first Franco spy who showed his face in our camp."

During the conversation, the man pro-duced a pack of Lucky Strike cigarettes. Orwell would have supped with the Devil for one of those so there was no problem in exchanging a few thoughts with a Papist.

"You seem familiar enough with my writ-ings to know that I'm a stiff-backed Protes-tant Atheist."

"Yes," said Alex, cupping a match to his cigarette. Then he used his cigarette to light

Orwell's as the hesitant flame of the match had already died in a gust of cold air. Their discussion produced another kind of current.

"And I suppose you know that I view the Church as an obstacle to freedom of thought?"

"Yes. But Mr. Blair, I also know that when you were a young man you greatly admired Chesterton."

Orwell coughed at the remark. Despite growing troubles with his lungs, he wasn't about to pass up a deep drag of good American tobacco. Hell, considering the almost poisonous black shag he rolled into cigarettes and insisted on smoking, the cigarette in his mouth at that moment was like a baby's pacifier.

"You know a lot about me," he told the Ukrainian. "I like Chesterton for much the same reason I like Oscar Wilde. I'm British. I have to admire our eccentrics, especially when they're gifted at paradox and epigrams. But I don't accept Chesterton's theological arguments as anything but clever poetry."

Oscar Wilde

"Well, I'm here because of his politics," said Alex. "I'm a Distributist. I hope to end up joining Augustin Ortiz of the Agorists! Ortiz is receiving a lot of support from America. We hope to form an Anarchist front with Durruti. We may even see a combined Agorist-Distributist brigade."

Orwell watched the smoke from his cigarette lazily encircle a tree branch over their heads. "There have never been more factions in a war, never in history. So the more, the merrier. Can I thank the Agorists for these cigarettes?"

"Yes."

"Then three cheers for Agorism," said George Orwell. "But you still surprise me with your religious views. Aren't you concerned about the gutting and sacking of the churches and monasteries?"

"No!" said Alex emphatically, surprising the Tory anarchist. "The Church in Spain has brought this on itself. It isn't Rome's fault. Did you know that during the Spanish Inquisition Rome tried to hold the Spanish Church back from its excesses?"

Orwell let smoke trickle out of his nose. "I think I've heard something to that effect but I've never looked into it. I have trouble imagining a reasonable and cautious Inquisition."

"Point taken," said Alex. "But as for the world of today, the Spanish Church has supported the worst of the landlords and been one itself. It

has done things here that can only be for-
given by a higher power. We need to cor-
rect the idea that all Catholics support
Fascism. The Church needs to resist evil in
the world, not encourage it. Besides, you
have a growing number of Catholic fans.
We have to be worthy of our favorite au-
thors!"

"An excellent goal," Orwell conceded
with a chuckle. "I wish your movement
the best of luck. But remember the risk.
Just as Stalin uses the Comintern to advance the power of his narrow nationalist interests, so too the Church can have narrow interests behind its universal rhetoric."

"Yeah," admitted Alex, spitting at a
lizard that scurried past his boot. "But what are you gonna do?"

After receiving a bad cut on his hand in March, Orwell was moved to
Monflorite until he recovered from the infection. He spent the time writing, as
well as finishing a box of cigars Eileen sent him. She also let him know that she
intended to come to Spain herself. Spring was coming and he became opti-
mistic again. He wasn't even coughing very much.

Alex wasn't there when he got back to the front. At first he was worried that
the eager young man with the sandy hair had died for the cause but instead he
had been transferred. Orwell hoped he would finally be with one of the groups
close to his heart.

One of the POUM newspapers reported that Chesterton had returned to

London because of declining health. The fact that
the old scribbler had come at all, especially after
another near-brush with the Grim Reaper the
previous year, impressed Orwell.

He was delighted that one of the heroes of
his youth hadn't let the side down. And who
could say but that the presence of the old gentlemen, and the fighters he inspired, might have
kept a few Spanish priests from being hanged
with their own intestines? Even the revolution could
show a little Christian charity.

But Orwell reminded himself that one could
carry sweet reasonableness too far. Debates and

fine distinctions should really be postponed for the return of sanity. Now was the time for battle.

He had come to see action and there simply wasn't enough of it. So it was with great delight when he heard the news from his Irish comrade, Paddy Donovan, that they were going to make a night raid on the Fascist positions.

The battalion commander had worked out a plan for a two-pronged attack. Orwell would be responsible for fifteen Englishmen and fifteen Spaniards. The patrol made it past the barbed wire but before they could throw their makeshift grenades over the enemy's fortifications, a sentry spotted them and sounded the alarm.

Orwell and Paddy were caught between the fire of their own men and the Fascists. Tossing a grenade, Orwell tried to change the equation. Others followed suit.

Despite Paddy's cries for Orwell to stay low, the tallest man in the assault stood up and charged. They took the position and Eric Blair finally had a taste of what he had come to Spain for in the first place.

Unfortunately, the Fascists mounted a successful counter-attack. Heavy fire forced them to relinquish the ground just taken, and they made a retreat through rain and mud and blood . . . .

Now it was May and he was back in Barcelona, performing sentry duty on the roof of a movie theatre. He was haunted by the memory of how quickly victory turned to defeat in this war. The official version of the night assault was that it had actually been a success because it drew attention away from a more significant attack by Anarchists. Maybe Alex had been part of that militia.

Orwell hoped that the story was true. Already he had learned that in this conflict that it was almost impossible

to be certain of anything outside of your own immediate range of personal experience. A nice, sane war had two sides. At least that's how he thought back when he was ten years old.

There were so many sides in this conflict that he was losing track—and he was supposed to be the political professional. Watching a city already famous for street-fighting transform into a scene from Dante's *Inferno* was a sight to drive the most pigheaded optimist into morbid depression!

In retrospect, even the disorderly retreat in Aragon seemed like a total success compared to what was happening at this moment. He wished he could be back there, cold and hungry in the mud. Anything was better than watching the dream destroy itself before his eyes. And worst of all, how could this be happening in May, the month of worker's celebrations all over the world?

The event that lit the fuse that set off the disaster in Barcelona seemed an unbelievable catalyst to all concerned. The government had decided to take over the telephone exchange from the CNT. It was like a bad joke, actually. Did you hear the one about the Anarchist phone company?

But Orwell's analytical brain never limited its analysis to only the surface details. The conflict between Anarchists and Communists had to erupt eventually. His mistake was to assume that Stalin would want a decisive defeat of Franco first. Tonight he knew better. One day the whole world had to learn the truth.

Thousands of foreign Communists had been coming into Spain, all of them under Party (Soviet) discipline. Ever since the Anarchists proved to be a military force in the summer of '36, the Reds were more open about wanting to disarm them. That was another bad joke. Did you hear the

one about the Commie who tried to take a gun away from the Anarchist?

The Catalan President was a fool. He underestimated the resolve of the Anarchists. But one man who would never make that mistake was Josef Stalin as his heavy hand moved pieces on the chessboard. Orwell understood this as certainly as if he'd seen that giant hand reach all the way from Moscow and grab the Telephone Exchange.

As a political writer, Orwell fully appreciated the power of propaganda. He studied the techniques of both Dr. Goebbels and Madison Avenue. He knew better than most men how the British influenced the news services of India. And he knew exactly what it meant, a few days ago, when he came across a poster showing a grinning Adolf Hitler hiding behind an Anarchist mask.

When Stalin started telling his big lies, he didn't stop. The pictures and words came first but he always ended it with bullets. If this was the Party line against the Anarchists, it didn't take a lot of imagination to realize that the POUM was next. His comrades wouldn't admit this to themselves until it was too late. They hated Stalin, but they didn't hate him nearly enough.

Orwell knew that Stalin's methods were the same as Hitler's. No matter how different (or similar) their ultimate objectives might be, the inescapable fact was that they used the same methods. Not enough people understood. Not on the right. Not on the left.

He would have to write a book about that. Maybe a couple of books.

As for now, in May, he remained on the roof of an old movie theatre and guarded his position. He worried about his wife. He worried about his friends. He wanted this insurrection to end. He also wanted to get back to the *real* war, back to fighting the Fascists again. Just one more time. Just for the hell of it, if he could manage a return to the front.

But he didn't know how much time Stalin would give him. Tonight in Barcelona he knew the dream was dead. Stalin had killed it. He would be more vicious in destroying the POUM than he was with the Anarchists. The POUM was closer to him and therefore the greater danger.

He'd drag out all the old libels and slanders about "social fascism." He'd say the POUM was behind an insurrection against the Republic. He'd insist that the Anarchists weren't organized enough on their own and had to be manipulated by the Devil of Reaction himself, Leon Trotsky. And the POUM was his infernal instrument.

Before Stalin was finished, he'd be telling the world that Franco was giving orders directly to the POUM. As for all the young, brave soldiers of the POUM who died with Fascist bullets in their heads and hearts, why, they were sacrificed so that Fascism's fifth column could enjoy the final victory.

Orwell was not a man who cried. He considered it weak and effeminate. But tonight he wanted to let loose and weep. He could see Stalin's intentions as clearly as if he'd been given the assignment to write the

propaganda himself. He could hear the words thundering in his brain: "The POUM was never an ally. All true revolutionaries have always been at war with the POUM. We have always been at war with the POUM."

Orwell fumbled around in his pocket for a cigarette. He was fresh out. But the man who was going to relieve him had promised to bring some Lucky Strikes. Life was still worth living.

While watching the world collapse about one's ears, there was always time for irony and contemplation. Orwell realized that Stalin was the quintessential manipulator of weak individuals and strong organizations. Stalin understood the power gained by manipulating the masses, but his machinations might suffer if his collectivist past led him to underestimate the inherent dedication underlying the plans and organizations created by people who were attracted to anarchy.

Stalin believed in order, the same as the capitalist regimes he sought to overthrow. He counted on people acting in a predictable manner, the same as any miserable banker. Basically, he underestimated anyone who was not like himself.

Probably the only thing Stalin knew about anarchist theory was that Marx hated its great Russian advocate,

Karl Marx

Bakunin. When it came to radical politics, Stalin was too busy trying to outsmart and murder other Communists to waste any time on involved strategies against those of an anarchistic inclination.

Mikhail Bakunin

Orwell prided himself on not avoiding a logical conclusion. Perhaps the future of Spain was in the hands of the Anarchists. But how could they prevail against all the forces that would be arrayed against them?

It would take a miracle.

CHAPTER 8

June 1937

The Perfect Plan

He never expected that it would end like this. He had been too careful. He was too powerful and too feared for it to end like this. He'd been entrusted with a mission that couldn't possibly fail. The plan was foolproof. There were just too many men and too much equipment and too many weapons for an enemy force to prevail.

For once in his life, he had felt completely secure about an operation. But now Alexander Orlov (also known as the dread "Nikolsky") sat in a small room on the top floor of the Soviet Embassy. It was a lovely, sunny day in Spain. But there was nothing bright inside his soul.

He sat alone. He would never see another human being or hear another voice. His universe had been reduced to two objects on his desk: a picture of his wife and children, and an 1895 Nagant 7.62mm revolver. His eyes drifted back and forth between them.

The gun held no fear for him. He counted himself fortunate to have it right now. He'd heard that officers in the POUM often had no revolvers and were forced to buy them on the black market from Anarchists. The poor fools of the POUM! Whatever happened in this war, they were going to lose. Then the officers of the POUM would need those revolvers so they could do what a hand-picked agent of Josef Stalin

Alexander Orlov

was about to do in this room in a few minutes. Orlov would set a good example for those enemies of Stalin. He was a friend of Stalin and he had enough sense to blow his own brains out.

Thank God he had the gun. It was the key to his escape from this unbearable nightmare. When Stalin found out what had happened to the gold shipment, the Soviet leader's reaction would be an imaginative retribution that would impress even Adolf Hitler. Orlov, a general in the NKVD secret police, had an imagination as well. He had made a considerable contribution to the cause of human suffering. He was very good at it.

But he considered himself a rank amateur compared to his boss. What tortures could possibly compensate for the loss of 460,516,851 grams of refined gold worth 518 million U.S. dollars? That was precisely what the general had managed to lose.

Transferring the accumulated wealth of Spain to the Soviet Union was no small affair. They had postponed the operation several times since it was first proposed. They were so careful about everything. When rail lines between Madrid and Cartagena fell into the hands of Anarchists, the project was postponed. The least little thing had them backing and filling and rethinking the plan. They figured that the Anarchists were the least of their problems despite a lot of wild talk about Durruti as some kind of superman.

But the Anarchists finally abandoned their positions. At least it looked that way. And even if they hadn't, there were too few of them to stop an operation of this magnitude. How could mere brigands stop the trains and remove nearly eight thousand boxes of gold?

The final plan was perfect. It had been perfect when it was first developed in 1936. And it was still perfect when it was finally, at long last, implemented in May and June of 1937. It took a lot of work and a lot of time. There was a lot of gold to consider.

They couldn't put it off any longer. Stalin had surprised everyone when he extended credit to the Republic. But all that had come to an end! No more credit was available from the great banking institution known as the

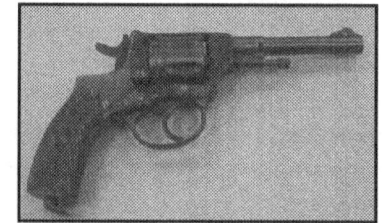

1895 Nagant 7.62 mm Russian revolver

International Communist Conspiracy. The wealth of centuries was to be transferred from Spain to what most Spaniards still thought of as Russia instead of the U.S.S.R., brain center of human progress. The ghosts of the Czars had to be laughing in their Summer Palace in Hell. They would recognize a victory for the Russian Empire.

Part of the gold was payment for what Stalin had already provided in his unaccustomed burst of generosity; the rest would be held as advance payment for the ongoing supply of armaments and men. The way the war was going, even this vast sum would have been soon spent. Then Spain would be forced to dig even deeper until Stalin had not only its soul, but its last doubloon.

It was a perfect plan! The Soviet Union was planning to do to Spain what Spain had done to the Aztecs and the Incas. The ghost of Karl

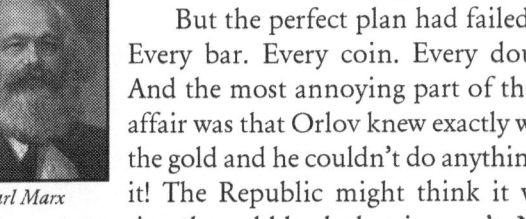

Karl Marx

Marx could share a laugh with the ghosts of the Czars.

But the perfect plan had failed. The gold was gone. Every bar. Every coin. Every doubloon. And the most annoying part of the whole affair was that Orlov knew exactly who had the gold and he couldn't do anything about it! The Republic might think it was getting the gold back—but it wasn't. No gold

Nicholas II

for them and no gold for Stalin either. No gold for Franco. No gold for Orlov. It was a killer of a joke on everyone, especially Orlov. It was truly amusing.

Maybe if the situation in Barcelona hadn't occurred when it did, things might be different. Hard to say. Who knew it would be such a mistake to anger the Anarchists? They were *nothing*. Merely pawns. Fools and pawns. They weren't supposed to have magical powers.

It wasn't fair. Nobody told Orlov about the magic. How do you plan against magic?

Stalin wasn't the sort of man who appreciated the ironic humor of bad news; unless it was bad news for his enemies. He certainly was not the sort of man to whom one brought bad news without expecting repercussions. Even minor alterations in one of his schemes put Stalin in a bad mood. For example, in this case he had kept insisting that no receipt should be given the Spanish official when the gold was delivered.

The lack of a receipt would make the Spanish official very nervous. He might be assassinated over something like that. He might have ended up where Orlov was right now, contemplating suicide. But that pros-

Josef Stalin, 1936

pect hadn't bothered the NKVD general. Putting people in untenable situations was part of Orlov's job.

Staying out of situations like this was also part of his job. But he told himself, yet again, that it was unfair to expect him to plan for the impossible. He wasn't supposed to be facing the black abyss. The plan had been a very good one.

At any rate, Stalin's reasons for not wanting to issue a receipt made perfect sense. He didn't want a paper trail. He didn't want any scrap of evidence that might get back to Hitler proving such a deep level of Soviet involvement, and profit, in the Spanish situation. That might make Hitler very angry. The leader of the Third Reich was touchy about things like that.

Stalin was not yet ready for a showdown with Hitler. Well, the Soviet leader didn't have to worry about that any longer. There would be no receipt. But there would be no delivery either.

Lifting the gun, Orlov put the business end of the barrel to his head. For some reason the small circle of metal against his perspiring skin reminded him of the wedding ring he gave his wife. He hoped that maybe, just maybe, his family would be spared Stalin's wrath. But he knew that was impossible.

The trouble was that there was nothing he could do about it. Maybe his wife and children would even agree that they should be tortured to death. They might even apologize to Stalin with their last, bloody, gurgling breaths.

460,516,851 grams of gold worth 518 million dollars was, in the current circumstances, all the money in the world. Orlov felt sorry that he could only commit suicide once. At the very least, he'd willingly do it a hundred times.

He pulled the trigger and listened to the heavy click on the empty chamber. He wasn't playing Russian roulette. He didn't think he deserved that much pleasure. He simply hadn't loaded the gun yet.

He wasn't through agonizing.

The plan had been beautiful. He'd never seen a better plan. They had thought of every contingency that made any kind of sense. They worried about reasonable things like the Fascists taking over Madrid. Events that might actually happen.

The smartest part of the plan was the secrecy. Russians were always good at secrecy but this one was especially well done. The citizens of the Republic could understand removing the gold for safe-keeping because there was a war on and they didn't want it falling into Franco's hands. They might imagine the gold was going to America. That would be a nice, safe place.

But no one would believe the gold was going to the Soviet Union for safe-keeping. That was like sending it to the Moon on a one-way trip. That was like sinking it in the deepest trench at the bottom of the

Francisco Franco

ocean. The average Spaniard wouldn't be very happy about that idea, whether he was a Nationalist or a Loyalist.

So the operation had to be carried out in complete secrecy. Only a handful of nervous bank officials in Madrid were informed and even they did not know everything. The majority of the bankers thought the gold was safe inside naval caves. Soldiers would be kept guarding the empty caves so as to maintain the illusion.

Of course, the finance minister knew. Orlov wondered what sort of suicide that splendid fellow might be selecting for himself at this very moment. People who said they didn't believe in suicide were dreadfully ill-informed about just how untenable life could become, given the right circumstances.

Anyway, Orlov reflected, it had been a lovely plan. For a brief moment, the richest man in the world would have been the Russian economic attaché. Very amusing.

During the course of three moonless nights, the gold was loaded onto trains. At the other end of the pipeline, Soviet freighters waited for their heavy cargo of bullion. There were even Spanish warships to protect the Russian ships; and the best part was that the Spanish captains didn't even know what cargo was to be loaded onto the Russian freighters.

The plan got even better. Thirty high-ranking NKVD agents posed as longshoremen to receive the shipment at its first stop in Odessa. There were hundreds of special troops. The gold would be checked and weighed along the way to its final destination at Moscow's Special Metals Deposit. They had even developed a procedure to separate the rare coins with historic value from the rest of the treasure because these coins were actually worth more than the gold-by-weight. Such attention to detail!

Orlov wondered, idly, how valuable that rare coinage would have been when added to the grand total he lost for Mother Russia and the glorious Communist Revolution. Not enough for Stalin to wish him any worse an end, he decided.

Could the historical dialectical process guaranteeing the ultimate victory of world Communism survive his blunder? He tried to cheer himself up with the thought that he was providing just one more test to prove the historical inevitability of scientific socialism.

Sure he was.

His mind kept returning to Stalin's big plans for a celebration at the Kremlin where the general secretary of the Communist Party would announce that the Republic would never see the gold again.

Actually, Stalin was right about that.

Stalin certainly must have planned a sumptuous banquet. Orlov hated to spoil everyone's evening with bad news. Even worse than bad news would be a story no one believed. That made everything so much worse.

If Orlov could go back in time and warn himself about anything at all, he would tell his earlier self to take more seriously the wild rumors about the "wonder weapons" that were used against the German planes in Guernica. He'd dismissed the stories at the time because if such marvelous devices really existed, why had so few of them been used? And why was no evidence found afterward, except for the wreckage of several Condor Legion planes? And why did the Basques know nothing about it except to circulate crazy rumors that Durruti was behind it?

A weapon of advanced technology was the last thing one would expect in the hands of Anarchists. If they had such a marvel, why did they only use a few in Guernica? It had been easy to dismiss the stories.

Orlov also shrugged off warnings that Durruti used to rob trains in South America and had designs on the gold shipment. What train robber could do anything against the marvelous metallic juggernaut that Orlov was setting into motion?

Besides, if the Anarchists had magical weap-

Buenaventura Durruti

ons, they would cost a lot and they had
probably used them all up in Guernica anyway.

Yes, all these thoughts seemed reasonable at the time but for one thing. If you
have magical weapons that cost a lot, you
might as well spend everything, and use
up everything, if you are going to seize all
the money in the world. In for a ruble, in
for all the rubles!

There were other factors, as well. If you
have every disaffected Anarchist in the
whole of Spain itching for a fight after the

uprising in Barcelona, you might manage to gather enough of them for
one giant offensive. That could mean an army big enough to move a lot
of gold. Assuming they could get their hands on it, of course.

That was precisely the body of men that descended on the gold
train.

General Orlov was not a man to roll over and surrender. The surprise attack was not beyond his abilities to repel. The numbers of attackers were unexpected but still manageable. Durruti was always cranking
out pamphlets bragging about a million Anarchists and proclaiming
how they were the great lion of Spain. But there were only several hundred of his followers who descended on the gold train, a far more serious assault than anyone had anticipated but still a foe that could be
resisted. The defenders might have prevailed.

So what if the Anarchist ranks were swelling with foreign volunteers, the same as Stalin bringing in thousands of Party members? There
were more Communists in the world than Anarchists. Soon there would
be more Communists than Capitalists. It was only a matter of time.

All the general had to do was win one unexpected battle. That was
how Stalin would see it. It's how Orlov would have seen it, had he not
encountered the "Horns of the Bull."

It was only at the very end that he learned the name of the weapon
that so easily defeated him. A dozen of the double-rocket devices came
at the trains from all directions. It was like being caught in the middle
of a Chinese New Year except there was no papier-maché dragon. Instead there was a real dragon and the general felt its hot, scorching
breath.

They never had a chance. The general tried to die in battle. He tried

very hard but they wouldn't allow him that dignity. The final insult was that they didn't even take him prisoner.

Durruti came up to him and announced that he was free to go. He'd never in his life seen a man like the hero of the anarcho-syndicalists. He truly had piercing eyes. Orlov thought he was in the presence of a resurrected Rasputin.

"Everything changes now," said Durruti. "To hell with Stalin. To hell with Franco. To hell with the false Republic."

Orlov kept up with the twists and turns of Spanish politics from his unique perspective in Stalin's secret police. The frankness of Durruti disarmed him. The general had even thought the Anarchist leader would continue allying himself with the Republic despite the unpleasant incidents in Barcelona that everyone in the NKVD had worked so hard to bring about.

"Aren't you going to kill me?" asked the general hopefully.

"No."

"And you're not placing me under arrest?"

"No."

Anarchists could be very annoying people. They didn't have any concern for other people's feelings, that was the trouble with them.

"We'll blindfold you and let you think about the future as one of our drivers takes you on a tour of the countryside. Too bad you won't see any of it. Eventually you'll be returned to your side."

These were the last words the Syndicalist leader said to him as he was turned over to someone named Sammy. The general's driver was apparently an Agorist. Orlov had never heard of that before but he was given an earful. Agorism must be some new mutation of social fascism, he supposed. The baleful influence of Trotsky must be everywhere.

As he loaded the revolver, General Orlov reflected on his decision to accompany the train. If he'd stayed behind he would have killed

himself a day sooner. He would have had a pleasant day, a good meal and a few drinks, and then the news would have come. He would have done the same thing he was about to do now but he would have been more relaxed.

On the other hand, he wouldn't have seen the aerial torpedoes that ruined his life. He would have doubted the veracity of the reports. He might have shot the bearer of the bad news with the very gun he was about to turn on himself.

Oh, well. Live and learn.

Learn and die. That was the way of the world.

His last thought before the darkness came was: "What in the hell are they going to do with all that gold?"

Meanwhile . . .

Back in Hollywood

This would be Hedy Lamarr's last Hollywood party for quite some time. Nobody else in Hollywood knew. Tomorrow she would tell Louis B. Mayer. She owed him that.

He would be angry with her and he would threaten her. He'd tell her she needed to stay in town and promote *Red Pawn*. Even though principal photography was finished on *Algiers*, they might need her for looping. The publicists would insist that she and Boyer do something like "go to the Casbah" more times than they ever did in the film. And then there would be all the plans her Uncle Louis had for her now that he was finally ready to put her in a prestige MGM production!

He would read her the riot act and lay down the law. But it wouldn't make any difference. Within a few days she would be on her way to Spain.

Poor Mayer. Suddenly he was in the position of all the men who ever tried to hold her against her will. He wouldn't see it that way. In his mind, the only salient fact was that he had a contract.

In her mind, the important thing was that she wasn't defecting to another producer! She was running away from the land of make-believe to the reality of Spain.

She had to go. Von Braun was with the Anarchists. His letters had been revealing, with tantalizing specifics that made her want, even more, to be there and experience the entire story as it unfolded. She had suspected all along and now she wanted to know and participate in *everything!* There was no other explanation for the puzzled and confused reports from Spain about the "wonder weapons."

She had decided that *he* must have built the small rockets that changed the war forever by making the seizure of the gold train a success. Now, it seemed, he was ready to build something really interesting.

Since the heist and disappearance of the Republic's gold, the Nazis and the Soviets were taking the Anarchists very seriously. The battle between Franco and the Republic had moved to second-feature status on a double-bill whose "Feature Presentation" now starred the maneuverings of Hitler, Stalin and the Anarchists. Von Braun and Zuse wanted to cast Hedy as the leading lady in a surprise-filled drama that could change the world.

With Europe on the verge of another major war, there was no question in Hedy's mind about sitting on the sidelines in Tinsel Town. Not now. Not when von Braun asked her to join him in a manner that might not seem particularly touching to most people, but that Hedy understood as his own, unstudied and endearing version of true Romance.

After she decoded his last special letter and learned the amazing facts of her own contribution to the "Horns of the Bull" and the "Matadors" who guided the flying torpedoes from the ground, *nothing* could have kept her away. It was the most thrilling news of her young, tumultuous life.

Tonight, as she prepared to maneuver her way through the sexual and financial challenges of a cocktail party, she would have to try very hard to pay attention to the other guests. How easy it would be for her mind to return to the thrilling world described in the most recent letter from von Braun. Her spirit was already half a world away.

> Your ideas for frequency-hopping helped more than you know, my dear. Maybe that's appropriate. When it comes to hopping, I imagine you jumping from bed to bed now that you're a big Hollywood star. You are more than a wonderful woman and the goddess of my dreams. You are the smartest woman I've ever met. You are also the most honest.
>
> I don't know what is more surprising: your frank and honest attitude toward sex, or your sophisticated and ana-

Wernher von Braun with V2 Rocket

lytical mind. Frankly, I don't know many men who admit, with the your degree of candor, what they do to satisfy their emotional and physical needs. I have encountered even fewer who would appreciate the way Konrad Zuse and I adapted your idea of using sprocketed movie film—how perfect for you to think of that—for coding and decoding messages. The "Horns of the Bull" employs a device which sends an encrypted control signal. The signal has four limited commands: *Left* and *Right*, *Up* and *Down*.

Your letter made such an impression on me that I can quote what you said from memory:

Dear Wernher, I'm pleased by your report of the matadors' success with the "horns of the bull" devices. The loss of control, while there is still fuel and the rocket is still under acceleration, is certainly a serious problem. The operators need as much time as possible to hit their targets and must have control during the complete fuel burn. The current design has the film on the matador's radio-control transmitter unwinding by spring action at the same time as a spring unwinds the matching code film on the rockets' radio receiver. This has proven to be unreliable—just as the old hand-cranked cameras of early silent films recorded movement that appeared unnatural when projected on the screen. We don't need a fancy clock mechanism to keep the codes synchronized and effective because the fuel would run out long before such an expensive solution would stop functioning. Using the simple shutter of modern movie cameras, and only changing the codes on a frame-by-frame basis, should still prevent enemy jamming of the signal and give the matadors enough time to maintain control until the fuel burns out. Keep 'em crashing. Hedy

I'll forever be an adolescent with you. For example, when I think of the signal going up and down, I think of you! What we're doing over here feels like a school boy's dream. When we realized that we couldn't build a gyroscope small enough for these rockets, we solved the problem by using the double-rocket assembly. When they fly, the rockets carry the radio receiver with them. Two rockets are better than one because two provide enough lift to make the radio guidance possible and they are, as you know, the only way to steer. I long to see your slender, white hand holding and stroking the glowing column of the control device.

Sorry.

As you can tell, I miss you terribly. Konrad is aware that I'm sending you these coded letters. He'd have a fit if he knew the details I include. I explained to him that someone who can come up with frequency-hopping can handle the mechanics of using a match to burn sheets of paper!

Hedy, you are the only person I've ever met I find as exciting as my work. For the first time, I realize that it is possible to combine pleasure with the highest goals of one's life. I think about you more and more, even when developing solid fuel engines for the "Horns of the Bull." I have plans for an alcohol-based fuel that could be used in something larger, but that's all I have to say about that right now.

Konrad and I talk about you a lot. The men have acquired a print of *Ecstasy* and they watch it so often that it's getting scratches from the old projector we use. You are an inspiration to all of us. One day we'll name a *cohete* after you. Your name on one of my rockets, how appropriate!

There's nothing else to say now except that I'm writing a poem dedicated to you. It may not be very good but I like the title, *Days of Wine and Rockets*.

Love, Wernher

The letter had made her resolve to join Wernher in Spain even stronger as she burned everything in a neat little ashtray that Ilona Massey had given her. Mayer had made arrangements for the Hungarian blonde to become roommates with his Austrian acquisition. Hedy hoped that he wouldn't take his wrath out on her fellow European when she lowered the boom on him tomorrow. On the other hand, maybe her skipping town would land Ilona some more work.

Well, that was tomorrow. Tonight she would make herself have a good time. She'd try not to judge her fellow entertainers too harshly now that the German rocket man was opening up the universe to her.

Hedy Lamarr

The party was being thrown by the mother of Ginger Rogers, one of the most prominent Republicans in Hollywood. Hedy hoped she wouldn't get into any strident political arguments just because she liked President Roosevelt. On the other hand, she was disappointed that FDR avoided taking a stand on behalf of the Republic against the Fascists.

The social occasion was to celebrate the imminent release of *Red Pawn*. It was to be a more political event than the wrap party the studio had thrown earlier. That was the night she broke it off with the actor, Frank. His wife, the author of the screenplay, was coming back to Hollywood. Her Broadway play had finished its run and she was looking to sell the film rights to her new novel.

Frank warned Hedy to watch her step with his wife, Ayn Rand. Hedy loved that. It was the first time in her life that anyone had suggested a writer could be more temperamental than a star. Ayn Rand proved that she was not to be taken lightly when her invisible hand reached all the way from New York to blacklist an actress from appearing in *Red Pawn*. The actress, Noelle-something-or-other, was a member of the Communist Party. Ayn Rand declared the Noelle person to be "a force of the anti-mind." Still, there didn't seem any way the girl could sabotage the production. She was merely cast in a small part, playing the role of a whore. The studio fired her just the same.

Ayn Rand was already holding court as Hedy entered the living room, but the moment those lustrous Russian eyes—the largest Hedy had ever seen—fixed on her it was as if everyone else in the room vanished. Rand approached the actress, brandishing her cigarette like a German director.

Hedy prided herself on her lightning-fast ability to make accurate appraisals of people. She was not surprised when she found that many Europeans in Hollywood shared her skill but this Russian émigré was unlike anyone she'd ever met before.

"They tell me that you have a good mind," Rand said in a thick Russian accent.

"I've heard the same about you," Hedy an-

Ayn Rand

swered, lighting up her own cigarette so that she was equally well-armed. She marveled at Rand's severe pageboy haircut and clothes that would have been the height of fashion in the Roaring Twenties.

Suddenly Rand surprised her by coming off as typical Hollywood. "They showed me *Red Pawn* last night. You were marvelous, darling."

"Thank you," said Hedy and really meant it.

"Perhaps you would consider playing Kira if a film is made of my first novel which has just been published, *We the Living*."

"Is it another piece about the Soviets?" Hedy inquired.

"Yes," she replied, her body beginning to tense. No performer could work in a film of Rand's without realizing her depths of loathing for Communism. Her husband Frank had spoken of Rand's hatred of Reds and their ideology. This knowledge had helped Hedy turn in a better performance.

"I feel the much the same way about the Nazis that you feel about the Communists," Hedy replied. "We both come by our dislike fairly. We've both been in close contact with evil men."

"Yes," Rand agreed. "That's well put."

Josef Stalin

Part of Hedy's ability to size up people came from her sense of sexual adventure. When she found men or women who excited her, she acted on her feelings. She couldn't figure out Rand. At first she thought she might be bisexual as well, but now she wasn't sure.

Adolf Hitler

Hedy ran a little experiment. Walking toward them was a gorgeous young, blonde actress Hedy met when filming *Red Pawn*. She was Portuguese and her name was Paula LaBaredas. Hedy hadn't learned the girl's proclivities yet.

Paula was with a charming young man at the party, of course. Whether she was the wholesome girl next door or the Queen of Sin, Hedy found Paula exciting either way. She wondered how the girl would impress Rand.

"Hello, Paula, I'd like you to meet the author of our movie," Hedy made the introduction.

"A pleasure," said the girl as she took Rand's hand.

"You had a small part but you understood your character," Rand replied.

"Doesn't she have lovely skin?" Hedy remarked to Rand. "I just love this girl's complexion."

The author turned her gaze back on Hedy. It was as if she had dismissed Paula from her mind entirely. Hedy and Paula hugged each other goodbye and the young actress ran off to rejoin her date.

Ayn Rand

"I think we have more important matters to discuss than skin," said Rand.

"It's one of my favorite subjects," Hedy answered sweetly. The experiment had failed. She couldn't read the older woman's sexuality. She wondered if Rand knew about her affair with Frank.

"Is your husband here tonight?" Hedy asked.

"He's indisposed," Rand said. "I thought the two of you worked well together."

"He is a surprising man," Hedy said. "One minute he can be very forceful and yet the next so quiet and gracious, so undemanding . . ."

"Stop!" Rand held up her hand. "You are speaking of matters you can't possibly understood. Frank is my ideal man, my highest value."

"I understand," said Hedy quietly. "I feel that way about a man myself."

Rand softened. "May I ask who he is?"

"A genius," said Hedy.

Something changed in Rand's face. For the first time, Hedy felt a flicker of something like friendship from this very difficult woman.

"Would I know his name?" asked Rand.

"He's not part of the history of the world yet but he will be."

Rand nodded. "I understand the feeling. It derives from a commitment to reason. Do you love him?"

This evening certainly was full of surprises. Hedy's resolve not to think about the man of her dreams went up in smoke with the plumes of tobacco. She expected to have downed three drinks by now but she hadn't even had a sip of champagne.

Ayn Rand projected a luminous quality quite unlike anything Hedy had encountered before. Either the woman was brilliant or a bit mad. Maybe she was both. Rand made the art of thinking seem sexy. No wonder it was difficult to read the ebbs and flows of her sexual energy. This woman was in love with the mind!

"Yes, I love him."

Rand patted the actress on the arm. Hedy felt as if she'd received a friendly caress from a man. But there was nothing remotely sensual in it. Some people might take a first look at Rand and assume that she was a dyke. They'd be gravely mistaken.

H. G. Wells

"Maybe one day you can tell me all about your young man," said Rand, jumping to a correct conclusion. "But you're holding out on me, darling. I know you had a long intellectual conversation, only last year, with someone the world considers a genius. Word from this town gets around, especially in New York."

For the life of her, Hedy couldn't fathom what Rand was driving at. Then she remembered.

"You must mean the Englishman, Wells!"

"Yes."

"H. G. Wells," Hedy echoed herself. "He most certainly is a genius. He was in Hollywood last year when Korda was doing the big push on the British film version of *Things to Come*. Wells and I met at a party, just as we are doing now."

"How did he impress you?"

"He said he'd like me to appear in one of the film adaptations of his works."

"That proves he hasn't gone blind in his old age," said Rand with a smile.

"Don't you like him?" Hedy asked, noting the tone of disapproval.

"He's a socialist," Rand said simply.

For a moment, Hedy had hoped she could avoid politics. She remembered now that Rand was part of the minority still arguing for Capitalism even in the middle of the longest economic depression in U.S. history. No wonder that H. L. Mencken was a fan of her new novel.

"Well, at least he stood up to Stalin," Hedy said, searching for common ground.

"When was that?" Rand asked.

Now it was Hedy's turn to show off. Wells had personally given her a clipping from *The New York Times* of his

1934 interview with Stalin. She related the high-lights of that account.

"Wells told Stalin to his face that propa-ganda for violence was out of place and out of date. Wells came off as the defender of man-kind and civilization in opposition to Stalin!"

Rand clapped her hands in delight. "You are an intellectual, aren't you? Your delight in matters of the mind shows in your voice and shines through your eyes. Bravo! But, your story makes a good case for my position. I didn't say that Wells was a Communist. He has some good ideas and has always been a defender of science and progress. Like him, I'm an atheist. But his ideas on socialism are also out of date. One day you must allow me to convert you to Capitalism, darling!"

Hedy called over a waiter. She was ready for her drink now.

CHAPTER 9

Howard and Hemingway

An Afternoon in Murcia

"We are going to Murcia," announced Ernest Hemingway.

"We are?" echoed Howard Davidson. "I'm invited?"

"Of course," Hemingway insisted. "You're part of our intrepid band of writers. You crank out those magazine serials about, let me remember, the Bat and the Robin."

"The Turtle and the Dove!" Howard corrected him.

"Yes, indeed. Well, stick with me and I'll introduce you to some new subjects."

Davidson was delighted with this turn of events. He thanked the unexpected appearance of Chesterton during his first meeting with Hemingway for thawing out the great man to the American pulp writer. The mysterious appearance of the Anarchists' "wonder weapon" seemed to have further turned the tide in his favor. This latest invitation went a long way toward making Howard a believer in the change in Hemingway's attitude.

Hemingway's tendency toward combative display of his manly virtues had one major shortcoming, though, so far as Howard Davidson was concerned. Hemingway was more likely to go after something if one of his competitors also wanted it. He saw every other prominent writer as someone with whom he'd have to get into a boxing match sooner or later.

Ernest Hemingway

As a good American, Howard believed in the rough and tumble of fair competition. The main reason he hated dictators was that they weren't on the square. They weren't on the up and up. They cheated in the game of life and made millions of people suffer in the bargain.

But it was possible to have too much of a good thing. The more Howard experienced the great writer, the more obvious it was that the man was competitive in all sorts of small and petty ways. He pushed the boyish charm to the brink of a dangerous bravado.

It's not that the man didn't have guts. God knows, his courage was well-known as the equal of his tremendous talent. Whereas, in all the time that he'd been in Spain, Howard felt that he hadn't done anything requiring courage. Mainly he'd been lucky.

Howard recalled the night that Hemingway left the Hotel Florida, unwilling to tell anyone what was up. Until his mission was safely concluded, he was no blabbermouth. But after he returned, safe and sound, he resumed the role of the raconteur. Thanks to his contacts in the Comintern, he had been allowed to participate in a mission against the Fascists.

Again everyone was reminded that Hemingway was more than a writer. Like the Englishman George Orwell (a hero to every writer in Spain), Hemingway actually put his ass on the line.

However, unlike Orwell, Hemingway seemed to do his bit a few times and then it was back to being the celebrity. Orwell was actually serving as an officer on the line. There was another distinction between the two big names, as news traveled fast in Spain. The

George Orwell

word was out that Orwell didn't trust the Comintern any further than he could throw the White Cliffs of Dover.

Howard wished that Hemingway would cast the same jaundiced eye he reserved for publishers on the shadowy figures of the Comintern. By the simple expedient of keeping his eyes and ears open, the author of "Dripping Daggers of Doom" (all-time reader favorite of *The Inquisitor* series) was doing a lot of growing up in Spain. It wasn't always easy to separate the heroes from the villains in this war. But, as Chesterton had pointed out to everyone in the bar of the Hotel Florida, it really wasn't

possible to get away from issues of right
and wrong.

Christianity was most insistent on
that point, to the annoyance of virtually everyone. At some point Howard
intended to do a thorough investiga-
tion of Buddhism.

But here and now, the American
pulp writer faced the burden of choos-
ing sides in Spain. He wasn't going to
abdicate the responsibility by pretending there could be moral neutrality on
anything this important. There was no
moral neutrality in a world that had
Nazis in it.

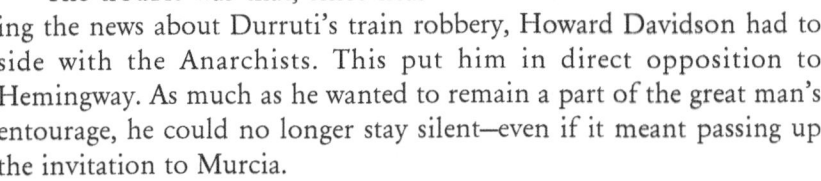

The trouble was that, since hear-
ing the news about Durruti's train robbery, Howard Davidson had to
side with the Anarchists. This put him in direct opposition to
Hemingway. As much as he wanted to remain a part of the great man's
entourage, he could no longer stay silent—even if it meant passing up
the invitation to Murcia.

"You can't trust anarcho-syndicalists," said Hemingway before tilt-
ing a hefty wine skin in the direction of his mouth and squeezing out a
fine, red stream.

The moment of truth had arrived. Howard said what he really
thought. "They may be the ones who'll win the war."

"How?" Hemingway wanted to know. "By stealing the Republic's gold?"

"We would never have known about the gold if Durruti hadn't
published pamphlets admitting it," said Howard. "Your pals in the
Comintern kept it a secret. The Republic kept the secret. The truth is
known only because the anarcho-syndicalists are telling everyone that
they took it."

"Don't fall for that line," said Hemingway, which really pissed off
Howard. "You shouldn't believe the Anarchist story. Obviously the Republic was moving the gold to a safer location so that it wouldn't fall
into Franco's hands. If Stalin provided help it's only because he sup-
ports the cause of the workers."

Howard tried to answer but he was too busy sputtering for anything
coherent to come out of his mouth. He finally understood how Dos

John Dos Passos

Passos felt the other night when Howard heard him arguing with Hemingway about his lost friend, Robles. The
walls were thin in the Hotel Florida.

Dos reported that Robles was dead. Hemingway said
he already knew and had been waiting for an opportune
time to break the bad news.

Because Robles had a
brother who fought on the side
of the Fascists, he was himself suspect despite
his unquestioned loyalty to the Republican
cause. The Communists snuffed out his life just
to be certain that he wouldn't let anything slip
to a family member. They were as casual about
the matter as one might be about erasing a
smudge on a ledger. Dos was enraged.
Hemingway didn't help by making another of
his cracks about the fortunes of war. The other
man slammed the door behind him. It sounded as though it might be a
permanent break between them.

Until hearing that exchange between Hemingway and Dos Passos,
Howard had always thought of the author of *Men Without Women* as a
true individualist. Sweltering in a badly ventilated hotel room far from
home, Howard decided that the books he'd loved for such a long time
were as good as ever. But from this point on, he'd have to take a certain
author's political judgments with a grain of salt large enough to go with a
Margarita the size of Lake Michigan.

Martha, official lady friend of the great author, seemed to operate in
the same unethical mental universe as her lover. "How do we know there
was any robbery at all?" she asked. "Officials right here in Madrid say they
still have the gold. The whole thing sounds like a propaganda hoax to me."

"Like the rumor of the wonder weapons?" asked a little ferret of a
man who was part of the Hemingway group but whose name forever

Hemingway and Martha

eluded Howard.

"That brings us back to our science
fiction author," said Hemingway with a
grin. "Do you believe that the Anarchists
have such weapons?"

"Someone has them," said Howard.
"Unless, that is, you don't think they really exist."

Hemingway became serious for a moment. "There are too many reports to ignore. For now, I prefer thinking of these things as Unidentified Flying Ordnance."

The ferret suddenly popped up with, "We keep saying *science fiction* all the time. Isn't the correct term *scientifiction?*"

Oh my god, thought Howard, *maybe this guy's a fan!*

"I don't want to bore anyone with this," Howard began, noting Martha's yawn. "But I do know the answer. Hugo Gernsback coined the term 'scientifiction' to go with the first regular magazine of this type, his brainchild *Amazing*. But when he lost control of the magazine, the special term went with it. He then started using another one of his coined phrases and it

Hugo Gernsback   has caught on."

"I like the original label," said Hemingway. "Scientific Romances! That sounds as if the hero might get his arms around something other than a polka-dotted monster."

"There are many kinds of monsters," said Martha, encircling her own choice of menace. Hemingway returned the favor.

"All right then," said the author of *The Sun Also Rises*. "We aren't going to solve the issues of the war today. I have a treat arranged for us. I like one aspect of an anarchistic state of affairs. No one is issuing stupid edicts against bullfighting!"

"The Matadors are the real rulers of Spain," muttered an old man listening to the conversation.

"As I've always believed," said Hemingway. "So we go to the Plaza de Murcia. We'll have breakfast and reach the town by afternoon or early evening. Tomorrow we're promised a most special bullfight."

"What about the war?" asked Howard.

"They'll put it on hold for us," chuckled Hemingway. "Nothing is happening right now anyway. Madrid will be here when we return. And now that we enter the month of July we have to do something to celebrate being American! We won't be home for hot dogs and fireworks on the 4th. So we'll have our own party."

Howard had to admit that there were certain ad-

vantages to Hemingway's contacts in the government of the Republic. The Comintern did more than see to it that he met Russian-trained generals. (One of whom was even a Pole, further proof of the international dimensions of Marxist-Leninism!) The Reds wanted Ernest to have a good time. They almost seemed to be in competition with his New York publishers to see which organization could guarantee Hemingway the largest profit.

Well, Howard Davidson was no fool, so he joined the gang of thrill-seekers on the road to Murcia.

The weather was good. The Spanish countryside could grow on a man. The rolling hills soothed Howard's tensions *much* better than the wine that members of his party insisted he guzzle with the rest of them.

Their truck was in good condition and didn't even lose a wheel when the driver failed to avoid a shallow crater resulting from a recent shelling. Deeper holes ahead would have crippled their axle but the driver was alert by then. Howard was grateful that the man hadn't joined them in their endless drinking bout.

Hemingway didn't speak for most of the journey. He even managed to take a nap despite the swaying of the vehicle. The example set, Howard joined his fellow writer in a snooze.

A barking dog awakened him to the sight of a beaming Hemingway. "We made great time!" he crowed.

It was late afternoon and the sun was in everyone's eyes. "We don't have to wait until tomorrow to catch our first fight," he said. "Let's go now and we'll grab a bite to eat later."

There was no arguing with the master of ceremonies. In the short time he'd known the man, Howard had never seen him so excited. Every literate person in the world recognized Hemingway as the poet laureate of the bullring. But, it was still surprising that he would be this eager for a second-rate bullfight.

There must be something else going on. The man had something up his sleeve.

Hemingway enjoys a quiet moment with the bulls.

Having never attended one of these spectacles before, Howard was in no position to judge the preliminaries. But he detected a touch of nervousness in the girlfriend. She must be an old hand at this and either sensed that all was not right in Murcia or she'd been tipped off to expect something unusual.

Howard didn't have to wait long for his suspicions to be vindicated. No expert was required to pronounce the sight before them "unusual." It was a spectacle worthy of the Roman games.

"The customs here are unusual," said Hemingway, relishing the obvious.

Either that, or the war had driven the country into a state of insanity. Howard felt a primitive emotion that he had described in the soul of his villain in many an installment of *The Inquisitor*, but he never expected to feel it himself.

Howard had expected to be above it all. He wasn't going to root for the Matador to torment the poor beast in the arena. Nor would he go in the other direction and hope that the man suffer a goring. He would sit calmly through the dance of death and chalk it up to quaint customs, all the while feeling vaguely superior to the brown people wearing their big sombreros and their big grins. When it was over, he would solemnly thank Hemingway for the experience, proud that his own heart had not beaten faster when the blood began to spill.

But the psychological game he played with himself was predicated on a human being entering the arena. There was no Matador below to take off his hat and receive flowers from admiring women.

There were only two animals. The bull was there. Of course there had to be a bull. But what maniac had thought of including a large, full-grown tiger?

"I don't believe it," gasped Howard.

Hemingway didn't say anything. He was too busy snapping pictures. Martha's breathing was loud enough for Howard to hear. The other members of the group strained forward exhibiting various responses ranging from disbelief to eye-popping horror.

The bull stood its ground, staring at the striped feline that began to pace back and forth.

The tiger didn't try to go around its prey. In the closed circle of the unnatural confrontation there was nowhere to go. No possibility of surprise.

Howard felt every bit as trapped as the animals. There was nowhere for him to go either. He hated himself for being fascinated by the imminence of carnage. *Damn* Hemingway for dragging him into this. *Damn* the man for being so right about human nature.

"They're taking their sweet time about it," Martha muttered just as the tiger made its move.

The crowd surged forward as if a third animal had joined the fray, exhaling its hot breath and quivering in anticipation of the deep, rich aroma of spilled blood and torn flesh. A collective gasp accompanied the tiger's leap onto the bull.

But the first screams of bestial delight from the crowd quickly transformed into  screams of laughter. It took a momob to realize ment for the the change in the program, in its entirety.

The tiger did not claw the bull. It did not bite and maul. Instead, the large feline began licking the bull's ponderous testicles. The bull didn't seem to mind. After the novelty wore off, the crowd began to mind very much.

Where was Nero when you needed him?

When Hemingway began to laugh, there was no stopping him. Well, he had promised an unusual event and he had most certainly delivered. Martha soon joined him and then everyone else in his group did the same.

But Howard didn't laugh. He was preoccupied with the seething emotions of the crowd. Somehow he didn't think they'd be satisfied with the absence of carnage.

He was right.

Men finally entered the ring. Not one wore the dashing costume of the Matador. Howard was actually glad about that. It didn't seem right for a fine Spanish gentleman of the cape and sword to prod at dumb beasts with long poles in an attempt to enrage them when the blood lust simply wasn't there.

A bull was always ready to fight the Matador. In an earlier time, a hungry tiger did not hesitate to attack the gladiator. But on this hot and sticky afternoon in Spain, two animals staged their own revolution against the entrenched authority of *Homo sapiens*.

The people would not have it. They jeered and taunted the men in the ring for not doing a better job of angering the beasts. One man either grew tired of the insults or else he became careless. He jabbed too hard and too fast and struck the tiger in the eye.

The tiger did not content himself with licking the man's genitals. Shortly after pouncing upon the helpless peasant, the big cat ripped out his throat and left the head dangling like a blood-filled balloon. The other men screamed and ran at which point the bull acted like a bull.

Howard had the weird sensation that the animals were acting in unison, completely impossible but a perception that he felt had a certain, darkly poetic, resonance— considering the turn of events. These nervous literary musings were not shared by the hapless men suffering the wrath of the combined attack of the enraged carnivore and the aroused herbivore. To these men it must have felt as though they were the first victims of the animalo-syndicalist union.

The bull's horns were strong and sharp. His neck was as solid as the hills the Hemingway party had traversed to come here. His nostrils flared and he breathed in the horror of the screaming man as he was lifted easily and gracefully on the bull's natural weapons.

The horns of the bull. The fangs and claws of the tiger. These instruments did their work and covered the white sand in deep, red blood.

The mob enjoyed every drop but pretended not to. They pretended to be glad when the Civil Guards came in with the weapons of man, weapons that render the beauty and terror of natural horn and fang into something sad and trivial. Man, who can make horn and fang into fossils ahead of their appointed time.

The guards opened fire with machine guns. The bull fell quickly but the tiger stood its ground. When the first volley stopped, the men and the tiger faced each other as the bull and the tiger had done earlier. The big cat seemed unscathed although that was impossible. But it kept on standing.

The men fired again and this time the big cat howled its death dirge in contrast to the silence of the bull. It didn't try to attack them but collapsed like an empty sack next to the bleeding carcass of the bull.

Martha was crying. She started slapping at Hemingway. He didn't resist but sat impassively. Howard found himself liking the big bear of a man again.

Martha Gellhorn

"Why did you make me watch that?" she asked. There was no possible answer but she should have known better than put a question to an author.

"Watching those animals slaughtered reminded me of the time people were machine-gunned at Badajoz. I wonder why this disturbs me more."

"It's so unexpected," said Howard, having already proven himself no slouch at answering rhetorical questions. "Animals are supposed to die a different way. We reserve certain deaths for ourselves and call it war."

"Not a bad line," said Hemingway. "You should write your pulp stories like that."

"Shut up, can't you?" demanded Martha.

"You ask a lot," he admitted.

The little ferret of a man got into the act. "I think we've received an omen for the future of mankind," he opined.

"Now that's more typical of your old style," Hemingway said to Howard, ignoring the ferret. "You need to work on that."

"Oh, shut up," said Martha again but her heart wasn't in it this time.

Howard decided to move the conversation to a higher plane. "Oh, what are we so worked up about? Spain is going to hell in a hand-basket. The rest of the world will probably follow soon. What do we care about the death of two dumb beasts?"

"As you pointed out yourself, it was unexpected," said Hemingway. "I have an idea. How many of your wonder weapons would it have taken to kill everything in that bullring?"

Howard grimaced. "You know that they're called the 'Horns of the Bull.' This might be the right place for them."

"Are we leaving now?" asked Martha, standing.

"Ready for dinner?" Hemingway asked in his most pleasant tone of voice. She didn't like that.

As they exited the entertainment facility, they learned to their dismay that the promised excitement offered by Hemingway's memorable day was by no means exhausted. A lone bull faced them in the street. The crowd barely noticed at first, but then men started shouting and everyone got the idea.

How the bull got loose was a good question, but it remains unanswered. Apparently this day was simply marked for chaos. And the Hemingway party was just as apparently marked for that particular bull because it didn't seem at all interested in the milling throng of Spaniards.

As fate would have it, the bull was standing in such a way as to block Hemingway's small group from entering the larger square. Their only avenue of escape was down a narrow alley. The bull snorted and headed straight for Martha who was completely frozen in her tracks. Hemingway took off his jacket and distracted the animal by throwing it away from Martha—but the article of clothing caught on a red and blue display of political posters advancing the cause of the POUM.

Howard surprised himself by what he did next. Removing his jacket, he took his turn at distracting the bull. He did a better job than Hemingway. With a snort of what sounded like derision, the bull fixed Howard with its clear, shining eyes and charged.

Howard heard the voices of his friends (for at times like this any other human is your friend) shouting all kinds of advice but for Howard their voices had the same inconsequential background quality that one associated with falling rain on a distant rooftop. It was just as well because he wasn't going to listen to anyone but himself now. Mainly, he strove to hear, in his mind, what he'd been told about situations like this. Naturally, if ironically, the voice he heard in his mind was Hemingway's.

Of course, the one person in his life who had given him the most advice about what to do when being attacked by a bull was none other than Ernest Hemingway, just a few days ago. Remembering the advice given then was going to be more useful than trying to make out the words shouted at him now.

Unfortunately, as he recalled the conversation, most of the advice was about what to do when one was present at the *running* of the bulls. Running with the bulls meant *literally* running with the bulls. You wouldn't be caught under their hoofs if you joined with them. Great advice, but somewhat useless when being pursued by one bull down a narrow alley!

There was nowhere to escape. No doors or windows beckoned him to safety. And now that he was engaged in a life and death race with this one particular animal it was difficult to implement the rule about running *with*, not away from the bull!

He was left with only one course of action. He knew that he needed to distract the bull. You were supposed to distract the bull! He had already lost his jacket in his first attempt, which had worked well enough at distracting the bull from Martha—only to give it a fixation on him.

Maybe he would have better luck with his shirt. He hurriedly unbuttoned it and threw over his head. If luck were with him, the bull would try to gore the moving object nearest him. If he remained lucky the shirt might at least slow the bull down.

If he were even luckier, the shirt would cover the bull's eyes and the animal might stop in its tracks. Whatever the outcome, Howard would know soon because he was about to run out of alley!

Panting for breath, Howard Davidson reached the alley's dead end and the dull, brown walls that had been rushing by his sides were joined by an equally dull, brown wall in front of him, without even a single political poster in sight. For some reason he hadn't yet felt the horns of the bull ripping into his spinal cord. Had the desperate ploy with the shirt actually worked?

He turned around. His shirt hung off one of the horns but in no way obstructed the bull's vision. The big eyes continued to stare at their intended prey as the animal snorted in apparent frustration.

Howard had been so busy running for his life that he hadn't noticed that the alley had kept narrowing until it became impossible for the bull to continue. The animal was stuck!

Exhausted, Howard sat down as best he could in the narrow confines and counted his blessings. He heard the sound of men coming up behind the bull to perform the unenviable task of trying to back it out.

The experts finally succeeded. The sun had set by the time Howard Davidson rejoined the Hemingway party. He assumed that they'd be laughing over his close call, but also laughing over his deliverance and ready to ply him with good liquor for the rest of his life.

He could tell from their expressions that something was very wrong. "Whatever's happened, can it wait until we get back to Madrid?" he asked. "I can't take any more excitement."

"We won't be going back to Madrid," said Hemingway.

"You mean we'll be staying here longer than tonight?" he asked.

"He means we aren't going back to Madrid," said Martha. "Not ever!"

"Sleepless Sirens of Atlantis"
Unpublished Extract

"What have you done with her?" the Turtle demanded.

The Inquisitor chortled. "Wouldn't *you* like to know?"

"You mean you actually aren't going to tell him?" demanded the Dove.

"How long can we continue asking each other questions before some-one has to provide an answer?" queried the Turtle.

"Do you actually believe, for even a second that I will answer before you tell me where you've hidden my inertia bomb?" the Inquisitor growled at his two prisoners.

"Why should we even begin to tell you anything when you're too much of a coward to show us the face you keep hidden underneath that crimson hood?" the Dove asked, deflecting several of the previous questions.

"Are you such fools as to believe that my malign purposes or aesthetic appearance can be fathomed by your puny intellects?" sneered their captor, slowly turning the dial on his neutronic reactor.

"Why not? You defy the natural order of the universe?" said the Turtle through clenched teeth.

"That wasn't a question!" roared their infernal foe.

"Yes, it was," said the Dove.

"No," shrieked the Evil One. "It was a declarative statement."

CHAPTER 10

Aragon, June 1937

Orwell Meets the Anarchists

There were many kinds of silence in Spain. There was the silence of waiting for stalemates to end. There was the silence of hunger and disease. There was the silence of death and those who were past pain and only waiting to die.

But the worst silence was about regret and memories that haunted the living. The man the world knew as George Orwell did not want to be a pessimist. He had come to Spain with high hopes only to see them dashed by cold and calculating minds that were supposedly on his side.

Barcelona was the worst nightmare of his life. At least he had managed to find his wife and they had gotten out of the city before the general arrests began. Eileen didn't doubt that her husband would rank high on any list of enemies drawn up by the Comintern.

He told her that he wanted to return to the front but didn't think it was right to take her with him. She had a ready answer to his objections. After all, she'd be in danger if she stayed behind. Anyone with an association to the POUM was about to become a target.

So the two of them went to Aragon around the middle of June. The front was not as he had left it. When the Anarchists became a great power, they began to move on the map of Spain.

145

"Aragon is our base of operations for now," said Buenaventura Durruti as he shook hands with Orwell and his wife. "We are planning a major winter campaign."

Some of Orwell's old comrades had joined the Anarchists. Some were imprisoned or dead, thanks to the Communists. Some had gone over to the government side, or tried to. Orwell thought ex-POUM militiamen might fare as well offering their services to the Fascists!

"There are times I'm grateful for your fame," Eileen had said as they arrived at the Anarchist camp. Orwell didn't disagree. It was one thing for his sympathies to take him in the direction of the most radical of the radicals. But joining the Anarchists was a large step. It was nice to be trusted so quickly.

Eric Blair

He chatted with Durruti as old soldiers do. Orwell wondered if they had solved the problem of lice that drove him nuts back in April. They'd get into his trousers and nothing short of burning the pants would make a difference. The damned buggers were the only downside of the warmer weather.

Painting of Durruti with FAI/CNT..

Durruti boasted that what he had done to the lice only a short time before he would next do to the Fascists.

Eileen recalled that Trotsky had once complained that Durruti was the man who wanted to give Spain a raincoat full of holes. She tried to make a joke of that but stumbled over a few Spanish words. He helped her and then said in perfect English: "The idea is to stop the rain when each rain-drop is a bullet intended to destroy the people's freedom."

"Thank you for driving the Fascists away from here before my husband returned," she said. "I always fear that he'll run out of luck and get himself shot!"

Eileen Blair

Durruti made it easy for his distinguished, but slightly nervous, guests. He so much wanted to put them at their ease that he served them tea. It was, in fact, around four p.m. when he invited them into his tent. Eileen quickly revised her opinion of a man she'd heard was as likely to cut a throat as put a bandage on a wound. Although his face was hard, it wasn't cruel.

"I've been a robber and a criminal," he said. "Prison did not teach me to improve my trade. Instead, I learned a different lesson when I recognized the similarity between criminals and the State. I decided I didn't want any part of either."

"I know what you mean," agreed Orwell, slurping tea out of a saucer in the style of an English working man. His wife smiled inwardly, always amused when her husband labored so hard to distance himself from his Etonian background.

"I've read your work," said the leader of those who sought a world without leaders.

"Brutal conditions make for brutal men," said Orwell. "It is what I most hate about Fascism. I've always wanted to live in a cooperative society but not if it comes at the price of whips and barbed wire."

"I share your opinion. I want a libertarian communism for the people but the important thing is liberty first! While you are among us, you will meet individualist libertarians. If it had not been for this war, I would not even dream such people exist. Many are from America and England. You will also meet Augustin Ortiz, the world's first Spanish Agorist."

"What's that?" asked Orwell.

"You'll have to ask him. The idea still confuses me."

Eileen cheered. "These are truly revolutionary times! I love that your side is acquiring individualist recruits from America. It makes up for so many Party members joining the Abraham Lincoln Brigade."

Orwell finished his tea. He always had a healthy appetite. "I like fine theories as much as the next man," he said. "but they don't amount to much when you're in the ground."

"We intend to *take* ground rather than go into it," said Durruti.

"How much ground?"

"The whole of Spain before we are finished."

Orwell pursed his lips. "A tall order."

"Yes, but inevitable. We always had support among the people. Now we have so much more!"

"The gold train?" Orwell always spoke what was on his mind.

Durruti was more than willing to address the topic. "We have plans for that money. First, we are

Buenaventura Durruti at the Front.

buying weapons. A lot of them."

Ever since his arrival in Spain, Orwell had been cursing the inadequate supplies. He could stand going without a meal or a smoke but there was no excuse for not providing fighting men with the tools of victory. He'd even been forced to buy a pistol on the black market. Some of the rifles he gave his men were antiques. One blew up and put a man out of action, although he survived.

"Before I left Barcelona, I saw something you should know," said Orwell. "The government's Assault Guards had new rifles, nothing like the junk I've been forced to use. They called them Russian rifles but I suspect they were really made in America."

"Don't worry about that," said Durruti. "Soon we will settle many old scores. As for the weapon situation, we have excellent sources of supply. Later I'll introduce you to an American who is invaluable to our future arsenal."

He stood and went over to the little table where he kept his kitchen supplies. Eileen noticed that he made tea the British way by first warming the pot before adding the tea. As their beverage was brewing, he resumed his litany of good news.

"Second, we will be making more of our special weapon, the Horns of the Bull. You are no doubt aware of the impact it has had so far."

Orwell nodded. Everyone had heard of this miracle. "How did you come by such a device? I'd love to see one."

"You will, my friend. You will also meet the German wizard who makes them for us. Which brings me to the third point. This wizard isn't through making weapons for us yet! He has a friend back in Germany who will join us soon. Together they will do things you can scarcely believe when price is no object."

"Germany?" Orwell asked with a surprised look of concern and puzzlement.

"Of course. You have no doubt met German radicals of all persuasions. Who is better qualified to fight Hitler than those who know him best?"

January 1937, Orwell (rear), Barcelona with POUM.

Aragon, March 1937, Eric Blair (tall) and Eileen (seated).

"True," said Eileen. "But you said that one of them is still in Germany."

"In the underground. He comes and goes, but it is becoming dangerous for him. The next time he leaves it will be for good. But enough talk! Come with me now and you will meet my Teutonic friend. Our tea can wait."

They left his tent and followed him up a ridge to where a small, ramshackle construction jutted out, an alien artifact protruding from the stark hillside. The barren branches of an ancient tree clawed at its roof. Orwell could almost believe that a wizard was inside. There was nothing remotely military about the appearance of the shack.

There was a large metal tower next to the shack. Slowly rotating on top, with a groaning sound of metal on metal, was a bizarre contraption which resembled a gigantic metal box-kite. The small party stopped in its tracks and marveled at the spectacle before entering.

Orwell was a tall man. He'd become accustomed to towering over many of his comrades. So, the first thing he noticed about Wernher von Braun was his height. Even bending over a tangle of conductive wire, the man seemed to need far more space than the shack afforded. He almost bumped his head when he snapped to attention upon seeing Durruti.

"Cut that out, Wernher," said the Anarchist, good naturedly. "I've worked all these years to convince my men not to salute or bother with any other military nonsense. You've got to stop being such a good German."

Von Braun laughed. "You can blame my Prussian background. And thank you for bringing such a distinguished guest to my humble cabin."

"You know me?" asked Orwell.

"Everyone knows you," he answered.

"Your English is excellent," said Eileen,

extending her hand. Von Braun delighted her by taking it in the most formal way and yet kissing it with the passion of a cavalier.

"You must have Spanish blood in that gangly body of yours," said Durruti, approvingly. "But you must work on your accent. In fact, all three of you speak my native tongue quite well but with the most abominable accents."

"What are you doing?" Orwell asked Von Braun, gesturing at various components strewn across a rough wooden work bench and the control panel that he used to aim the beam antenna on the tower.

"Attempting something that my good friend, Konrad, could handle with far greater ease. I am building a radio receiver. We are at such a high altitude that we should be able to receive a static-free signal if we only use the proper equipment."

"We can never have too many radios," said Orwell, in agreement. "It's disgusting that the Republic outlawed all amateur radio sets since the uprising."

"They become more like the Fascists every day," added Durruti. "Our lovable comrades in the Communist Party want a monopoly over all radio transmission in the Republic."

"Practical anarchy begins at home," muttered von Braun as he fiddled with a dial.

"You will build a magnificent short-wave radio receiver," said Durruti. "I have total confidence in you."

"I should be able to do this," agreed von Braun. "Even if it's *not* rocket science."

"Who's this?" asked Eileen, holding up a framed picture of Hedy Lamarr. "She looks just like a movie star."

"She is," he said. "She's just starting to hit it big in Hollywood but she worked in Europe first."

Eileen's eyebrows shot up. "Somehow I don't see you as a movie fan."

"We're friends. She believes in the cause and will be joining us."

"My, you are full of surprises!" Eileen was positively beaming. "Is she German, too?"

"Austrian."

"So is Hitler," said Orwell.

"I wish he'd go into acting," said von Braun.

"Does he ever do anything else?" asked Durruti. Everyone laughed.

Von Braun told them some more about his makeshift receiver and how he built the four-element beam antennae to pick up frequencies from Spanish broadcasts. He promised to have his device finished within forty-eight hours.

He even started to tell his new friends about how various Anarchist brigades were already benefitting from acquisition of the German Teleprinter but Durruti waved him off from that subject. Orwell reflected that even decentralized syndicalists had to keep a few bureaucratic secrets.

"Wernher, why don't you admit why you're in such a rush to finish your radio?" Durruti's tone suggested that he was teasing the scientist.

Von Braun shrugged. "I'll confess," he began with a smile. "We don't have enough radios here. Daily we go through a little revolutionary struggle over which station to tune in."

Durruti found the situation amusing. "Usually Von Braun wants to listen to EAQ which broadcasts in different languages. And sometimes he switches over to Radio Debunk so he can hear samples of the more blatant Nazi propaganda."

"But many want to hear what comes over the station in Burgos," von Braun complained. "That's where you tune in to hear the Republic badmouth us!"

"The best entertainment is from Seville," added Durruti, almost as an afterthought.

"So you see how it is," said von Braun. "Some of our comrades even want to listen to obscure Catholic stations reporting all the different processions in little villages to honor the Virgin Mary."

Orwell snorted in sympathy. "Everyone needs his own radio!"

Von Braun scratched his head. "We could carry this idea too far, I suppose. But if something vital comes in over the airwaves, the von Braun studios certainly will be open to this wonderful company."

"Speaking of company, you are all invited to dinner," said Durruti. "No dull beans for us tonight. I offer an excellent cod and Spanish rice."

As they followed him to the feast, Eileen reminded him that she was still waiting for her second cup of tea.

Aragon, July 1937

The Poisoned Dwarf

Dr. Paul Joseph Goebbels

On July 4 the same group convened in von Braun's shack to hear a radio broadcast. The receiver had been working well for two weeks but nothing had yet come over the air waves that was as important as today's news.

The Nazis had taken Madrid in a lightning-fast attack that they dubbed *blitzkrieg* or "lightning war." The world stood aghast. As for what Stalin's reaction would be, everyone's imaginations were running overtime.

During this attack on Madrid the Anarchists had struck an unexpected blow against the Nazis. One of Durruti's men had been in town with a "Horns of the Bull" rocket assembly. He sent it straight up at a Stuka dive-bomber coming straight down. The results were most satisfactory.

Since the completion of the short-wave set, Orwell spent many an evening with von Braun sharing a bottle of brandy and trying to figure out what Dr. Paul Joseph Goebbels was up to. For months, the Propaganda Minister of the Third Reich seemed to be taking an inordinate interest in Spain. Orwell thought that was a bad sign.

Goebbels employed a standard trick. He oversaw broadcasts from Salamanca that appeared to be standard Spanish radio programming, having no connection to Germany. Each of these supposedly "Spanish" broadcasts was carefully designed to include a single false impression on

Joseph Goebbels

matters of import to the Republic. The innocent listener would never know that embedded in each, otherwise factual, broadcast was one propaganda lie designed to undermine the Republic.

But now the game changed. With the occupation of Madrid, the Nazis could come out of the propaganda woodwork and drop the subtle approach. To hammer home this change in tactics the German Propaganda Minister himself took a plane to Aranjuez where he insisted on making a broadcast to the world. It was common knowledge that the "poisoned dwarf" (as his enemies called him) was considered, in many quarters, to be the most persuasive speaker in Nazi Germany. As far as Hitler was concerned, Goebbels was the number-two orator, which was all his sycophantic cheerleader needed to be considered in a state of grace.

Tonight Goebbels would read the same speech in both Castilian and Catalan for the native population. Then he would do the honors in English, French and German. The show-off!

Von Braun wondered if the good doctor really spoke that many languages or if he was reading from specially prepared texts written out phonetically and carefully rehearsed to give the impression of a fluent command of all the languages. Orwell said he didn't give a rat's ass but intended to listen to the speech in every language he understood. Martha and Durruti said nothing.

The speech was the same in every version. It would have been the same in Esperanto. The voice was sonorous and reassuring.

Men and women of Spain, we come as your friends. The liberation of Madrid from the coils of Judeo-democracy is a victory for European culture. You have been fighting among yourselves when you should have joined against the common enemy of your noble civilization.

From the beginning of our movement, the National Socialists of Germany have seen the possibility of a new Europe where no important nation is excluded from its place at the table. We admire the greatness of Spain and have been heartsick to see the Bolshevik assault on your most sacred traditions and the integrity of your folkways.

Naturally we wished to extend a helping hand to General Franco and the Nationalist forces under his command. We had no other choice when your brave and persecuted nation faced a despicable attack from Bolshevik agitation from the east and an economic war against you conducted by western banking institutions. It's an old story. But only now is the world beginning to recognize the truth.

The pattern is always the same. The poison is always the same. Your nation has been infected and we offer our services as a doctor who, generously, makes house calls.

As in the case of so many others, you have a nation that wants nothing more than to put its house in order. You want to run Spain your own way. And we of the Third Reich want nothing less for you.

We have the same goals. We want you to have a healthy nation in which your children can grow up clean in mind and strong in body. We are here to help you achieve this worthy goal. The cause of your calamity is the same as all the troubles of Europe. You are the latest victims of the Jews.

Our occupation of Madrid is a temporary measure. This was necessary because of the dimensions of the threat you face. General Franco cannot clean the house all by himself. He is a good man who does the best he can. We will help him to the best of our ability.

Consider what three groups of Jews have done to your country. Jewish Communists, Jewish Capitalists, and Jewish Anarchists give the Spanish people no chance for survival as anything but slaves. The enemy fight among themselves only when they can afford to do so. Let a strong and uncompromising force challenge them in their dens of vice and iniquity and then you shall see the true face of the Hebrew.

Don't think for one moment that a Jewish Capitalist is going to let a Jewish Communist starve. On the other hand,

let the so-called revolution come to a grasping, usurious center of finance capital and
watch what happens. The Jewish Capitalist
will not be dispossessed or imprisoned by
the Jewish Bolshevik. They never know when
they will need each other again! As for the
Anarchists, they are Jews with the gloves off.

Spain would never have been pushed
to the brink of absolute destruction without the involvement of the worst conspiracy in human history. We have entered

Paul Joseph Goebbels

Madrid because it is a beachhead in the fight to reclaim Spain
for the New Culture of a revived European people. We would
save you from the three-headed dragon that devours your children. Centuries ago, Spain inquired into ways of solving the
problem but failed. We will now finish the job.

Men and women of Spain, join us in this noble crusade.
Join us in a campaign of racial hygiene for which your children
and children's children will be eternally grateful in the eyes of
the Almighty.

We will use our power to save your great heritage and we
will also help you rebuild. We will stop the destruction of Church
property. We will do this in the name of history and the patri-
mony of Western Civilization. This has nothing to do with
religion but everything to do with that which springs from your
blood and soil.

Consider one fact that you have probably never heard before. The Jews have been the bane of the West long before the

advent of Christianity. The proof is
overwhelming but here is but one example. In the First Century B.C., the
Roman statesman, Cicero, complained about the usurious practices
of the Jews and proclaimed them to
be a dark force in the world. A century later Christ drove the money
changers out of the Temple.

It is a great mistake to see our
movement for racial hygiene in the
antiquated terms of a religious con-

Paul Joseph Goebbels

flict. This is a mistake common to your country in all classes because you have never been shown the scientific basis for a vigorous anti-Semitism. Never fear. We will provide you with everything we have discovered. We intend to share our knowledge and progressive methods with all the countries of Europe until this great continent is pure once again.

Only some of you are hearing my voice at this time but that, too, will change. We intend to give Spain a gift of thousands of radio sets, the *people's* radios, so that we may do a better job of keeping in touch. The peasants and the workers need to know what is going on in their own country. We do not mean to fault the Fascists of Spain who have done the best they can under trying circumstances, but they don't have our techniques. We will help teach them about the importance of modern communications.

Now I specifically address the people of Madrid. The curfews are temporary until we have rooted out the enemy in your midst. The Gestapo is here to help. If the task is beyond them, we may also expect assistance from the SS. Everything at our disposal will be made available to you. Please remember to complete your paperwork carefully and carry your identity cards with you at all times. The price of security is eternal vigilance.

In conclusion, I want to make a few remarks about the historical significance of this date, July 4th. This is the date they celebrate Independence Day in the United States of America. We think it wholly appropriate that, on this same day, we establish our policies to liberate this vital and important city from the parasites.

You know, some people think we Nazis don't have a sense of humor. But so far I've resisted making the claim that we performed this military operation to liberate the German minority in Madrid. Oh, I made a joke after all! Maybe we *can* find a few Germans if we look hard enough.

But, to end on a serious note, we are

proud to draw a parallel with the American
fourth of July. That is because there are two kinds
of revolutions. The Russian revolution was a victory of parasites on a nation's blood. The eternal enemy tried to do the same thing to you here
in Spain. In contrast, the American revolution was
against foreign parasites who infiltrated the com-
munities they exploited. These blood-suckers were finally cast out.

That is exactly the kind of revolution our great Leader, Adolf
Hitler, has brought to Germany. He is ridding us of our parasites. He is willing to do the same for you if you will only take
the hand he is offering in friendship.

After they listened enough times, von Braun switched off the set. They
sat in silence for a long time.

There are many kinds of silence in Spain.

"Was it real?" asked Martha.

"I take it as a personal reminder," said
von Braun. "I must finish my greatest project
as soon as possible."

"I take back my suggestion that everyone needs a personal radio," said Orwell.
"Not if they get it from the little doctor!"

"How will our American friends respond
to the comparisons with their July 4th?"
asked Durruti.

"With horror," said Orwell.

"I take this speech just one way," said
the man who was, in effect, commanding
General over all the Anarchist brigades. "The
worst Fascists in the world have seized

Madrid. Now we will take a city of our own. The plans are in place."

"May we know?" asked Orwell, holding hands with his wife. He was
not characteristically a man who showed public affection.

"You will approve, my friend. It is the only logical choice. We are
going to take Barcelona."

Early Summer, 1937
Franco and von Ribbentrop

Francisco Franco

General Francisco Franco couldn't believe the gall of the man. He thought the Jews had a word for it. They called it *chutzpah*.

Of course, it was expecting too much for Hitler's foreign minister to see himself as any sane person saw him. None of the Nazis seemed to have a clue or care about that. All that mattered to Joachim von Ribbentrop was that he had taken time out of his intensely busy schedule to actually meet with the Spanish leader personally. Such an encounter should be taken as a signal honor. Further, when one considered that von Ribbentrop was deigning to have *breakfast* with Franco, well, that should raise the visitation to Olympian heights.

That was as close as Franco could get to seeing the world through the Nazi official's eyes. He did not desire to be any closer. But he had to complete this discussion, however painful the experience. So he sipped coffee and watched the German wolf down his eggs.

Von Ribbentrop had a high forehead. He probably thought he was a genius. Franco wished that the Third Reich didn't have quite so many smirking geniuses.

"I was not informed," the general complained.

"You already said that."

"How could Germany take such a precipitous action as to occupy Madrid without first consulting with me?"

"I already explained. There was no time. Besides, we're doing you a favor."

"How do you conclude that?" asked Franco, already dreading the answer.

"Your Fascism is out of date, general. Your heart is in the right place and you can always count on our assistance, but you fail to see the broader picture."

"I don't understand," Franco frowned. But, of course, he did understand. All too well.

"Look, you have no popular support, not really. The rich are behind you and some romantics

Joachim von Ribbentrop

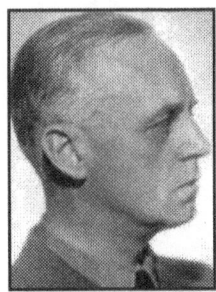

Joachim von Ribbentrop

who miss the good old days. You also have the clerics. You'd be better off without them at all!"

"But that's the old order," said Franco. "When have I ever pretended to be attempting anything other than the restoration of the natural *order* in Spain?"

Von Ribbentrop held up his hand, signaling Franco to wait while he finished swallowing a mouthful of toast. It looked as though the man was *Sieg Heiling* Franco.

Would this terrible meal never end?

"It's this way, general. A few big, feudal land owners do not form the basis of a lasting regime. You have to inspire the masses. Even the damned Reds know that much! We're going to help you become part of the 'larger' European picture. And, before we're done, we'll remake the world."

The general shook his head. "But it's precisely because I don't *want* to remake the world that I led the rebellion against the radicals in the Republic."

Von Ribbentrop gobbled down a sausage. "Ha! They think they're radical. Wait until they see what we have in store for the future. We're challenging the false cultural traditions of thousands of years."

"I don't want to challenge anything like that," said the general with a sigh. He stared at his plate of untouched food. He doubted

Adolf Hitler salutes the German troops.

that he would ever regain his appetite.

"Don't worry about it," said von Ribbentrop. "Did you know," he added, "that a lot of people say you're more brutal than Mussolini? Did you know that?"

The general nodded. It was suddenly hard to speak.

"Well, you just keep being brutal and leave the driving to us," said von Ribbentrop.

German military magazine: "Condor Legion at the Front," and
"German Volunteers Fight for Spain."

CHAPTER 11

Aragon, Summer 1937

Orwell Meets the Capitalist

George Orwell was looking forward to meeting Chuck Hammill. He hoped the man would live up to Durruti's endorsement. Hammill was one of the few Americans with whom the anarcho-syndicalist leader did business. Although Hammill was a famous capitalist, Spain's most prominent exponent of anarchistic communism thought he was "the cat's pajamas," to employ a bit of American slang that had recently caught on with the brigade.

Leaders of other Anarchist brigades were also showing up for Hammill's appearance. The American Agorists would be there and the British Distributists. Regarding the latter, Orwell learned that not all of Durruti's adherents thought of themselves as anarchists. But, evidently, those that did not were content to be considered fellow travelers. Apparently Hammill was not an Anarchist either, but called himself a libertarian. Orwell had never met so many variants of libertarians in his life. He was fascinated.

From the time of his first meeting with Durruti, Orwell and Eileen had been honored to sit in on select meetings of the Iron Column, the anarchist's inner circle. Today was something brand new. The Iron Column was sponsoring a presentation by Hammill that was even open to

161

Emma Goldman

select representatives of the radical press. It was the sort of stunt that only Anarchists would dare to pull. It also demonstrated the confidence of this new force growing in Spain.

Up until this point, Hammill had conducted his business with a low profile. He was apparently some kind of New York banker. Orwell wondered how someone in his position could do business with certain International Brigades. The answer exploded from Durruti's mouth: "Guns!"

The New York banker turned out to be the most successful gun runner in the entire world. But Hammill insisted on selecting his customers carefully. He claimed never to have made a direct deal with Communists or Fascists. He joked that so many millionaires were doing business with the dictators that it only left Hammill a niche market with freedom fighters.

The anarchist's business relationship with the gun runner preceded the "acquisition" of the gold. Now that Durruti was one of the richest men in the world, the deals would become even more important and sweeter.

Orwell and his wife were introduced to the prominent visitor prior to his appearance at the Iron Column presentation. "I understand that you know Emma Goldman," said Orwell as he shook hands with Hammill.

"Yes, I first met her back when the Wilson administration succeeded in having her deported," he replied. "Henry Mencken and I tried to stop that miscarriage of justice but, I'm sorry to say, we failed."

"Well," volunteered Eileen, "if America hadn't exiled her to Russia, we never would have received her criticism of Lenin in *My Disillusionment with Russia*."

"Stalin has been working hard ever since to disillusion everyone else," added Orwell.

H. L. Mencken

V. I. Lenin

Hammill was dressed for the mountain terrain with an all-weather jacket, heavy boots and a rumpled old Fedora hat. The only photograph Orwell had seen of the man was taken at a swank New York private club specializing in pretty girls and stage magic. One item from the picture stayed in the Englishman's memory, however, and he saw that Hammill still carried it: a silver-headed sword cane. The most notable feature was the silver head which

Lysander Spooner

had been fashioned into a mermaid, her top half charmingly bare and posed so that any hand grasping the hilt must be in full contact with her torso. Truly this was an *objet d'art*.

He must watch his step with Hammill. The man was charming, but Orwell had been a critic of capitalism for too long to be converted by a few friendly words. The tragedy of his life was his honest recognition that every attempt to achieve Socialism that he'd examined turned out to be a jackbooted disaster. That was why he remained an independent man of the Left, still searching for an equitable path to a more egalitarian society.

Now he was meeting a new kind of libertarian from America. Hammill chatted amiably about some of his influences: Lysander Spooner, Benjamin Tucker, H. L. Mencken, Albert Jay Nock—and there was someone new on the scene he found promising, a woman named Ayn Rand. Apparently she was developing a theory of libertarianism that was the precise opposite of Orwell's egalitarian

Benjamin Tucker

spirit.

Orwell was in for an even greater surprise when Hammill said, "I saw a sneak peek of a movie she wrote against the Communists. It's terrific. There's a splendid, new actress in it named Hedy Lamarr."

Albert J. Nock

Eileen pulled at Orwell's sleeve and gave him a can-you-believe-this look. Von Braun had left the night before to arrange details about Hedy's imminent arrival in Spain. Getting the prominent actress safely to Aragon was no small task.

They shared the news with Hammill and his reaction delighted them. "I always trust my instincts. No wonder I'm her biggest fan! So she's going to join your band of heroes! I regret that I must leave tomorrow and won't be here when she arrives. Will someone get me her autograph?"

Durruti volunteered for the welcome task. Orwell chewed on the end of a pretty bad cigar and marveled at how strange everything had become since people who believed in a communal life were suddenly as wealthy as King Midas. Would they make a film while she was here, starring Hedy, to keep up everyone's morale? Would she entertain the troops? Apparently anything was possible in this brave new world.

Ayn Rand

Chesterton, Distributist

Tables had been set up outdoors and the guests enjoyed a fine meal. During this picnic Orwell met the mysterious Ortiz, the Spanish adherent of American Agorism. As best as Orwell could make it out, the theory consisted of the notion that all the good guys should disappear into the black market and stay there. This would cause serious problems for the bad guys. End of story.

The Distributist leader, a fellow Englishman named Rod Bennett, questioned the Agorist theory of absentee land ownership. Orwell started feeling right at home and was about to comment when Hammill beat him to the punch.

"Landlords in a free market are the opposite of those who exercise brute force though a monopoly of State and Church. Your lovely country is only now emerging from an era of feudalism. The road to freedom requires a respect for individual rights and private property. Landlords provide a useful service in a truly free society."

Orwell couldn't help intervening at this point. "What happens, then, when private property interferes with individual rights?"

Hammill swatted at a fly that had landed on his mutton-chop whiskers. Then he dabbed a napkin on his mouth after taking a sip of the best wine Durruti had to offer. "My dear Orwell," he said, "the rights of private property *are* individual rights in a free society. When Kings and priests and dictators dole out the property, then you get into trouble."

Orwell sampled the wine although he would rather be drinking a beer. "I think the Fascists are doing a job for the Capitalists," he said simply. "If we achieve a free society in Spain I fear that the British Navy might sail an Armada over here and set things to rights."

Hammill nodded. "I appreciate your sarcasm and I agree with it. But the problem with the British Empire is that it's the British Empire. Times are changing. Progress, you know. Maybe your country should try Capitalism just for the hell of it!"

Durruti laughed first. "He's really a character, isn't he? The only man I've ever met who's even more bizarre is Konrad Zuse, Von Braun's chum. He's always going on about mechanical brains. Jesus Christ! I used to think I was strange."

"Tell him about your time in prison," Eileen goaded their host.

"Which one? I've been in so many. Maybe Mr. Eric Blair over there will do an essay about the period when I was locked up in Catalonia."

"I might do an homage to that," Orwell agreed. Meanwhile, he felt the tension escaping like air rushing out of a balloon. He was no stranger to factionalism and varying theories among radicals. But the curse of Stalinism was that it ultimately stifled debate by concurrently embracing some ridiculous theory of internal criticism. Here, with *these* people, George Orwell experienced the bracing winds of freedom without a Big Brother looking down and telling them not to veer from the orthodox position.

Thank God.

Besides, he had only recently seen the other side of factionalism in the streets of Barcelona. Disagreements ended with murders and arrests. It was like an insane alphabet soup with the working class vaguely represented by the CNT and the FAI and the POUM, in opposition to

the PSUC. It was a lot better here and now at Durruti's picnic with the capitalist.

When everyone was well fed and slightly drunk, Chuck Hammill gave both a lecture and a demonstration. Orwell took notes.

Hammill's Presentation

"Let's talk about the Good Old Days," Hammill began. "Psychological warfare has always been with us. Once upon a time during a siege of a walled city in Europe, the defenders of the city got a bright idea. The attackers assumed that the defenders were almost out of provisions and must therefore be on the verge of surrender. Guess what? That was the truth but the defenders of the city didn't want to let on. So they took their last pig and their last handful of grain, went up to the top of the

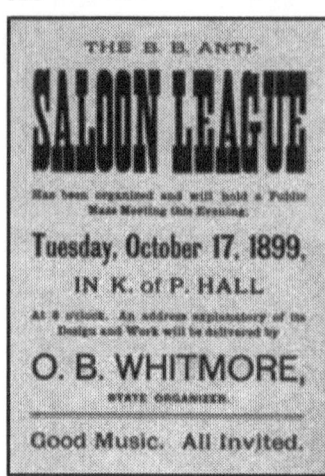

tallest tower where the enemy could see them nice and clear. They fed the pig the grain and then tossed the animal over the wall!"

"What happened?" asked an eager young Distributist.

"The enemy threw in the towel and went home," said Hammill. "They gave up on the siege because they assumed that the city must have more than enough food to outlast the attack!"

There was a thunderous round of applause. Orwell thought that he might be back in London, attending a Music Hall programme. The show wasn't over.

"Now let us discuss the *Law of Unintended Consequences*," said Hammill, "with an illustration from my own country. If it had not been for the insanity of the Volstead Act, now thankfully repealed, our gangsters would never have turned the streets of our big cities into a war zone to rival what you've experienced in your Civil War. I suggest that you think of these gangsters as incipient Fascists instead of heroic freedom fighters."

"Why don't we just call them capitalists?" asked Orwell with a smile.

Hammill cleared his throat and went on. "The point is, that by

1928 Thompson Submachine Gun

attempting to outlaw a widely-used, easily-produced commodity like alcohol, the State only succeeded in militarizing the criminal class. Machine guns were as legal as any other firearms for years, with no particular problems of criminal misuse, for the simple reason that they were not cost-effective for most crimes. Representing the cutting edge of the gunmaker's art, they were fantastically expensive compared to more conventional weaponry. You could equip an entire criminal gang with rifles, pistols and shotguns for less than the cost of a single machine gun."

"Are you going to sell us machine guns?" asked one of Durruti's oldest compadres.

Hammill grinned. "Even better," he promised. "I am also going to teach you how to *make them* yourselves. Out of scrap-car axles when alloy steel is scarce,

and on lathes powered by beasts of burden where there is no electricity. Since the right to own weapons is the right to be free, I want to see weapon-making technology distributed as widely as possible.

"But please allow me to finish making my point, which is that, in general, markets trump governments. Arresting and shooting sellers of the popular drug, alcohol, did not drive it off the market, but only drove its price high enough to cover the risk of being arrested or shot. All of a sudden, ten bucks worth of sugar and yeast could be easily turned into a thousand dollars of product—but product that the police and the legal system cannot be called upon to protect from rival gangs. Most perversely, the police (themselves well-armed) are now the most serious threat of all. Overnight, Prohibition created a new criminal class with both the need for heavy weaponry and the funding to acquire it.

"And, finally, don't think it's only sinful intoxicants that provoke the State's displeasure. Those Americans who disobeyed Franco Roosevelt—excuse me, *Franklin* Roosevelt's recent order to exchange all of their gold for pieces of green paper money, find themselves in the same position as the bootlegger. If they don't turn their gold coins over to the State, and ordinary criminals threaten to steal their gold, the armed might of the State will not protect them. Its own extraordinary criminals will not only steal, i.e. confiscate the gold themselves, but then lock its owner in a cage for ten years in the bargain."

"I have an idea!" shouted a young girl whose father was unable to stifle her. "If we collectivize our property, then we protect it with guns the same way any member of the bourgeoisie protects his house."

"Right," said Hammill. "It's up to you to decide how many people are in your family or trade association or defense organization. So long as it's voluntary, there's nothing preventing cooperation between individualists and syndicalists. Can't we all just get along?"

This inspired more applause, followed by a vigorous exchange of questions and answers.

Finally the orgy of spontaneous order was too much for Durruti and he regained control of the supper meeting as if he wielded a hefty club.

"Don't you have a surprise for us this evening?" the Anarchist leader reminded the speaker.

"Oh, yes," said Hammill. "Revolutionaries do not live by the gun alone. Allow me to demonstrate."

He waved at two men in the back who brought forth a box. After clearing away several plates and cups, they put the contents of the box on the table. Hammill stretched his hands over the metal objects as if they were sacred relics. Then he started making gestures worthy of a stage magician.

"This is the first delivery," he said. "More to come! Here you see a lathe and 3-axis milling head. It's in good condition and dirt cheap. In the hands of a skilled machinist, of which you have several, this equipment is sufficient to fabricate essentially any metal object bounded by straight lines and circular arcs."

Now Orwell was really impressed. As Hammill paused in his delivery, there wasn't a sound to be heard except for the chirping of crickets and far off the howling of a dog, or perhaps it was a wolf.

"For starters," said Hammill with a grin as big as a Cheshire Cat—"for starters, you can use this to make *another* lathe and milling head!"

"And guns?" Ortiz asked the obvious, already knowing the answer.

Hammill was an a roll.

"You can *make* all the weapons you will ever need. Since machine tools are used in every shop that builds or repairs automobiles, trains, boats, motors, agricultural equipment, and a hundred other things, there is simply no way that any government anywhere can outlaw, or even meaningfully regulate this, without exorbitant costs that would put themselves out of business! Wherever people are in cities—or where there is a decent supply of electricity—this phenomenon will grow exponentially."

Orwell looked at Durruti's smiling face.

They would have their own city soon enough.

Hammill wasn't finished. "The lathe principle was used when the only power source on earth was wind, water and beasts of burden. That's a source of power no one can take away from you in Spain! Just tap off the village water wheel, or grain mill, and you'll have enough energy to spin your drive shaft.

"The big advantage is that since you're not trying to become a general purpose machine shop, you don't require the specialized equipment of a shop lathe. You can get by with a stripped down outfit dedicated to your particular weapons-manufacturing needs.

"But here's the hitch. The one weapons-part you can't manufacture, without exotic and specialized equipment, is properly rifled gun barrels. I will be providing those items on my next trip over here! And never mind what our good friend Durruti will be paying. But in the meantime, you don't have that serious a handicap. I've brought several crates of gun barrels instead of complete weapons. You can make the rest of the parts yourself and never worry about defective weapons blowing up in your face ever again."

Orwell applauded. For a moment he was alone but then everyone else joined in.

Hammill nodded and continued: "If push comes to shove, you can build a whole gun from scrap metal. Hell, you could take an old car axle for the chamber, barrel and bolt. The other parts aren't that crucial."

"And this is only temporary," Durruti interjected. "We will be upgrading our purchases during our winter campaign. Besides, we are building other things than just guns."

Hammill performed a mock salute. "I may want to place an order for a few Horns of the Bull, myself!"

"You can conquer everything but the lice," said Orwell, thinking out loud.

"That, too!" boasted Hammill. "My associate, Rick Blaine, will be providing portable, fuel powered washing machines very soon. Now *there's* an item no one has to smuggle! Other stuff you shouldn't have to smuggle would in-

clude a hacksaw, file, and a welding torch. You'd be surprised to learn what weapons you could make with those."

"It's in the can," Eileen blurted out. "You're not holding out on us!"

Hammill laughed. "Where did a nice English girl like you pick up our big city slang?" he said. "You're not from New York."

"And how!" she answered with a smile. "I read *Black Mask*."

Hammill shrugged. "Our American pulp magazines are the real revolution."

He retired a short time later. Apparently the man hadn't slept in three days. But before departing to his well-earned slumber, the American became wistful over the next leg of his journey. There were crucial contacts to be made in Amsterdam, which also happened to be his favorite city.

He left a pamphlet with Orwell, a classic essay by Lysander Spooner, drawing the distinction between crimes and vices. Apparently Amsterdam lived up to this high standard, according to the American, who recommended window shopping in the *Oude Zijds Voorburgwal*.

Orwell decided to stay up for the rest of the evening. Eileen finally went to sleep. He didn't even make the attempt. He was too excited; and it wasn't from thinking of the lovely female wares on display in that celebrated street in Amsterdam.

Nor was he experiencing the intellectual raptures of a schoolboy. Political debate long ago lost the power to light a fire in his soul. The prospect of getting back into action was something else again. He knew full well what Durruti was driving at when he mentioned the winter campaign. Hammill's presentation was one more reason to believe that the genuine war had only begun.

Orwell had come to fight the Fascists. Now he would also have a chance to fight the Stalinists.

Dear John #2
LETTER FROM HOWARD DAVIDSON

Dear John,

I wouldn't blame you for being angry with me. After promising to write regularly, all you've received are a few postcards. It's amazing that you managed to get a letter to me. It was the last item of mail I received at the Hotel Florida before I accepted an invitation from no less than Ernest Hemingway to attend a bullfight.

Let me assure you that it was no ordinary bullfight. Remind me to tell you the whole dreadful story some time, but you'll have to get me

drunk first. Speaking of which, I hold my liquor better than I used to. You can thank Hemingway for that. I'll show off the next time we attend the Pulpmeister's Club.

I can't be sure that you'll receive this letter before you see me again. At least I had the sense to take your letter and the enclosure with me when I went to Murcia. My crystal ball was broken and I didn't realize the Nazis would make it impossible for me to return to Madrid.

Even if they declared an open city, I wouldn't enter Nazi-occupied territory for obvious reasons. Hemingway would have dared it on his own even though they certainly have a file on him. But the Comintern wouldn't help one of their advocates put his neck in a noose. That neck is too valuable where it is.

In addition, Hemingway was with friends and he worries about them. That is one of his best traits. Spending time with him has changed my mind on a number of points but a lot of the details will have to wait until we see each other in person. For now, let me say he's a good man but also a great fool. Maybe

Ernest Hemingway

that is the ideal combination for an artist of any kind.

But I wouldn't say that my other celebrity "discovery" lacks wisdom. The last postcard you received was the one where I spilled the news that I met Chesterton!!! You write that you find that encounter

more amazing than shooting the breeze with Hemingway. I totally agree about the extreme good luck that put me in the right place at the right time for that encounter.

I'd completely forgotten that one of your favorite short stories is Chesterton's, "The Angry Street." I had a lot on my mind. (An aside: I've learned that Lenin's favorite writer was one of ours, Jack London. Turns out that Stalin's favorite movie star is also one of ours, Charlie Chaplin. And get this one: Hitler apparently loves Mickey Mouse cartoons and Busby Berkeley musicals!)

Where was I? Oh, yeah, doing my usual name dropping. The truth is that meeting and talking with these two writers made the whole journey worthwhile. And I also met Dos Passos, although I never had a real conversation with him.

Yes, I have regrets. It's not like I ever joined in the fighting. I could still do it but I'm coming home instead. The only action I saw was running from a bull in Murcia. Yes, it's the awful truth; all part of that story I'll tell you after I'm stinking drunk.

To answer you on another matter, I never tracked down a single Stirnerite anarchist. Don't laugh. There are so many varieties of anarchists all over Spain at this point, you'd think I could have found one of them.

Weirdly enough, I did locate a whole box of their magazines at the Hotel Florida. I was going to bring back that collection of *Iniciales* (a monthly journal for true individualists, nudists and vegetarians) as a trophy. But the box is in my hotel room in Madrid which means that the Nazis have it by now. Maybe they sent it to Hitler since he's a vegetarian and claims that he'd like to see Wagner performed in the nude. Not a bad idea if a movie studio does the casting and they dub in the voices later!

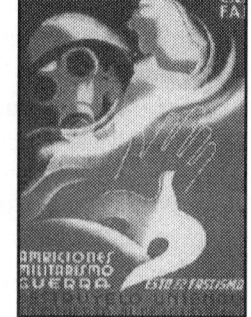

Hem has no use for any anarchist. (I think I've earned the right to call the great one Hem. He says I should stay in touch.) His attitude might have made sense at the start of this thing but it doesn't any longer. It looks to me like the only forces able to resist the Fascists and the Nazis will be these Anarchist brigades. The independent Marxist POUM is finished. The Republic is coming apart.

Stalin seems to be losing his grip. I'm sure you heard about the fiasco of the tank corps he sent over here. The military excuse was that they were considerably under strength because Stalin wouldn't pay for any more than what they had, which wasn't nearly enough!

Then there's the subject of the incredible shrinking thug, Franco himself! Now that he's turning into a lapdog of Hitler, we're almost forgetting that he's the one who started the war when he wouldn't accept the results of the popular elections. What an idiot! He's losing everything. But as the smaller evil shrinks, he is replaced with far greater evil.

If I had any guts, I'd stay and fight. But I've already covered that. I came to Spain only to find out that I'm a coward. You told me to stay out of this thing. Well, if events continue on this way, we'll all be drafted into fighting the Nazis eventually. Then issues of personal cowardice won't matter, will they?

The last time I saw Hemingway, we argued about nearly everything. He keeps talking about the Germans as if we're getting ready for a replay of the Great War. He doesn't seem to recognize Adolf's special qualities. Sometimes Hem sounds like a Nazi himself when he says that if the Germans cause another world war we should sterilize them!

But with Hem, that's just the booze talking. But the Nazis mean it when they preach eugenics. I'm remembering Chesterton's warnings about that sort of thing as far back as the 1920s. He may be a fat old Papist and a bit of an anti-Semite himself but he also sees the same danger I recognize in Adolf Hitler.

John, when you spend your life making up fictional super villains at pulp-word rates, you sometimes lose the ability to recognize the real thing. But I trust writers like you and me to see the real monster before our brethren in the slicks notice any change in society at large.

The Nazi carpet bombing of Guernica was a science fiction prediction.

The rockets the Anarchists are using was a science fiction prediction.

As for the Chancellor of the Third Reich, he is the sort of megalo-

The Nefarious Fu Manchu

Sherlock Holmes

maniac resisted by Holmes when fighting Moriarity or Nayland Smith going up against Fu Manchu. Naturally, Hem doesn't think this way. He kept me around for comedy relief.

But Hem is wrong about the Nazis. They are far more than a reincarnation of the Kaiser's Germany and far more dangerous than other Fascists. As for Hitler, a lot of people make fun of him and think he won't amount to much. He scares the shit out of me.

Sax Rohmer, creator of Fu Manchu

Hem is also wrong about the Anarchists. The last time I saw him, he complained that Anarchists are lazy drunks, full of criticism about the Republic but unable to do more than belch and roll over on their cots. The sad truth is that Hemingway was describing himself when he performed his diatribe. He was too intoxicated to get out of bed and bid me farewell. He did tell me to stay in touch, however, and I appreciate that.

Before I sign off, I'll tell you about the contents of that letter you enclosed. Frankly, I'm surprised that it got past the censors. But the postmark was from a little town in Spain and it was sent to my publisher in New York. You were really taking a chance in sending it back to me. That's when I figured that the censors would have taken a peek. On the other hand, they may share my attitude that it's a stupid joke and not worth bothering over.

Supposedly the letter is from a Spanish priest. It's the strangest fan letter I've ever received. This priest claims to have left the Church because of reading my *Inquisitor* stories! So I should refer to him, I suppose, as an ex-priest.

This must be some kind of practical joke. The padre would have us believe that he was given the task by the Vatican itself of keeping track of my humble literary efforts!!! What am I supposed to be here, Martin Luther?

Now I'm supposed to buy the idea that my art so "overwhelmed" him that he took off his collar and joined an Anarchist unit! He would be using an assumed name now, and so would be impossible to track down.

Someone in the Pulpmeisters Club must be behind this. Play detective for me, will you? All your stories in *Black Mask* must have taught you something, my old friend.

See you soon, I hope. Or as the Turtle and the Dove are wont to say

Not the blackness of interstellar space nor the gray void of the corridors of time will stay our hands from meting out justice!

—Your obt. svt., H. D.

P.S. One last thought. After I left Guernica, the Nazis attacked the city. Then I took my leave of Madrid, and the Nazis grabbed the city completely. Now I'm in Barcelona and about to make another dramatic exit. What do you think will happen to this poor burg?

I'm glad to leave. I've given up the idea of being a war correspondent. It's too damned dangerous.

Somewhere in the Spanish Countryside
Hedy and Wernher Reunite

They didn't say a single word but let their bodies communicate. There would be plenty of time for words later.

Hedy Lamarr didn't even know the name of the town they were in. The dirty little hotel room seemed like a suite at this glorious moment. After they made love, she would accompany von Braun to the mountains. She'd stay the winter, probably in a tent or a hovel. Then she could think back to this hot and dusty day in the close little room where it was hard to breathe and the sweat poured off their bodies. She'd think back to this moment and cherish it as pure ecstasy.

The long time they'd been absent from each other had built a mounting tension—it broke like a dam, releasing all the pent-up furies of their struggle with the world. Fortunately the old bed didn't break, but the springs screamed at the combined weight of their heaving bodies.

His tongue was like a red flame, burning her body wherever it touched her. Her hands were just as unstoppable, wanting to hold him before the blissful moment when she had to let go.

As they made love, he gave her gentler kisses, close-lipped and softer. She wanted more of him inside her and opened her mouth to take his tongue into her hungry mouth. They stayed like that until the moist explosion that would put any rocket's blast to shame.

He broke the spell first. "Thank you for coming." They shared a quiet chuckle and fell asleep entwined in their renewed intimacy.

CHAPTER 12

Barcelona, Fall 1937

Durruti Attacks

One million people in Barcelona!

Orwell couldn't stop thinking about that number. A certain percentage wanted to be liberated by the machine Durruti set into motion against the city. A certain percentage remained loyal to the governing bodies Orwell despised. But for the majority of the city's residents, the working and suffering majority, they only wanted peace.

When Anarchists involved themselves, however marginally, with the government, they only succeeded in poisoning the well. Their rhetoric continued promising fresh, clean water but the people remembered the muddy compromises. Orwell didn't fault the radicals for any of this. He'd been guiltier than they when it came to practical concessions. Now they were all comrades because it had turned out that practicality was only so "practical" after all.

But Durruti faced the problem of convincing the tired, paranoid population of Barcelona that this time they weren't going to be screwed. Maybe he was even telling the truth. Orwell would like that.

Eileen noted his increased sense of confidence. She even accused him of flirting with optimism. His unchangingly dour expression made her laugh. But she painted a long frown on his features when she sug-

Eric Blair

Eileen Blair

gested that she might take up a rifle and join him in the final assault. In many respects, Eric Blair was a most conservative man. No wife of his was going to join him in combat.

Some things were just beyond the pale. She asked him not to go. She was nervous that his luck might run out. But she didn't nag him or even elaborate on her request. He'd made up his mind.

Typically, he didn't sleep the night before the attack. Instead, he studied how the Nazis succeeded in Madrid. They counted on air supremacy. Between newly invented radar and the ME-109 they made their point. Ground troops supported by a few state-of-the-art tanks finished the job. But the army still had to listen to Goering boast that the heavy machine guns and cannon of the ME-109 left the soldiers with little to do.

Franco

As far as the foreign press was concerned, the only one with nothing to do was General Franco and his Nationalist Army. Ever since that day, the Spanish Fascists became obsessed with proving their mettle. They were thwarted in this because Hitler kept sending in more of his troops to "provide assistance."

Orwell concluded that Hitler had a better deal in Spain than Stalin because he was out in the open. The Soviet dicta-

Adolf Hitler

tor had painted himself into a corner with all his secrets and post-war plans to follow imaginary victories. The government in Barcelona's leadership might be foolish enough to believe that Stalin cared about their revolution.

To George Orwell, there was no right-wing nationalist more reprehensible than Josef Stalin.

Josef Stalin

Durruti made one last rousing radio broadcast to alert the citizens of Barcelona that they were about to be freed of every kind of nationalism under the sun, both foreign and domestic. He reminded his listeners that he had always been a voice on the anarchistic side against acts of random sabotage. In the early days of left-wing solidarity, he stood shoulder to shoulder with all comrades and sang out the official slogan of the Republic with gusto, "They shall not pass!"

But times had changed. Stalin changed them with one too many knives in the back. And Hitler forever rendered the slogan of "they shall not pass" superfluous after what the Nazis did in Guernica and Madrid.

Durruti also warned anyone listening to take shelter if they could not evacuate the city. It wasn't only the Nazis who relied on air supremacy.

The Anarchists had several dozen "Horns of the Bull" assemblies. Although every effort was being made to limit civilian casualties, the realities of collateral damage were an accepted cost of the operation. To someone on the receiving end, Anarchist militia was the same statist enterprise as any other army.

Life was a series of Lenin omelets.

And for breakfast on this fine, cold day in Spain, Orwell treated himself to a fried machine gun nest.

He regretted that the enemy was so

V. I. Lenin

young. They were JSU, the youth league of the PSUC. Taking a forward position placed Orwell in the direct line of fire and he had no choice but to radio in the location to a Matador. As he hunkered down and waited for the firestorm to descend, he heard one of the young men scream over the pop-pop-pop of the rattling machine gun, "Death to CNT counter-revolutionaries!"

Somehow that made it easier to take when they were wiped out. This close to a target, the Matadors achieved a far greater accuracy. A piece of shrapnel cut Orwell's ear but he didn't notice until much later.

Immediately he faced another problem. A spray of gunfire had only one thing to recommend it. The indiscriminate nature of it meant that he wasn't in a sniper's sights. In the case of the latter, he wouldn't have to worry about it because he'd be dead if the man was any good.

But he couldn't make out where the bullets were coming from. Abandoning his position, he made a zig-zag line for better cover. Wherever the enemy was located, Orwell's erratic movements made it harder for him.

There were so many bullets that the weapon had to be another machine gun. He was glad of that, figuring that a shooter with a decent rifle would have taken him down by now. As one of the bullets nicked the heel of his boot he fell to the street and tried to flatten himself in the gutter. The situation was quite frustrating because he had no opportunity of returning fire.

Suddenly the attack stopped. He heard an explosion that sounded like a simple grenade instead of an elaborate rocket. *Hooray for our side!* He was back in the fight.

As he stood up, he found himself only inches away from a man he
knew to be a Comintern thug. The
man had threatened Eileen once and
he wasn't about to forget him.

The bastard pointed his gun at
Orwell instead of shooting. His first
mistake. They were at close quarters.
His second mistake. Orwell pro-
ceeded to instruct the enemy about his third mistake.

The man didn't expect his target to move parallel to the gun and
grab the barrel from underneath. Before he knew what was happening,
Orwell had his entire hand around the gun. He broke the man's finger
on the trigger by pushing on the gun with one hand and pulling up on
the wrist with his other hand.

As the man howled in pain, Orwell put him out of his misery with
a solid punch to the jaw. That was the last thing Orwell remembered for
some time because another grenade went off nearby. Orwell's opponent
was right between him and the blast. The other man took the brunt of
the explosion which saved his life.

But Orwell's personal war in Spain was finally over.

Both Eileen and he feared that he might have gone deaf but his
hearing finally returned. He was receiving the best of care in a hospital
in Barcelona.

The city had fallen in record time.

Durruti celebrated the restoration of his new friend's hearing by bringing him a portable radio so that he could listen to the remarkable news.

Goebbels was in the middle of another harangue ". . . and so the

two great people's movements of true Socialism form
this alliance against the perfidy of the Anglo-American
banking conspiracy that hides behind the false mask of
Jewish anarchy . . ."

"What the hell is going on?" Orwell sat up in bed
and demanded to know.

Joseph Goebbels

Durruti produced, as if by magic, a fairly recent edition of the *Times of London*. "We've scared them to death,
ever since we took Barcelona. Ribbentrop took time off from torment-
ing Franco to arrange a Hitler-Stalin pact."

"I don't believe it," said Orwell.

"Stalin doesn't want Hitler to devour all of Spain. Hitler wants to

hold Stalin at bay. One day the titans will fight but for now they have
drawn the line here. Maybe they think
they can put us out of action if they
combine resources and act together."

"Can they?" asked Eileen.

"Never again will we be neutral-
ized," said Durruti. "For years I have
insisted that the Anarchists are like a
lion wasting time in front of a rat
hole when the whole jungle beckons.
Von Braun has everything he needs
here in Barcelona to finish a project
he's been working on with Konrad
Zuse. Soon the lion will roar!"

Spring 1938

Hedy and the Rocket Man

The spring of 1938 was a good time for anarchy.

The Orwells were back in England, now serving in the role of am-
bassadors-at-large for the "sovereign" community of Barcelona. They
managed to generate a lot of press, most of it very favorable to their
cause. Prime Minister Neville Chamberlain hailed them as visionaries
for peace.

Back at the war, Hedy Lamarr insisted on entertaining the men
who held the line for freedom. They couldn't get enough of her. She
even attended showings of *Ecstasy* and did a question and answer session
afterward.

These men were sincerely grateful to the woman who had become
their battlefield angel. An angel, yes, but not a Saint.

For the ones who harbored bourgeois attitudes towards their wives and sweethearts, they strained not to apply old-fashioned standards to her. Word got around that a special and (dare one say it) monogamous relationship existed between the movie star and the wizard who aimed at the stars.

Sometimes she and her Wernher would go a whole week without seeing each other. Far from generating a single spark of jealousy, these periods of absence only enhanced the desire they felt for each other.

Tonight they shared an early twilight which brought out a sliver of moon and the spot of white fire that was the Morning Star.

"I can't look at Venus without thinking of you," he said as she let her slender fingers dance around his shoulders.

"You're more Romantic than I am," she said. "Tonight's sky only makes me think of an Islamic flag."

He squeezed her shoulder. "That's only because you made *Algiers*," he said. "Have you seen it yet?"

"No," she said. "Let's not talk about pictures here, not when I'm with you."

Von Braun had never been one to tease women before his relationship with Hedy but she brought out a whole new side in him. "All right then," he said. "Do you miss the social life in Hollywood?"

"What do you mean?"

"Well, do you miss those handsome movie stars?"

She embraced him and moved her lips against his shoulder. "What do I need with pretty boys pretending to be what they're not when I'm in your arms? You are the reality. You are one of the motors of the world."

He enjoyed the strength of their relationship in a manner different from that of any actor. He accepted the situation as perfectly natural. With any other man Hedy would have assumed he was taking her for a ride. But not with Wernher. He was the exception to all her rules.

"I still can't look at Venus without thinking of you," he said smiling, as he embraced her.

"Your whole life is dedicated to the study of Heavenly bodies," she said. "That's your trouble."

"It's no trouble," he said. "You're my Venus di Milo."

"But with arms!" she said, taking his face in her hands and kissing him hard.

When she let him come up for air, he whispered in her ear: "I've solved the rocket fuel problem."

"You have?" she said excitedly.

"The last details are finally ironed out. We have our less-toxic alcohol-based fuel. You remember how the regular oxides were the main problem? Well, I'll never have to use a petroleum-based fuel again."

"Oh, Wernher," she said. "How exciting for all of us!"

A while later, she reminded him, "You still owe me a poem, you know."

He sighed. "I wish you'd forgotten about that."

"A woman never forgets when she's promised a poem."

"I know, but I'm no poet! I'm not happy with *Days of Wine and Rockets*. It needs to be a lot better."

"Maybe I could help you with it," she suggested, toying with his ear.

"That's ridiculous! Who ever heard of the subject of a love poem helping write it?"

"So it's a love poem," she said, tracing a finger across his chest.

"What did you think? I was going to give you a circuit diagram? Well, never mind. I have a much nicer gift for you."

"And what's that?"

Now it was his turn to be mysterious. "You'll know soon enough."

From their hill, they looked down at Barcelona. "It's such a beautiful city," she said.

"Yes."

"Madrid is a lovely city, too."

"Unfortunately," he said.

Spring, 1938
Konrad Zuse Joins the Forces

One week later they greeted a ship docking at the port. She thought that Konrad Zuse looked the same as the time when she'd met him on the train when escaping from Fritz Mandl. No matter how he combed his hair it stood out from his head at all sorts of angles giving the impression he'd just received a massive dose of static electricity. He wore huge glasses and seemed also to wear a permanent grin. If she owned her own movie studio she'd cast him in the role of the mad scientist.

Konrad Zuse

Zuse came bearing gifts; his ship was full of German technicians. "The final contingent of your ground crew," he told von Braun. "I've also finished the electronic guidance system. I'm throwing in a ridiculously oversized gyroscope just for fun."

"Thanks, Konrad," said von Braun. "You remember Hedy, don't you?"

"Of course," said Zuse. "I liked the French Maid costume better," he said, as if he'd last seen Hedy only the other day. She was too amazed to say anything. It would have been difficult, in any case, to get a word in edgewise.

While he kept up a running commentary, he managed to oversee the unloading of the boat and the signing of various papers attached to various clipboards. Suddenly he announced, "Oh, did you receive my telegram?"

"I don't think so," said von Braun.

"No matter. I may have forgotten to send it. Anyway, you should be the first to know we have a winner in our contest for the best super explosive. A *Spaniard* came up with it. I'm sure you see the political advantage to that. Everything can't be German, can it?"

Zuse tapped Hedy on the shoulder, "Or Austrian, my dear," he added. "Anyway the explosive will be delivered by land. The man is with your Agorist group, Ortiz I think."

"Augustin Ortiz served in Teruel over the winter," said von Braun. "He's been trying to warm up ever since."

"After suffering frostbite, he'll bite the Nazis hard!" said Zuse. "His brain never stopped working. When a fuel container ruptured, he got the idea for a 'fuel-air explosive.' Later, he did his experiments in a more congenial climate. By mixing the fuel with a perfume atomizer inside a sturdy container, the overpressure was overwhelming when ignited. Although some of my friends are working on splitting the atom, I have a lot more faith in this right now! We can thank Teruel for providing inspiration."

"It was the last brutal campaign our side will have to suffer," said Hedy. "We hope."

"Something changed in Ortiz after Teruel," von Braun continued. "Some of his men froze to death. Machines froze. They say the cold would freeze the balls off a polar bear. The Nazis missed out on that one. The enemy was the Nationalist army."

"How nostalgic," said Zuse. "We can only hope that the Nazis experience something like that eventually. Meanwhile, we'll warm things up for them. Thanks to you, Wernher! And also thanks to Ortiz for coming up with his sweet little explosive."

"He lost two fingers off his left hand in the cold," said Hedy.

"Well, it's a good thing that he writes with his right hand," Zuse replied cheerfully. And that seemed to be the extent of his sympathy.

"After you're settled in, we have a lot of figures to go over," said Wernher, mildly.

"I'll bet Hedy has been helping you in that department," he said, wiggling his eyebrows and sounding just like Groucho Marx.

"It's nice to be appreciated," she said with a tired smile.

"Before I leave you two love birds, I must pass on one last, crucial fact," said Zuse. He now had their undivided attention. "Remember when Goebbels slipped propaganda into his radio broadcasts from Salamanca?"

"Which one?" asked Hedy.

"Any of them! Well, here's something you must know. There is a Catholic school of Free-Market theory in Salamanca. That school is an influence on von Mises and the Austrian school. And the Austrian school is an influence on the Agorist brigade!"

"What is so crucial about that?" asked von Braun.

"Just goes to show that life is full of little ironies. And no matter where the National Socialists go, they still can't learn anything."

He left them without saying goodbye, then thought better of it and yelled back at Hedy. "We've got to discuss my plans for thinking and computing machines. Your ideas about frequency hopping could revolutionize radio communications."

"What the hell was that about?" she asked.

"I'll tell you later."

Madrid, July 4, 1938

The Lion's Roar

In another month it was showtime. Hedy felt the kind of excitement usually associated with attending a Hollywood premiere. At dusk, Durruti, Ortiz and she went up to the site together. Von Braun and Zuse were already there at the blockhouse.

The giant rocket stood fifty-feet high. Airport searchlights illuminated its gleaming surface. What were Stuka divebombers compared to this? It was a hammer from the gods. Durruti insisted on calling it the Lion's Roar. She couldn't resist telling him that the lion was also the symbol of MGM Studios at which she was, as a matter of fact, still theoretically, under contract.

Like all gifts from the gods, the rocket would make no distinctions when it came crashing down on mere mortals. Spaniards would die along with Germans. There were no civilians in this war.

Durruti did what he could. He'd dropped pamphlets and made appeals over the radio until he was blue in the face. He was now the blue division all by himself! He begged the people of Madrid to evacuate the city.

But to no avail.

Interception of German messages, courtesy of the captured Field Teleprinter, indicated that the enemy didn't believe the threats. Durruti chalked one up to German pomposity.

Hedy felt strangely calm as *Zero Hour* approached. She noticed a stray cat wander by, ribs showing plainly, reminding her of the skeletal hand of the Grim Reaper. Lately she was becoming superstitious. She hoped the cat was not an ill omen.

"Lucky puss," she said, squatting down and offering her hand. But it ran away. She couldn't help wondering how many attacks the cat had already survived from Fascists, Nazis, and various defenders of the Republican ideal. Politics didn't matter to the cat. Humanity became its enemy the moment that food became scarce. But things were getting better. She wanted to tell the cat that it could give up its own private war. She'd offer it something to eat.

The cat was going to be all right. It wasn't in Madrid.

There were no clouds tonight and there was a full moon. Hedy felt like switching off the artificial lights. They didn't need them now.

If only the Nazis knew what was in store for them. In wartime, a

full moon was considered almost the same as broad daylight. The Nazis could attack now, while preparations were still underway.

But the Germans didn't know. The few attempts they'd made at infiltrating the Barcelona group had failed utterly. The Nazi spies had not made very convincing anarchists.

She couldn't get over how tall the rocket was. No one could believe that anything this massive was ever going to leave the ground.

She almost didn't believe it herself.

As she marveled at the tall rocket, her tall lover strode over and took her hand. "Did I ever tell you that my parents wanted me to be a musician?" he asked.

"I don't think so," she said.

"Join me in a toast," he said, producing a brandy flask. She wondered if the liquid fire sliding down her throat might not be a kind of rocket fuel itself. She passed the brandy to Durruti.

Von Braun couldn't stop looking up at the deadly needle piercing the sky. It was imposing even at rest.

"Maybe I did fulfill the dreams of my parents, after all," he said to all his assembled guests. "There is a music to mathematics. But the truth is that I only studied math because I needed it to make my dream come true."

Durruti passed the brandy on to Ortiz who asked, "Do you really think a rocket may one day reach the Moon?"

"Yes," he said. "What's more, I've already drawn the first set of blueprints and christened it the Princess Hedy!"

"Oh, Wernher," was all she could think to say.

"So tonight's rocket is named for someone else?" asked Zuse.

Von Braun nodded and placed his hand on Zuse's shoulder. "I refuse to name an engine of destruction after the woman I love. She is to inspire the first spaceship! But for the action we take here tonight, I dub this the *Lion's Roar!*"

Durruti's eyes seemed to shine and Hedy didn't think it was the brandy. "But you really think you are doing more than building weapons?"

"The Moon is only the beginning," continued von Braun. "After that, we will reach the planets. Then we'll go beyond to other solar systems and touch the universe."

Hedy felt the hairs on the back of her neck stand at attention. She was sure it was the closest she'd ever heard him come, in public, to expressing the powerful emotions underlying the unswerving rationality that was more often the face he showed to the world.

"Yes, I aim at the stars," concluded Wernher von Braun, "but we begin with Madrid."

Durruti reached into his pocket and extracted a gold coin he'd kept from the gold train robbery. He'd made it his good luck piece. "I want you to have this," he said, passing it to von Braun.

Von Braun hesitated. "You've poured so much gold into my rocket already," he said. "I can't take this."

"Of course you can," said Zuse, having just finished off the brandy. "*This* is the piece of gold that matters."

"When do we launch?" asked Ortiz, as nervous about his fuel-air explosive as von Braun and his ground crew were about the rocket.

Von Braun touched his imposing brow with a well-manicured hand. He never gave the impression of a man at war.

He summoned his head technician and they conferred. "In a few hours," was the verdict.

"It's all about timing, isn't it?" asked Durruti. "Everything is. We stole the gold at the right time. You German geniuses were born at the right time and turned against Hitler in time!"

Ortiz touched von Braun's shoulder with his good right hand. "Let's do this right," he suggested. "Let's hit them at dawn."

"By dawn's early light," said Hedy Lamarr. "A phrase I picked up in America."

No one slept that night. They drank wine and ate cheese. At dawn, the moon was still visible as the sun joined it in ushering in a new world. These were the perfect witnesses for their fiery chariot.

They went into the blockhouse with the main technicians. The ground crew took up their protected positions further back. Everyone had a good view.

Flame started at the bottom as the rocket began to rise slowly. It was so very slow. Exhaust fumes welled up and the sound vibrated in their heads along with the sturdy walls of the blockhouse.

The sound was a deep thunder, a bone-cracking exclamation. Their hearts beat faster, keeping time with the pulsing of the rocket engines.

Then there was a white contrail, a column of pure white cloud to mark the passing of death's own messenger. The rocket shrieked to its goal on a clear and sunny day.

There was no way to tell exactly where it would strike Madrid. No one in the blockhouse knew the precise point of impact. No one on the ground could tell either.

But through some vagary of the gods, von Braun's giant rocket, Durruti's *Lion's Roar*, fell right on top of a swastika flag, gently rippling in the morning breeze—now transformed into a bull's eye.

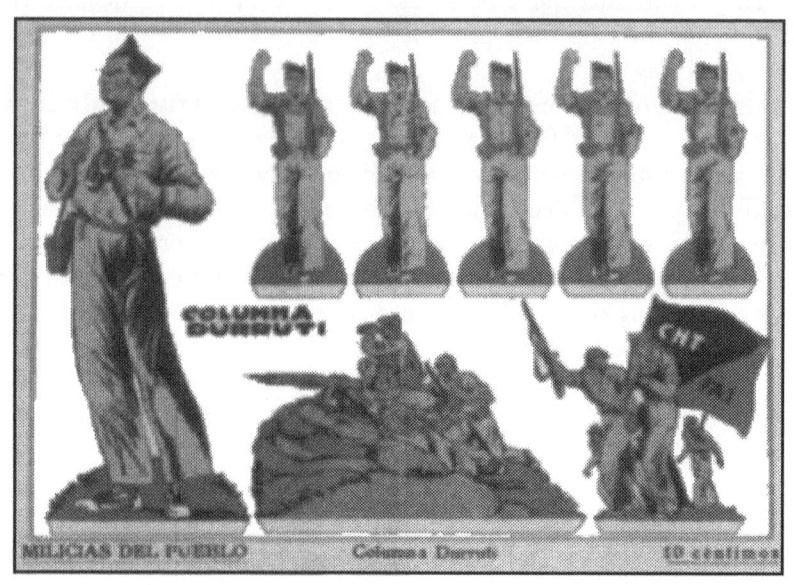

CHAPTER 13

Hollywood, USA

Confidential Memo From Louis B. Mayer

A lot of people around town say Hedy is ahead of her time and that actresses in the future will be just like her. Can you imagine how many ulcers, heart attacks and strokes would result in our industry? We can only hope that God, in his infinite wisdom, draws the line somewhere!

We're talking about actresses who don't mind doing nude scenes, are blatant about riding side saddle (fooling around with girls as well as boys) and insist on negotiating their own contracts. How can the good name of Hollywood survive such scandal?

Negotiating their own contracts?

We won't even get into politics. Everyone has been crazy on politics since the stock market crash. The only voting that should matter to us is keeping the EPIC Socialists from ever bolshevizing our beloved state. End Poverty in California? Can you imagine what would happen to this state if social spending outstrips revenues? It would be the end. We might as well turn the state over to the Reds.

Getting back to the subject of Hedy Lamarr, it's not true that I said she'd never work in this town again. I only said she'd be punished if she ran out on us. Now it is true that she currently has more box office appeal than any other actress in pictures. That stunt in Spain is responsible.

The bottom line is that she got away with it. That kraut she was in love with, von Braun, did a genuine Flash Gordon number on the Nazis and she was right there through the whole escapade. You can't *buy* publicity like that.

I actually believe she was in love with the guy. That's why I think she's on the square when she made that ridiculous statement to the French press. Who but an actress says that she'll never act again because she's found the man of her dreams and will devote the rest of her life to him? That statement is so dumb that only an actress would say it in the first place. The dames never can tell the difference between real life and melodrama anyway.

I'll admit it's different when she hooks up with a fella who actually does change the world! Shickelgruber was forced to go along with that.

Speaking of which, did you hear what Hitler said after the King Kong rocket (as David calls it) pasted Madrid? The destructive radius was almost a *mile*. He said that rockets are unnatural weapons and the work of the devil. He warns that the Third Reich will develop an anti-rocket defense to be known as the Vengeance Weapon. I don't see how that's possible. Well, whatever he develops, the great dictator sounds like a sore loser to me. The Nazis have left Spain with their tails between their legs.

But getting back to Hedy, I really believe that she actually believed her silly ultimatum. Actresses can't help themselves. Consider it an occupational disease.

I'm not so sure what happened to her kraut lover. Once von Braun proved he was a super genius, all the governments in the world got into a bidding war to buy his services. For a smart guy, he was pretty dumb when he broadcasted how Durruti set him up for life. Of course, the Anarchist leader is still busy fighting the remnants of Franco's army in Seville.

Hitler doesn't want anyone to have Wernher von Braun if Germany can't grab him! Stalin is always Stalin. And let's not kid ourselves about other world leaders. President Roosevelt is in the same boat as Prime Minister Chamberlain. They all want him!

Von Braun told everyone to take a hike and figured that he was safe with the Anarchists.

Maybe he is. Maybe he isn't.

The world thinks he was killed by a miniature rocket, the Banzai Missile, cooked up by that captured Japanese scientist. The Jap is supposed to have been held since the Sino-Russian war! Well, the man had a credible story about being kept in Siberia and forced to work for the Soviets. I'll never understand how he escaped. The world is still looking for him just as they're looking for Wernher.

But the point is that Hedy believes all this. She thinks her Wernher is dead. I don't go along with the idea that she's part of an elaborate cover-up and he's hiding out somewhere. She's a good actress but I don't think she's good enough to fool me.

So she's back in pictures and I've got her! I don't even feel like punishing her for running out on me, just so long as she behaves. If von Braun is alive, I don't think Hedy knows a thing about it so we ought to be safe on that score.

Besides, I've landed her a part that no actress would ever walk out on. Yeah, I admit it's strange that I keep lending her out to build her up and then fail to find her a part in an MGM picture. But this new deal builds her up like nobody's business. It's the best part in the world. And even though David has gone independent, I'll always think of him as part of the MGM family.

Hedy's got the accent down. Our last worry is kaput. When you realize all the major stars who wanted this role, from Kate Hepburn to Bette Davis, you realize what a *coup* this is? Did you know that Larry Olivier's wife almost got the part?

Hedy is riding the greatest wave of publicity I've ever seen. I'm even in negotiation with Korda about putting her in an H. G. Wells science fiction epic in 1940 if they spend the million pounds they did on *Things to Come*. There's nothing wrong with capitalizing on our rocket girl!

But for 1939, there is only one picture and Hedy is in it. Now that we have her playing Scarlett O'Hara in *Gone With the Wind*, can we finally keep her down on the plantation? If you know what I mean . . .

Readers Please Note:

The Back Matter for *Anarquía* consists of
the following sections:

List of **Significant Characters**
in *Anarquía*
(real and larger-than-life)

Afterwords:
Commentary about
Anarquía by six writers

The following sections concern
the *actual events and timelines*
of the *real* Spanish Civil War
and/or contemporary participants:

Map of the Spanish Front 1936

Glossary

Brief Chronology

Miscellanea

To learn about the creators of *Anarquía*, see
About the Authors

Anarquía Significant Characters
In Order of Appearance

Hedy Lamarr (Hedwig Eva Maria Kiesler)

Austrian actress who first came to world attention by appearing nude in the European film *Ecstasy* and who became a major Hollywood star in the films *Algiers, Boomtown, Comrade X, I Take This Woman, Tortilla Flat, White Cargo, Samson and Delilah* and many others. During WWII, she sold millions of war bonds and shared with Marlene Dietrich the distinction of actresses who had seen the Nazi beast up close. In 1942, she shared a patent for a frequency-hopping radio secrecy system to maintain control of a guided torpedo despite enemy jamming. In later years, her contribution was recognized by the Electronic Frontier Foundation (EFF), an Internet privacy rights organization. Hedy's idea is used in PCS cell phones and other popular wireless data systems today. In her autobiography, she tells stories of her adventurous sexuality. Basically, she's the ideal heroine for an alternate history science fiction novel, with the added bonus that she was real!

Fritz Mandl

European munitions magnate who married Hedy Lamarr but couldn't hold her. He was a friend of Adolf Hitler.

Adolf Hitler

One of the two most evil and dangerous dictators of the twentieth century not to live in China.

Howard Davidson

The major character in *Anarquía* who is complete fiction. He and his friend John Staples are composite creations of various pulp fiction writers of the 1930s. Street and Smith published all the magazines attributed to them in *Anarquía* except for *The Inquisitor*. We made that one up so Howard could have a series of his own. If there are times when Howard seems to have a viewpoint closer to our era than his own, it is explained by the simple expedient of his being a science fiction writer. We all know that sci-fi guys are ahead of their times, right?

Francisco Franco

In our history, the general was the only Fascist dictator who was still in business until his death in 1975. After winning the Spanish Civil War, he had the sense to stay out of the wider conflict of WWII. Things don't work out so well for Franco in *Anarquía*.

Louis B. Mayer

Famous MGM producer who made his fair share of Hollywood stars, among them Hedy Lamarr. Except for his final, signal triumph, the differences between Mayer in real history and our history are too trivial to mention.

Wernher von Braun

The most famous rocket scientist of all time and the man who helped put Americans on the Moon. In our world he was on the wrong side of WWII, but nobody's perfect. (Truth in advertising requires the admission that author Brad Linaweaver was a speaker for the National Space Institute during the period of the Viking Mars Lander missions. The NSI was founded by von Braun. Upon von Braun's death, Brad provided one of the obits in the NSI newsletter along with Arthur C. Clarke and other fans of the great man's work. Naturally Brad jumped at the chance of working on an alternate history where von Braun was never involved with the Nazis.)

Frank O'Connor

Husband of Ayn Rand whom she first met when they were both working for Cecil B. DeMille. He was immortalized by Peter Fonda in the film adaptation of Barbara Branden's *The Passion of Ayn Rand*. He never had the personal and career opportunities his character experiences in *Anarquía*; but to paraphrase Aristotle, he ought to have enjoyed the life we imagine for him in this Romantic novel.

Father Palma

Not all village priests in Spain at the time of the Civil War were the illiterates the radicals thought they were. Our imaginary priest finds himself in a complicated situation because he can read.

Cardinal Celi

We hope that no one like this really existed at the Vatican . . . but you never know.

Josef Stalin
One of the two most evil and dangerous dictators of the twentieth century not to live in China.

Konrad Zuse
Now recognized worldwide as one of the fathers of modern electronic computers. Zuse was also a pioneer in binary digital processing and programming languages. In other words, he created both hardware and software. (Truth in advertising again: Kent Hastings confesses to an enthusiasm for Zuse similar to Linaweaver's thing for von Braun. As Kent watched Brad transform Zuse into one of his mad scientist types from *Moon of Ice*, he consoled himself by watching Bela Lugosi as a mad scientist in *The Devil Bat*.) The really cool thing is that Zuse and von Braun knew each other in genuine history. They were two extremely sane scientists.

Orgaz
This poor Spanish farmer symbolizes every victim of every war. He also was unlucky to have this particular name.

Ernest Hemingway
Ask not for whom the bell tolls, it tolls for Hemingway. In *Anarquía* it tolls good and hard. The authors of this modest effort take a back seat to no one in admiring this man's artistic genius—we are disgusted by literary revisionists who would diminish his importance as a writer. But when it comes to his politics, especially regarding Spain, we must shout to the rooftops that he was a damned fool.

G.K. Chesterton
One of the greatest Catholic writers of the twentieth or any other century. He would add spice to this project for his wildly imaginative fiction but he is included more for his contributions to "Distributism." Although the movement didn't amount to much in the modern history of England, the ideas resurface now and again in the politics of land reform that avoid socialist and Marxist models.

Wolfram von Richtofen
Condor Legion general who was the kind of officer the Nazis had to mislead.

Ernst

Imaginary pilot of the Condor Legion who represents all the young, True Believer Nazis who couldn't wait to sacrifice themselves for Hitler.

Durruti Column Members

Representative sampling of some of Spain's best.

Martha Gelhorn

Hemingway's real life girlfriend during the time of this novel.

John Dos Passos

Noted author whose friendship with Hemingway ended in Spain because he could see through the Communist lies.

George Orwell (Eric Blair)

A real hero of the twentieth century and one of the heroes of our novel. The first big Orwell scene in *Anarquía* draws heavily on his *Homage to Catalonia* and other historical accounts. After Orwell returns to the Aragon front (post the Barcelona May uprising) we suck him further into our alternate history. In real life, he was shot in the neck in a battle in Aragon but other things happen to him in our story. Researching his part in the Spanish Civil War helped us better understand what drove this independent man of the Left to write *Animal Farm* and *1984*.

Alexander Orlov (a.k.a. The Dread Nikolsky)

Stalinist agent who masterminded secret gold shipments to Russia. Some would call this theft. He gets what's coming to him in *Anarquía*.

Buenaventura Durruti

Leader of the anarchist militia which fought Franco, Hitler, Mussolini, and, after the Bolshevik's power grab, Stalin and the Republic as well. Durruti was killed in action in late 1936 and a million people attended his funeral in Barcelona, but we decided to keep him alive. We needed a native hero of his stature.

Ayn Rand

A fine novelist, gifted screenwriter, great advocate of Capitalism, and one of the bravest anti-Communists the world has ever seen. If her life had taken a slightly different direction, perhaps she would have avoided being the fountainhead of a cult.

Eileen Blair

George Orwell's wife and a brave woman. She was with him in Spain.

Dr. Paul Joseph Goebbels

Hitler's Propaganda Minister and the main character in Linaweaver's award-winning novel, *Moon of Ice*.

Joachim von Ribbentrop

Hitler's Foreign Minister and not a character in *Moon of Ice*.

Chuck Hammill

The character who represents Libertarian "Minarchy"—property, contracts and the essential right of self defense. If people like Hammill had provided guns to the Spanish anarchists, history would have been much better.

Augustin Ortíz

Leader of a Spanish brigade who builds his entire life on the economic theory of "Agorism" as expounded by Samuel Edward Konkin III. Ortíz is a completely imaginary character.

Afterword: Anarquía
By J. Neil Schulman

Look, anyone who can read can blurb a novel.

Anyone who can write can write an Afterword for a novel.

But aside from the authors, themselves, the only man who can touch me in his commitment to this novel is James A. Rock, publisher of Sense of Wonder Press, who is issuing the first edition.

Nevertheless, with all due respect to Mr. Rock, he only bought rights to this book once.

I've bought them twice.

In 1999, when *Anarquía* was nothing more than an outline, I obtained the book-publishing rights to *Anarquía*—and paid the authors an advance to write it—in my capacity as publisher and editor-in-chief of Pulpless.Com.

A couple of years later I reverted those rights to the authors so they could accept Jim Rock's publishing offer.

Then, within 24 hours of the manuscript's completion in July, 2003—after reading only the first four chapters—I made an offer to purchase the movie rights. Within a week, the contract was signed, money changed hands, and I had an option on those rights.

You may reasonably conclude that I consider *Anarquía* an important work of literature, and one which, additionally, has great commercial potential both as a book and a movie.

I'll go further than that. *Anarquía* doesn't read to me like science-fiction, of which the alternate history is a subgenre. Neither does it read to me like an historical novel. *Anarquía* reads to me like a contemporary novel written in the late 1930s, about the time that Ernest Hemingway wrote his 1938 Spanish Civil War stage-play *The Fifth Column*. But *Anarquía* reads to me not like flat-beer reporting by the newsman Hemingway, but a rich brew by his far-more talented contemporary, and fellow Nobel laureate, John Steinbeck.

My inside track on this book goes all the way back to its conception . . . and I'm going to reveal a few secrets for the first time.

In 1992 the idea for *Anarquía* originated in the mind of J. Kent Hastings . . . but Kent's inspiration for the novel was Brad Linaweaver's 1988 novel, *Moon of Ice*, an alternate history of World War II in which the United States remains neutral, Nazi Germany uses nuclear weapons to conquer both the Soviet Union and Europe, and the Cold War is not between the United States and Russia but between the United States and Germany.

Kent asked himself, "What would have happened if even before World War II started—if even before Nazi Germany had made its first conquest—the anarchists in Spain had prevailed in the Spanish Civil War?"

It was a rich vein to prospect for literary gold. The Spanish Civil War was in many ways a prologue to World War II, and the literary lions associated with it include not only Hemingway (who covered it) but also George Orwell (who fought in it).

By 1995 Kent had outlined the novel with three personal heroes as its main characters: the father of the moon landing, rocketeer Wernher von Braun; the mother of spread-spectrum communications, movie-star Hedy Lamarr; and the father of modern computing, Konrad Zuse.

By 1998 Kent had reached the limits of research about the Spanish Civil War written (or translated into) English, and was studying Spanish so he could read documents and books in their originals.

Kent and I briefly discussed my collaborating on the novel, but in 1999 my adventures in book publishing shoved my life as a writer aside, and Kent went back to the source of his inspiration and offered the collaboration to Brad. I offered them a contract and their collaboration was official.

The rest is history.

Yes—after I bought the movie rights for my production company, Jesulu Productions—I did finish reading the novel. Actually, Brad read me the second half on a long weekend he and Kent spent at my house in Pahrump, Nevada, where we signed the option contracts. It was fair revenge since I'd read aloud to both Brad and Kent the full text of my latest novel, *Escape from Heaven* . . . then read aloud to them my screenplay adaptation as well.

And when I expressed my dismay at the abruptness of the novel's ending, Brad let me in on another secret, which I'll now share with you.

The last chapter of this novel is not an ending. It's a cliffhanger. The sequel is already in the works . . . and I'm already pumping Kent and Brad for deep background on my screenplay adaptation.

Here's the teaser for my screen treatment:

WE OPEN on a ten-year-old boy pulling a little red wagon through the streets of Berlin in 1922. Little Wernher von Braun has tied six Chinese firecracker-rockets to the wagon and is about to conduct his first experiment in rocketry. He lights the firecrackers and the wagon careens uncontrollably through the streets, narrowly avoiding disaster. A policeman grabs the little boy by the scruff of his neck and takes him home to his father, who takes off his belt, and the incident ends with nothing more than a little boy's yelps behind a closed door.

WE CUT TO July, 1969—Cape Canaveral, Florida—as Wernher von Braun watches proudly as Apollo 11 is launched . . . and a few days later the famous TV broadcast from the moon, as Neil Armstrong and Buzz Aldrin leave their footprints in lunar soil.

SUDDENLY WE ZOOM BACKWARDS IN TIME: the Apollo, Gemini, and Mercury missions . . . the launch of Sputnik by the Soviets . . . the liberation of Europe by the Allies . . . V-2 rockets bombing London and we're back to a little boy's wagon being pulled on a Berlin street in 1922.

WE REPEAT the rocket-propelled wagon careening wildly through the streets of Berlin, only this time the wagon knocks a well-dressed matron into oncoming street traffic. We hear SCREAMS and little Wernher von Braun watches his first experiment in rocketry end in tragedy.

And the rest is *alternate* history.

J. NEIL SCHULMAN is a Prometheus Award-winning novelist, screenwriter and author of significant non-fiction books on the Second Amendment and O.J. Simpson. He is best known for his script for the television series *The New Twilight Zone*, "Profile In Silver," as well as the novels *Alongside Night*, *The Rainbow Cadenza*, and *Escape From Heaven*.

Afterword: "The Horns of the Bull"
by Bill Patterson

We are going to inherit the earth. There is not the slightest doubt about that. The bourgeoisie may blast and burn its own world before it finally leaves the stage of history. We are not afraid of ruins. We who ploughed the prairies and built the cities can build again, only better next time. We carry a new world, here in our hearts. That world is growing this minute.

—Buenaventura Durruti

Anarquía is one new world—though it would have surprised Durruti, who was killed in November 1936.

The Spanish Civil War was a defining moment in the "Classic Era of Warfare" (Nietzsche's sardonic prediction for the twentieth century and beyond). The whole apparatus of Victorian cultural and political assumptions had been dismantled in the Torrid Twenties; *Goodbye to All That* was the spirit deconstructing the old age. And constructing the new age—?

That was what the Spanish Civil War was all about. The old monarch, Alphonso XIII, was long gone, and the Second Republic was off again-on again with the reforms that would get Spain out from under the thumb of the Catholic church and reverse the slow, centuries-long pattern of decay. In the 1936 General Elections, the Popular Front coalition of Communists and Socialists won a plurality of seats in the *Cortes* and formed a new government. A series of strikes and a monetary crisis put the coalition at risk, and within two months, Communists and socialists from all over Europe flocked into Spain to protect the Popular Front government. Fascist General (not yet "Generalissimo") Francisco Franco took up the blackfriars' mantle* and dedicated himself to keeping Spain safe for the Catholic Church: in July 1936 he led a revolt of the Army from Morocco, and the Civil War was on. Communists, Monarchists, Fascists, Catholic partisans, Republicans and Anarchists—anarcho-syndicalists—joined in Spain, in congress assembled. Franco invited Hitler, and Stalin followed (except that he was already there, directing the anti-fascists in his "united front"). You couldn't tell the players, even with a scorecard—and everybody was on the horns of the bull. In Real Life.

*Footnote: Caught you, didn't I? No one expects the Spanish Inquisition.

Anarquía takes a "what if" look at this confusing situation and imagines what if the anarchists had not been ground out between the Republicans (Communists) and the Nationalists (fascists)? What if the anarchists had won out? To realize this possibility of history, it would be necessary to make two assumptions: first, that the anarchists actually had acted like anarchists instead of trying to play coalition politics with their allies in the Republican POUM coalition of Communists and Socialists (this is a game anarchists never win, for all the obvious reasons); and, second, that they could evolve some weapon or strategy that would put them on a competitive footing with the German war machine, who were about to invent carpet-bombing at Guernica (April 1937).

Enter Wernher von Braun. In *Anarquía,* von Braun is derailed from his real-life path of making terror weapons for the Nazis, and he takes up making terror weapons—aerial land-mines—for the arguable good guys, the anarchists. Actually, there really were no good guys in the real Spanish Civil War, on any side (showing Francisco Franco as milquetoast fascist—a loyal Catholic fascist—was one of the books' boldest and most satisfying strokes). This is not so far from the way things turned out In Real Life: von Braun was brought to the United States after World War II and became Our Favorite Buzz Bomber. Of course, it helped that the Nazis had arrested von Braun for talking up interplanetary travel instead of buzz-bombing London. (Heinrich Himmler knew which planet he wanted the V-1 going to.)

At any rate, we can cheer von Braun's terrorizing Communists and Nazis in *Anarquía*. Once again, art imitates life and once again von Braun becomes Our Favorite Buzz Bomber. For this reason, Wernher von Braun may not have been the best choice to play John Galt to Hedy Lamarr's Dagny Taggart. (Though on looks alone, Jack Warner would probably have approved this couple coupling.)

Von Braun's double-rocket, gyroscopically stabilized aerial mine is called "the horns of the bull," and that is a wonderfully appropriate, flexible, and adaptable metaphor for the authors to have chosen. Not only does it recall the *corrida* and Spain's *other* national blood sport, but the bull is, after all, an aggressive *herd* animal, its aggression primarily directed to other bulls, and that, too, is what the Spanish Civil War was really all about.

Both Hitler and Stalin saw themselves as the cutting edge of Socialism. For a very long time, the ideal picture held by both Marxist and utopian socialists was of a centrally-planned, corporate-organized state. Hitler and Stalin were in Spain in 1936 to duke it out over who was going to be the top socialist in the world. Even Durruti's anarcho-syndicalists wanted to be good socialist idealists—which is why they were hated by Republicans (i.e., Communists) and Nationalists (i.e., fascists) alike. *Anarquía* plays with the imagination of *what if*, dream and illusion less than Hitler or Stalin did with their own illusions of mass movements and the total State, where planned famines and purges liquidating tens of millions of workers defined the "workers' paradise." And to join this play of reality and illusion, what better world, of will and of representation, than Tinseltown itself—where Hedy Lamarr waits out her exile? It's just too perfect.

The Great Socialist Future would be made by and for mass men. Except for a few crochety thinkers like American Pragmatist philosopher John Dewey, who was trying to reframe a new individualism for the Great Socialist Future, individualism was thoroughly identified with the Bad Old Days the Fabians were going to pave over with paper, the Progressives with Silver, and the CommuNazis with blood. The old Victorian cultural baggage was finally out; now, in with the new: the Spanish Civil War would sweep in the bright new world of the masses. In Spain, the authors of *Anarquía* at one point remark, even the anarchists were collectivists.

Messrs. Linaweaver and Hastings provided Durruti with a sprinkling of individualist anarchists, as the little leavening that leaveneth the lumpenproletariat. The *Anarquía* of *Anarquía* need not circle down the drain of mass-movement mania that tossed the whole of the world on the horns of a bull five years later—and ten and twenty and up to sixty years later.

Two fine books did come out of the Spanish Civil War—Hemingway's *For Whom the Bell Tolls* and Orwell's *Homage to Catalonia* (Catalan independence was one of the Republican's reform planks). To compensate this *dereglement* of history, Linaweaver and Hastings give us Howard Davidson and the pulp rhodomontade of his *Inquisitor* series, complete with a conspiracy of the Vatican. Davidson observes Hemingway—and Chesterton—and Orwell at work, and learns for us why Spain is the closest thing to Hell on earth. There should only be more of Howard Davidson!

The horns of the bull are not finished with us, yet, though. This graphic image has given us a classic metaphor: the horns of a dilemma.

Dilemma is choice, and *Anarquía* reminds us that we have, in every moment, a world growing in us. Between *our* world and the world of *Anarquía*, is Dante's vision: there is a way to heaven, even from the heart of Hell on Earth.

Bill Patterson
Santa Cruz, August 2003

BILL PATTERSON is the publisher/editor of *The Heinlein Journal*. With access to the official archives, he is writing the definitive biography of Robert A. Heinlein.

Afterword: "Planned Chaos"
by William Alan Ritch

At the outset I must tell you all how delighted and surprised I was when Brad Linaweaver asked me to write an Afterword for his latest novel, *Anarquía* (written with newcomer J. Kent Hastings). Brad and I have been friends, sparring partners, and each others' worst critics for nearly thirty-three years now. Our discussions cover every aspect of human life, and we have rarely agreed. How boring if we did. I was pleased to see many of the points that I have raised with Brad exhibited in this novel—although often from the mouths of the villains! I suppose that I expected no less.

In a word, I found the book fantastic. And you may interpret that word with *all its meanings*. Yes. I enjoyed the book very much. In fact, my only complaint with the book as a novel is that it was much too short. I wanted even more of the mesmerizing and fantastic (there's that word again) reality that Linaweaver and Hastings have constructed.

As many of you know, Linaweaver is one of the foremost practitioners of the fiction of parallel existence (often mislabeled "alternate history"). He made quite a splash with his first novel, *Moon of Ice*—set in the recent past after Germany has won a major war called "World War II." With this book, he returns to the well of his fascinating characters, "the Nazis" and writes about some of the events leading up to World War II, centering around a civil war in Spain. I suppose that *Anarquía* is a "prequel" (detestable word, that) to *Moon of Ice*, although there are inconsistencies between the two novels. (As a matter of fact, Hastings says that he was inspired to begin his alternate history of the Spanish Civil War because he was a fan of *Moon of Ice*.)

Linaweaver's vision of a world in which the European countries have not once, but twice (!) fought a vast, technologically enhanced war is both fascinating and frightening. Linaweaver has envisioned both these worlds with such clarity and detail that one would think he has lived in them. An independent country in the Americas, insane dictators in Germany, Russia, and England, philosophies in control of men's minds instead of allegiances to the crown—these are just some of the almost unbelievable aspects of Linaweaver's books.

Brad even stretches the bounds of credulity with his characters. In this book, for instance, he and his partner Kent have created the character of Hedy Lamarr—an actress who journeys from her European origins to live in the Americas. Early in her career she appeared nude in a "movie" (a sort of recorded play). She then becomes a celebrity as a movie actress in the Americas. I certainly find it unbelievable that a country founded on the Puritan principles of the Americas could ever celebrate so openly brazen a woman. But she is a fascinating character: beautiful, charming, brilliant. And degenerate, of course.

Her lover, Wernher von Braun, is another almost impossible character. With little training and a questionable background he adapts those cute little Chinese fireworks devices into a weapon capable of massive destruction. He even speaks of using them to launch a man into space. (Pull the other one, Brad!)

The secondary characters are just as interesting. Linaweaver must be the one who made it seem as if the civil war in Spain was fought almost entirely by English novelists. And they are all such larger-than-life characters. Not like any novelist I've ever met (Linaweaver excepted, of course). First there is Eric Blair, also called George Orwell—a passionate believer in one of Linaweaver's demon philosophies called "Socialism." His faith is often tested by the betrayal of fellow champions of his cause. Then there is G. K. Chesterton—a nascent anarchist—and a Catholic—in England. Three bizarre ideas rolled into one. And larger than any of them is an English writer from the Americas called Ernest Hemingway. We are told by all who meet him—and from his own mouth—that he is a great novelist. But he certainly is a flawed and deluded human being.

One nice touch is the appearance of Howard Davidson and John Staples. These two great New Amsterdamian novelists from the 1930s are well portrayed in the book—but they have been converted into writers of trashy adventure stories! I suppose that if I did the research I would discover that Hemingway actually lived in *our* world writing boxing stories for the tuppence magazines back then.

As wonderful as the good guys are, it is the villains who shine. The leader of Russia, a man coyly named "Stalin" ("man of steel"), is ruthless, heartless, and completely devoid of reasonableness. His opposite number in Germany is Adolf Hitler—seen here earlier in his life—before his successes chronicled in *Moon of Ice*. Stalin and Hitler are such wonderful comic opera bad guys that Linaweaver makes us feel sorry for Franco, the leader of Spain. He too is a villain, but he is fighting outside his weight class when he gets between Hitler, Stalin, and the anarchists. Of course we have another glimpse at Linaweaver's best fictional creation: Herr Dr. Paul Joseph Goebbels. The information minister for

Germany. Short, club-footed, articulate, and calculating—twisted in mind and body—there can be no better character.

Although Brad would not agree with me on this, the alternative worlds of *Anarquía* and *Moon of Ice* are cautionary tales. People like Hitler, Stalin, and even Goebbels could not arise in our world. It can only happen when the common man—the peasants and the trader class—is invested with political power. The world of *Anarquía* is the direct result of putting power and trust in man rather than in God and the King!

W. A. RITCH is Professor of History, emeritus, Liberal Arts University of the Americas, Boston, Massachusetts Bay, New England. (BILL RITCH in an alternate universe is a libertarian activist, contributor to *Free Space* and up to his eyeballs in work with the *Atlanta Radio Theatre Company*.)

Afterword: Sailing an Unplumbed Strait
The Singular Voyage of Anarquía!

By Victor Koman

I have to confess to reading *Anarquía* with an embarrassing handicap: I have a limited knowledge of history. It was always my worst subject in high school and even though time and age have given me a greater interest in the field, my early lack of enthusiasm has resulted in a vast sea of ignorance in which only a few islands of awareness can be found.

For the record, I knew there was a civil war in Spain in the 1930s. I knew that the communists were battling the fascists. I knew Hitler bombed the living hell out of Guernica. (I've seen Picasso's cubist commentary on the subject.) I even knew Hemingway drove ambulances in the Great War. What I didn't know was how pivotal the Spanish war was to shaping the course of World War II and the subsequent events of the remainder of the second millennium.

As one who read science fiction almost exclusively for much of my life, I can honestly say that the Spanish Civil War never struck to me as a subject of an alternate history story. Most alternate history I've read has centered on alternate outcomes of the Second World War, or sometimes to differing results in America's own civil war, the War for Southern Independence Against Northern Aggression. And nearly all SF written from an anarchist or pro-liberty, pro-individual-rights point of view has concerned itself with the American Revolution and where we went wrong (or where we didn't go right enough).

And yet, given that the Left has exalted the Spanish Civil War to a struggle of mythic proportions and has lionized every member of the Abraham Lincoln Brigade as a secular saint, it is astonishing to me that no novel-length treatment of the subject has issued from the pen of the numerous left-wing writers who populate the science fiction ranks, or any ranks for that matter. Certainly, there must be writers who think that a decisive Communist victory in Spain would have had a different effect on world history. There may even be a writer or two who has wondered what would have happened if famous leftists such as Ernest Hemingway had died in the conflict. What if *Animal Farm* and *1984* had never been written because George Orwell never made it out of Madrid? But of all the writers who might have put words on paper to describe their own dream (or nightmare) endings to the story of WWII's trial run, it came to pass that the firstest with the mostest are an unlikely pairing of a high-tech anarchist computer whiz known as J. Kent Hastings and a willfully low-tech minarchist, Hollywood-based Southern gentleman commonly referred to as Brad Linaweaver.

The fascinating aspect of the writing and publication of *Anarquía* is not that it is the first novel to deal with an alternate history of the Spanish Civil War, but that it should choose as the unlikely heroes of that conflict a rag-tag band of anarchists whom both the Communists and the Fascists (and nearly all historians) considered either an irritant, an impediment, or a joke. But anarchists are not to be taken lightly at any point in history. Not in the late 18th Century, where they clearly influenced the American Revolution, not in the early 20th Century, where they played a part in the Russian Revolution, and most especially not in the dawn of the 21st Century, where governments have demonstrated a serious vulnerability to forces that owe allegiance to no government, only to their own ideology.

It is important, then, to recognize the power of ideology, because as surely as it can lead to the Declaration of Independence, it can also lead to *The Communist Manifesto* and *Mein Kampf*. And as surely as the first has been an inspiration to centuries of liberation, the other two have been the rationalization for decades of enslavement and mass-murder. Only someone possessing a strong ideology can say, "Give me Liberty or give me death." And only someone possessing a strong ideology can suppress all human compassion and reason in order to kill themselves and thousands of others by flying hijacked airplanes into the World Trade Center, the Pentagon, and the Pennsylvania countryside. And only people with a strong ideology can liberate an entire nation from the hands of a murderous tyrant and idolater of Stalin, then fight to keep it from falling into chaos while facing death at the hands of an ungrateful minority of ideologues among the people they risked their lives to free.

It is the ideology of anarchism, then, that gives *Anarquía* its unusual slant and its powerful vision. The choice in the Spanish Civil War was not between the Scylla of Communism and the Charybdis of Fascism. As history has demonstrated in the latter half of the 20th Century, Communism and Fascism are two rocky shoals of the same strait of evil, two faces of the same, blood-drenched Janus-mask of tyranny. The real battle in Spain—and the true war fought endlessly throughout time—was and is the war between statism and liberty, collectivism and individuality, slavery and freedom. And in this battle, the most celebrated side—the Communists and their fellow travelers in the Abraham Lincoln Brigade—were squarely, albeit in some cases unwittingly, on the side of the tyranny of Joseph Stalin, the greatest butcher in all of history. To side with Franco, though, meant siding with Hitler, the second-greatest slaughterer the world has ever seen, though possibly only because Hitler didn't have as much time as Stalin.

What if, the authors asked, the third alternative had drawn the notice of a few critical people, such as the superlative rocketeer Wernher von Braun, the underappreciated cyberneticist Konrad Zuse, and the otherwise-famous spread-spectrum radio inventor, Hedy Lamarr? Might the winner of the war have been neither Fascist, with its assistance from Berlin, Rome, and Madrid, nor Communist, with its aid from Moscow, New York, and Hollywood, but rather Liberty, with the contribution of individuals dedicated to an ideology of human freedom?

What separates this novel from the majority of alternate history novels is that it deals specifically with the thorny subject of anarchists and anarchy, which most alternate history writers dismiss in their novels, and with a country other than the United States, which most libertarian novelists concentrate on almost obsessively. This is a rare and quite possibly unique novel, all the more to be cherished for its blend of wit and ingenuity amid the evil of the forces behind the horrific war it so brilliantly presents.

Along with *political* ideology, a gift for characterization and a deep understanding of the Golden Age of Hollywood (all areas in which Mr. Linaweaver excels), the story also posits that victory belongs to the side with the best *scientific* ideas, and in this realm Mr. Hastings wields a dominance of knowledge and genius. Using only the technology that was available at the time and postulating nothing more than the known brilliance of von Braun, Zuse, and Lamarr, Hastings has constructed a fascinating arsenal for Durruti and his band. The wish of every reader and writer of alternate-history fiction is to be a time-traveler, and nothing would be more thrilling than to go back and get these three together and over to Spain and see what actually happens. Unfortunately for the nascent time-travel industry, Linaweaver and Hastings have done that for us, and produced a novel as important to the field of freedom-oriented alternate history in the post-Soviet, post-9/11 21st Century as L. Neil Smith's *Probability Broach* was to the liberalism-soaked late 20th Century, over two decades ago.

VICTOR KOMAN is the author of the Prometheus Award winners *The Jehovah Contract, Solomon's Knife,* and *Kings of the High Frontier.* He is currently working on the next novel in his *Captain Anger* series of contemporary pulp adventures and can be reached through his website www.CaptainAnger.com.

Afterword: "Rolling Out The Red Carpet"
by Dafydd ab Hugh

The Jesuits—the Comintern of the Catholic Church—had a saying: "Give me the child until he is seven, and I will give you the man." The Hollywood Red would have understood this in his very soul, if he had one; since he'd long since traded it for pocket change and a good agent, and he lived only for the Materialist Now, he translated it as best he could: who controls the films controls the present, the past, and the future, all rolled together into one fat cocktail party in the hills below the Hollywood sign.

Like maggots infiltrating a loaf of bread, the Communists worked their way into cinema, eating their fill and reproducing, infecting the young and the listless. It was virtually impossible for the Red hunters to warn filmgoers of the danger without sounding like Kevin McCarthy, running around screaming about pod people and alien invasion ... a point that no doubt occurred to Fra Trumbo, Abbe Hellman, and the rest of the Red Cardinals: the best propaganda is too fantastical to be taken seriously, wriggling its way directly into the brain through the adventure or romance gateways, bypassing the critical faculties altogether. The program was one of the most successful of the Stalinist era, and it long survived the deaths of Stalin, Hitler, Franco, and every other mortal who fought in the clash of the titans, the Spanish Civil War. Even today, the viewer must be taken by the hand, like Adam in Eden, and shown, sometimes frame by frame, how *The Best Years of Our Lives* or *It's a Wonderful Life* corrupts and distorts the picture of the world, of capital, of the individual and his enemy, the hive collective.

Cardinal Celi and Comrad Stalin, mirrored antipodes of the endless struggle between the God of heaven and the god of earth, understood the power of bright dreams projected against a Judas-silver screen, puppet images jerking to the strings of whoever wrote the lines or directed the scenes. Stalin's fat, arachnid hand clutches at the map of Spain ... is it so different from the scores of Hollywood Reds groping for the hearts and minds of Americans through the commie movies they created?

The Hollywood Ten and their comrades and dupes, unconsecrated priests of Communism, knew their maggots of propaganda would thrive and wriggle so long as old classics were revived and new Soviet men like themselves made more. Stalin knew and urged them on; Goebbels knew and hired his own; and *Anarquía*'s Cardinal Celi knew, could see it as

215

clearly as he saw the body of Jesus descend from the cross: the image lasts long after the logos have faded to echoes in the ear. Lips crumble, but the seduction whispers on in the flicker of a blackened theater.

Men may go and come, but celluloid abides.

DAFYDD AB HUGH has written many *Star Trek* novels, historical novels, and a Young Adult series. In a moment of weakness, he collaborated on four (yes, four) *Doom* novels with Brad Linaweaver, who has been collaborating ever since (but not with Fifth Columnists). Naturally, Dafydd has focused on Stalin's role in *Anarquía* because of a new collaboration with Linaweaver, *Commie Movies.*

Afterword: "Report from the Front"
by Randall N. Herrst

In *Anarquía*, the Orlov operation fails because of von Braun's rocket weapon "the horns of the bull." During a conversation with Linaweaver and Hastings I pointed out that the operation could be explained better with a military paradigm. *Anarquía* is such an unusual project that the authors invited me into their world to describe one possible scenario and I was pleased to accept.

Perhaps some of you were wondering why Orlov was so confident that his gold train could not be stopped. And why everything went so horribly wrong.

Orlov knew that his gold removal plan could not be stopped because his military training allowed him to prepare for every possibility. It was an excellent plan, but it wasn't good enough to cope with a shifting paradigm.

Orlov knew that no light arms, not even the little wonder rockets, could destroy a train, so his plan was designed to preclude the concentration of large forces of men, tanks and artillery, while preventing explosive sabotage of the rail line. Orlov sent out covert patrols to guard the rails against sabotage. These patrols reported no explosives attached to bridges or rails, and no enemy activity within one-half km of the tracks on either side. The republicans sent low-profile patrols to nearby roads to prevent movement of tanks, heavy artillery and large numbers of enemy soldiers.

Orlov was pleased that the gold train looked like an ordinary freight train, but it was more like a Q-ship, heavily armed and carrying 172 soldiers. Just behind the engine and tender was a flatcar apparently loaded with several large crates, but the walls of those crates folded down to expose a mortar and a captured Flak 30 20mm cannon that spits out 280 high-explosive projectiles per minute—highly effective against charging infantry and unarmored vehicles within 700 meters. Next, two cattlecars whose slat-sides allowed the soldiers within to fire outward. Then, the seven boxcars loaded with gold. Then two more cattlecars with soldiers, followed by the final flatcar with medium machine gun and .50 caliber Browning M2 heavy machine gun.

Orlov also prepared a scout train to travel 30 minutes ahead of the gold train. The soldiers would scrutinize the rail line as they proceeded and watch for sabotage and ambushes. This train was also disguised to look like an ordinary freight train, even though it carried another captured Flak 30 rapid-fire cannon, two medium machine guns, and 67 soldiers. The two trains would be in radio contact with each other, in case the gold train needed help.

Orlov also knew that the Condor Legion posed a threat if the Fascists found out what Orlov was doing. But it had not escaped his notice that, after Guernica, the Condor Legion appeared to be frightened by the mysterious miracle weapon and was no longer conducting any low-altitude patrols or attacks. This was perfect for Orlov's plan, since he scheduled close air support by rotating patrols of low-flying Polikarpov I-16's of the republican air force operating out of a dirt airfield northwest of Valencia. The republicans could not afford to spare many planes, but five planes rotating through the region would leave one or two always within quick-reaction range of the train. An I-16 with its twin 20mm cannon and twin 7.62mm machine guns would provide strong firepower against enemy troops.

The coup de grace, just in case the wonder weapons were becoming widespread, was the brilliant work of his communications experts. Orlov's men had been monitoring the radio traffic during the battle of Guernica when they heard whines and clicks on 2 specific frequencies when the wonder rockets were in flight, apparently representing two different radio control sets. Orlov's radio experts realized that the rockets were guided by radio signals, which could be jammed. They were going to surprise the upstart anarchists and show them the superiority of Soviet science. Both trains and each plane received cobbled-together radio jammers that continuously broadcast strong random signals over the entire range of frequencies between those two.

What went wrong? Everything, including the paradigm shift that Orlov dismissed. He was even wrong about the vaunted Soviet secrecy. There were Anarchists working in the rail yard and they had been able to piece together enough of the plan to realize that the trains may transport a huge gold shipment.

He made excellent preparations against conventional attack, but for the first time in modern military history, accuracy supplanted raw power and volume of fire. Accuracy substitutes for quantity, so Orlov's preconception of the amount of materiel traffic needed for a big attack was high by a factor of 50. The Anarchists were easily able to smuggle several dozen Horns into the region via inconspicuous human, car and cart traffic.

Orlov "knew" that light arms could not stop a 180-ton train engine, but he did not anticipate a collateral attack on the bridges. After all, everyone knew that was a job for attached explosive charges, which he had efficiently precluded. Who would have guessed that missiles could accurately deliver small, adequate explosive charges to the bridge columns from a long distance? The Matadors were not detected because they set up their operational posts more than one-half km away from the rail line, outside the patrol zone. The Horns simultaneously attacked bridges in front of the gold train and behind it, trapping the train. Unfortunately, the scout train could not come to the rescue when Orlov radioed for help because another bridge has been destroyed immediately behind it, leaving the scout train 33 km away and also under attack.

Orlov's experts came to the wrong conclusion regarding the two frequencies they noted in the battle at Guernica. They assumed that they were two different remote control channels, but never realized that those were just two of the very wide range of hundreds of frequencies that the frequency-hopping guidance system used. Jamming the narrow spectrum between those two frequencies just degraded the accuracy a tiny bit. After the first Horns of the Bull was fired at a bridge column, Orlov activated the radio jamming equipment and was horrified to find out that it had absolutely no effect on subsequent missiles that hit his big gun dead center and then the machine guns and two of the cattle cars! How could these damned Anarchists be so far ahead of his radio and weapons experts?

Orlov called his air support as soon as the attack began, hoping that they could destroy the attackers. The first I-16 fighter arrived at high speed, but it is shot down after only two Horns are launched at it. The next I-16 arrives nine minutes later and it meets the same fate. Orlov realizes all is probably lost, but he continues to call for air support because it is his last hope. One by one, they arrive and go down in flames after providing only a few strafing runs to no effect.

Soon, Orlov had almost no troops who were still able to fight, so he signaled his surrender. Everything had changed and, as Orlov realized, too late.

RANDALL N. HERRST is the President of The Center For The Study Of Crime. A political consultant on self-defense issues, he is also a long time associate of J. Neil Schulman.

THE SPANISH FRONT IN 1936

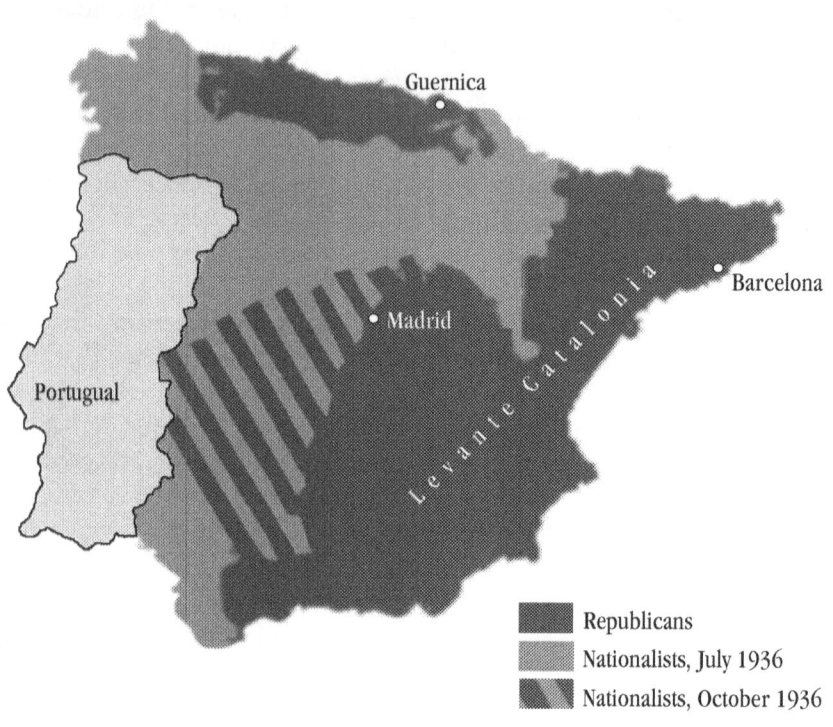

Guernica

Barcelona

Madrid

Portugal

Levante Catalonia

Republicans
Nationalists, July 1936
Nationalists, October 1936

Glossary

Abraham Lincoln Brigade: An International Brigade consisting of Americans who fought with the Republicans against the Franco and the Fascists in the Spanish Civil War. The first volunteers sailed from New York City in late 1936. The majority were members of the American Communist Party.

Acción Española: Monarchist party. *See also* Renovación Española.

Acción Popular: Catholic party, later a part of Confederacion Espanola de Derechas Autonomas.

Anarcho-Syndicalists: Confederación Nacional de Trabajo (CNT). Founded in 1911, this trade union, whose main support came from industrial workers in Barcelona, courted both peasants and unskilled workers. The CNT believed in the revolutionary overthrow of capitalism and was the largest trade union in Spain when the Civil War commenced. The CNT, like most political organizations during the Spanish Civil War, was constantly disrupted by factional differences. *See also* Federación Anarquista Ibérica (FAI).

Carlists: Founded in 1833 and named after Don Carlos, the uncle of Queen Isabella II. Group opposed to liberal secularism and economic and political modern movements. During the Spanish Civil War, Carlists favored a return to an ultra-Catholic monarchy. They led the opposition to the Second Republic in 1931 and later joined forces with Franco and the National Army.

Comintern: (Communist International) Organization founded in March 1919 by leading members of the Russian Communist Party and devoted to the creation, by all available means, of an international Soviet republic. Josef Stalin controlled the Comintern throughout the Spanish Civil War, using it as an arm of Soviet foreign policy.

Confederación Española de Derechas Autónomas (CEDA): Catholic party, founded in February 1933 by José María Gil Robles. For the most part, supported the Nationalist Army, however Franco dissolved CEDA in April of 1937.

Cortes: Spanish Parliament.

Elections of February 1936: An important prelude to the violence  that followed. The Popular Front won 34.4 per cent and the Conservative parties won 33.2 per cent. The remaining votes went to regional and centre parties. Despite these close results, the new government upset conservatives by instituting a number of left-wing reforms, outlawing the Falange Española and transferring right-wing military leaders such as Francisco Franco to posts outside Spain.

Esquerra Republicana de Catalunya (ERC): Catalán (Catalonian) left-Republican nationalist party which looked to the Republicans for support of their separatist agenda.

Falange Española: Spanish Fascist Party founded 29 October 1933 by José Antonio Primo de Rivera (executed November 1936). This group condemned socialism, Marxism, republicanism and capitalism and promoted the establishment of a Fascist state similar to Italy. Later became the dominant arm of the Nationalists. Offices  closed by the Popular Front following the February 1936 elections and banned in March. In 1937 Franco united the Falangists (now leaderless) with the Carlists and other small right-wing parties to form the Falange Española Tradicionalista y de las Juntas de Ofensiva Nacional-Sindicalista.

Falange Española Tradicionalista y de las Juntas de Ofensiva Nacional-Sindicalista (FET): Fascist party founded in 1937 by Francisco Franco when Falange Española Tradicionalista and Juntas de Ofensiva Nacional-Sindicalista merged.

Federación Anarquista Ibérica (FAI): Violent splinter group of the Anarcho-Syndicalists (CNT). In 1927 FAI members made several unsuccessful attempts to assassinate Alfonso XIII. The FAI was also credited with uprisings and numerous assassinations of Falange Española members in the 1930s.

Federación Ibérica de Juventudes Libertarias (FIJL): Anarchist youth organization.

International Brigades: Units comprised of foreign volunteers fighting with the Republican Army and established by the Comintern in July 1936. Nearly 60,000 volunteers from fifty-five countries served during the Spanish Civil War. *See also* Abraham Lincoln Brigade.

Izquierda Comunista: Left Communist (Marxist) party led by Andrés Nin. Later a part of Partido Obrero de Unificación Marxista.

Izquierda Republicana: Left Republican socialist party founded in 1934.

Juventudes Socialistas Unificadas (JSU): Socialist youth organization later dominated by the pro-Soviet Communists.

Legion Condor (Kondor): German Air Force unit fighting along the side of the Nationalist Army.

Lojalists: *See* Republican.

Los Amigos de Durruti: Anarchist opposition group within the CNT, FAI and FIJL.

Margaritas: Monarchist womens' organisation.

Mujeres Libres: Anarchist womens' organisation.

Nationalist Army: Forces led by General Francisco Franco  in July 1936, initially comprised of the Peninsular Army and the Army of African and two internal paramilitary police forces, the Civil Guard and the Assault Guard. Both Hitler and Mussolini assisted this force with men and equipment. Some number of officers and enlisted men supported, either openly or covertly, the Republican Army, the Popular Front or other political groups. Very few of these officers, however, refused to fight with the Nationalist Army.

National Front. Coalition of parties on the political right organized to  win elections in February 1936 which included CEDA and the Carlists. The Falange Española did not officially join but generally supported the National Front. They lost, narrowly, to the Popular Front. *See also* Popular Front.

Partido Agrario: Catholic party, later a part of Confederación Española de Derechas Autónomas.

Partido Communista de España (PCE): Pro-Soviet Spanish Communist Party founded in November 1921 by dissident members of the Socialist Party, the CNT and the UGT.

Partido Nacionalista Vasco (PNV): Basque separatist party founded in 1895 which looked to the Republicans for the support of its cause.

Partido Obrero de Unificación Marxista (POUM):  Workers Party of Marxist Unification. Anti-Soviet Communist party, founded September 1935 by Andres Nin and Joaquin Maurin, and strongly influenced by the political ideas of Leon Trotsky. The POUM was very influential in Catalonia but had little strength elsewhere in Spain. Membership in 1935 is  estimated at 8,000 members. Supported by the Popular Front, the POUM grew rapidly, having around 30,000 members by the end of 1936 with 10,000 in its own militia.

Partido Socialista Obrero Español (PSOE): Spanish So-  cialist Workers Party founded in 1879 and very influen- tial before the War. Supported by the UGT and FJS.

Partido Republicano Radical: Republican socialist party.

Partido Socialista Unificado de Cataluña (PSUC): United Catalán Socialist Party formed in 1936. Affiliated with Comintern and rep- resented the Pro-Soviet Communist Party.

Partit Comunista Catalá: Catalán Communist Party.

Popular Front: Coalition of parties on the political left organized to  win the national elections in February 1936. Included the Socialist Party (PSOE), Communist party (PCE), Esquerra Party and the Republican Union party. They narrowly won the election and formed a new govern- ment. Earlier, the name referred to advocates of the res- toration of Catalán autonomy, etc. Founded in October 1933 by Manuel Azaña. *See also* National Front.

Renovación Española: Monarchist party. *See also* Acción Española.

Republicans: Supporters of the Second Spanish Republic, broadly left- wing but covering all shades of political persuasion.

Republican Army: A force comprised of officers and sol-  diers loyal to the Republic as well as miscellaneous battalions formed by various political groups includ- ing the Anarchist Brigades, the Communist-controlled Fifth Regiment and the International Brigades (orga- nized by the Comintern). Further organization oc- curred in September 1936 and political commissars were created that October. The Soviet Union provided assistance in the form of tanks, aircraft and men. The lack of experienced junior officers greatly hindered the military successes of the Republican Army.

Requetes: Monarchist militaries.

Second Spanish Republic: Founded 14 April, 1931 following popular elections. Alphonso XIII resigns and leaves Spain.

Servicio de Investigación Militar (SIM): Political police force controlled by the pro-Soviet communists.

Unión General de Trabajadores (UGT): General Union of Workers. Socialist trade union originally established in Madrid by a group of printers and aligned with the Socialist party (PSOE). The more militant CNT broke away  from the UGT in 1911 to establish its own union.  The UGT supported the Popular Front following the 1936 elections and sided with the Republican Army. It was later dominated by the pro-Soviet Communist Party.

Unión Militar Española (UME): Conservative officers group.

Unión Militar Republicana Antifascista (UMRA): A small, left-wing group including Spanish Army officers who refused to fight with the Nationalist Army.

Unión Republicana: Republican socialist party.

Chronology

A Brief Chronology of Events during The Spanish Civil War

The Spanish dictator, Miguel Primo de Rivera is forced to resign, 28 January 1930

Provisional government calls for elections. Alfonso XIII goes into exile, 14 April 1931

Second Republic, Socialist Party (PSOE) and other left-wing groups win election, June 1931

Anarchist uprisings in Saragossa, Seville, Bilbao and Madrid, 8 January 1933

Gil Robles forms the Catholic Party (CEDA) 28 February 1933

José Antonio Primo de Rivera establishes the Falange Española, 29 October 1933

Spanish right-wing parties win general election over a divided left, 19 November 1933

Anarchist uprisings in Catalonia and Aragon, 2 December 1933

Andrés Nin and Joaquín Maurin create the Workers Party of Marxist Unification (POUM), September 1935

An electoral pact is signed by the Socialist Party and Communist Party, 11 January 1936

Manuel Azaña organizes the formation of the Popular Front, February 1936

Popular Front narrowly wins general election over Conservatives, 16 February 1936

General Francisco Franco is relieved of his command and sent to the Canary Islands, 22 February 1936

Civil Guard suppresses a left-wing rally at Yeste and kills nineteen people in the process, 28 May 1936

Over a million workers are on strike in Spain, 9 June 1936

Luis Bolin arranges for Francisco Franco to be flown to Morocco, 6 July 1936

General Francisco Franco issues manifesto that seeks to justify rebellion, 18 July 1936

Dolores Ibarruri makes her "No Pasarán" radio speech, 18 July 1936

Antifascist Militias Committee establish the Anarchist Brigade, 24 July 1936

Rebel forces capture Granada, 24 July 1936

Adolf Hitler agrees to give military aid to General Francisco Franco, 26 July 1936

Comintern agrees to establish International Brigades, 26 July 1936

General Francisco Franco and the Nationalist Army captures Badajoz, 4 August 1936

General Francisco Franco establishes his headquarters in Seville, 6 August 1936

Indalecio Prieto appeals on radio for an end to the Red Terror, 10 August 1936

The first International Brigades volunteers reach Spain, 12 August 1936

Nationalist forces bomb Madrid for the first time, 28 August 1936

Representatives of 27 countries form Non-Intervention Committee in London,
     9 September 1936

Alexander Orlov of the NKVD arrives in Spain, 9 September 1936

Alvarez del Vayo pleads the Republic's case at the League of Nations, 25 September 1936

The first aid from the Soviet Union arrives in Spain, 12 October 1936

510 tons of gold from the Bank of Spain is sent to the Soviet Union, 25 October 1936

Nationalist forces begin siege of Madrid, 6 November 1936

Republican government moves from Madrid to Valencia, 6 November 1936

Non-Intervention Committee concludes that there is no evidence of foreign intervention in
     Spain, 10 November 1936

Buenaventura Durruti arrives in Madrid with his Anarchist Brigade, 14 November 1936

Condor Legion, a squadron of the Luftwaffe, in action for the first time, 15 November 1936

Buenaventura Durruti killed while defending Madrid, 19 November 1936

Communists insist on the removal of the POUM from the Catalan government,
     17 December 1936

The Republican Army defeats the Italian Corps outside Madrid, 18 March 1937

Francisco Franco unites the Falange Española with the Carlists to form a single party,
     19 April 1937

The Condor Legion bombs Guernica, the Basque capital in Northern Spain, 26 April 1937

Anarchists and Syndicalists revolt in Barcelona against the authoritarian rule of government,
     3 May 1937

Juan Negrín outlaws POUM, 16 June 1937

Andres Nín, leader of POUM, is murdered by agents from the Soviet Union, 20 June 1937

The anarchist-dominated Council of Aragon is dissolved by Juan Negrín, 10 August 1937

Nationalists bomb Madrid for the first time, 28 August 1937

Republican government moves from Valencia to Barcelona, 28 October 1937

Nationalist aircraft bombs Barcelona, 8 December 1937

Italian Air Force bombs Barcelona, 16 March 1938

Juan Negrín proposes a thirteen-point peace terms, 1 May 1938

Juan Negrín announces the proposed withdrawal of the International Brigades from Spain, 21 September 1938

All foreign troops fighting for the Republican Army leave the front lines, 4 October 1938

Trial of POUM leaders starts in Barcelona, 28 October 1938

International Brigades parade through the streets of Barcelona, 15 November 1938

Barcelona captured by the Nationalists, 26 January 1939

President Manuel Azaña crosses the border into exile, 4 February 1939

Juan Negrín attempts to form a communist government on the territory he controls, 4 March 1939

Communist forces defeated in Madrid, 8 March 1939

Juan Negrín and his Soviet advisers fly out of Spain, 12 March 1939

Nationalist Army enters Madrid after a siege of nearly three years, 27 March 1939

Francisco Franco announces the end of the Spanish Civil War, April 1939

Republican

International Brigades

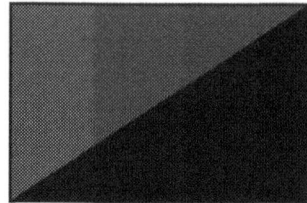

Anarchists

Carlists

Spanish Phalanx

Spanish Confederation Autonomous

230

Miscellanea

Agorism

From "agora"—the Greek word meaning "open marketplace"—agorism is both a free market ideology and advocacy of a peaceful black market (a "counter-economy") as the means of non-aggressive revolution. See also *New Libertarian Manifesto*, by Samuel Edward Konkin III, father of Agorism.)
—*from www.blackcrayon.com*

Alfonso XIII (1886-1941)

Born on 17th May 1886 in Madrid, Spain. He assumed full power of the throne in 1902 and married Princess Ena of Battenberg, granddaughter of Queen Victoria in 1906. He survived several assassination attempts, including one on his wedding day. He ordered the execution of radical, Ferrer Guardia, in 1909 and was generally resistant to liberal or democratic reforms. He was blamed for Spain's defeat in the Moroccan War (1921) and in 1923 supported a military coup led by Miguel Primo de Rivera. Upon Rivera's fall from power he agreed to general elections and lost to the Republic. Alfonso left Spain on 14 April 1931. During the Spanish Civil War he supported the Nationalists but in September 1936, Franco refused to return him to the throne. Alfonso XIII died in Rome in 1941.

Church of Christ the Savior

The original Cathedral was built between 1839 and 1883 by the architect Konstantin Ton. The structure stood in commemoration of Russia's victory over Napoleon. Stalin ordered the razing of this beautiful building in 1933. A committee was organized to help fund the rebuilding of the Cathedral and the construction was completed in the 1990s.

Condor (Kondor) Legion

The "Condor Legion" (*"Legión Cóndor"*), a unit of Nazi Germany's air force, was sent as a volunteer force in support of the Nationalists. The first units arrived in August 1936. In November the Legion consisted of about 100 airplanes and 5,000 men under the command of Hugo Sperrle (1885-1953). His chief of staff was Wolfram von Richthofen (cousin of the WWI flying ace). The *Messerschmitt Bf 109* fighter and *Heinkel He 111* medium bomber first saw active service in the Condor Legion. As the Germans realized that the days of the biplane fighter were over, the *Heinkel He 51* fighter was gradually switched to a ground attack role and then became a trainer. The Condor Legion would eventually total nearly 12,000 men. The group also included non-aircraft units including panzer crews with *panzerkampfwagen 1* and sailors who trained Franco's naval forces. The Germans also conducted early tests employing 88mm heavy anti-aircraft artillery which they used to destroy republican tanks, fortifications, and planes.

Distributism

An economic philosophy based on 19th and 20th century Papal teachings and developed by Catholic thinkers such as G. K. Chesterton and Hillaire Belloc. Holds that ownership of the means of production should be spread as widely as possible among the participants, rather than being centralized in the hands of the state. The system was designed to avoid the drawbacks to both socialism and capitalism. Chesterton once said that, "The problem with capitalism is that there are not enough capitalists."

Dos Passos, John (1896-1970)

Born in Chicago and left Harvard to join the Allied war effort in WWI where he served as an ambulance driver and later wrote *One Man's Initiation* (1920) and *Three Soldiers* (1921). Published *Manhattan Transfer* in 1925 which established his literary reputation. Joined the general effort of many to stop the execution of Sacco and Vanzetti in 1927. Published *The 42nd Parallel* (1930), *1919* (1932), and *The Big Money* (1936). Joined the campaign against Fascism in Europe and supported the Republicans during the Spanish Civil War but later became disillusioned with socialist causes as shown in his later novels *The Adventures of a Young Man* (1939) and *Number One* (1943).

Franco, Francisco (1892-1975)

His childhood was unhappy with a drunken and womanizing father and devout, overprotective mother. As a young officer in Morocco, Franco quickly gained attention; he was badly wounded at age 23 and became the youngest major in the Spanish army. In 1926 Franco became the youngest general in any European army. Not wishing to compromise his career, he maintained political "neutrality" in 1931 with the departure of Alphonso XIII. However, in 1933, when miners in Asturias mounted a rebellion, Franco sent the Moroccan-trained troops to halt the uprising. He was promoted to Chief of the General Staff but, following the close elections of 1936, was sent to the Canary Islands. He returned to lead his troops to war and in September 1936 he became *Generalissimo* of the Nationalist Army. He managed to unite all the warring right-wing factions under one banner and defeated the Republican Army in April 1939 (guerrilla resistance actually continued until the late 1940s). Franco then ruled as Dictator of Spain until his death.

Gellhorn, Martha (1909-1998)

Born in St. Louis, dropped out of Bryn Mawr in 1929 and began writing articles for the *New Republic*. She sailed for Paris in 1930, returned to the U.S. in 1934 and met Ernest Hemingway in Key West in 1936. In 1937 she traveled with Hemingway to Madrid to work as a foreign correspondent for *Collier's Weekly* covering the Spanish Civil War. She covered Russia's war against Finland in 1939, traveled across China (with Hemingway) in 1940, covered the WWII front and the D-Day invasion, the Java conflict and the Sino-Japanese War. Gellhorn and Hemingway were married in 1940 and divorced in 1944. Although chiefly known for her journalistic efforts, Gellhorn also wrote fiction including novels and short stories. She died in London at the age of 89.

Heinkel *He 111*

In 1922 Germany was finally permitted to manufacture commercial aircraft. The Heinkel *He 111* was one of the first medium bombers to emerge from these efforts. The prototype flew in 1935 and went into service with Lufthansa in 1936. The military version of this aircraft, the *He 111*, was used in the Spanish Civil War and in the early years of WWII it served as the Luftwaffe's principal bomber. An excellent early aircraft, it could not compete against the agile British fighters and by the end of WWII was used for transport purposes only. Over 7300 were produced.

Hemingway, Ernest (1899-1961)

Worked briefly as a reporter but joined the Red Cross in 1918 as an ambulance driver for the Allies where he was badly wounded and met and fell in love with his nurse while recuperating. After the war Hemingway worked in Chicago and became a foreign correspondent for the *Toronto Star*. While abroad he became associated with a left-wing group of radical American journalists. His first collection of stories, *In Our Time*, was published in 1925. His novel *The Sun Also Rises* (1926) brought him praise from literary critics and *A Farewell to Arms* (1929), based on his WWI experiences and his romance with his nurse, established his reputation as a major writer. *Death in the Afternoon* was published in 1932. Hemingway served as a war correspondent during the Spanish Civil War (1937) where he supported the Popular Front and spent much time with the International Brigades. He returned to the U.S. and attempted to raise funds for the Republican Army and returned to Spain in 1938 to tour those areas still held by the Popular Front. Hemingway published *For Whom the Bell Tolls* in 1940, a best-selling novel about the war in Spain. He won a Pulitzer Prize in 1953 for *The Old Man and the Sea* (1952) and the Nobel prize for literature in 1954. Hemingway committed suicide on 2 July, 1961.

Mandl, Fritz (*also* Mandel)
Fritz Mandl was an Austrian industrialist and CEO of the Hirtenberger Patronenfabrik, at that time one of the world's leading arms producers.

NKVD (1934-1946)
People's Commissariat of Internal Affairs or the Soviet Secret police. This arm of the Soviet government (and especially of Joseph Stalin) concentrated on tracking down counter-revolutionaries as well as establishing and running espionage networks, spreading communism and disrupting foreign governments. Also known as Cheka (1918-1922), GPU (1922-23), OGPU (1923-1934), MD (1946-1954) and KGB (1954-).

Orlov, Alexander (born Leon Feldbin, a.k.a. Alexander Berg) (1895-1973)
Participated in Russian Revolution of 1917, served as a officer in the Red Army, 1918-1920, studied law and became a ruthless prosecutor of "enemies of the state." Active in the OGPU from 1926 until 1936 when Stalin sent Orlov to Spain as an "advisor" to Communist forces. Concluding that the Spanish Republic was facing inevitable defeat, Stalin instructed Orlov to offer the "services" of the Soviet government to "temporarily" store the Republic's reserves of gold bullion with the promise that it would be returned immediately upon Franco's defeat. The government's gold was then moved to Cartagena where Orlov personally supervised the removal onto a fleet of Russian ships. He accompanied this priceless cargo to Odessa and then, by train, to Moscow. Astonishingly, however, and despite his overwhelming success, Orlov began to fear for his life when the bloody Soviet purges began. He and his family fled the country to Paris where they defected in the Canadian Embassy. He emigrated to Canada and later to Cleveland under his new name, Alexander Berg, where he wrote several books detailing his experiences and attacking the Soviet Communist regime. In *our* world, Orlov/Berg died in 1973.

Patent

Hedy Lamarr (then H. K. Markey) and George Antheil shared a patent in 1942 for a frequency-hopping radio secrecy system to maintain control of a guided torpedo despite enemy jamming. Antheil died in 1959, the same year, ironically, that the patent expired. Below is a portion of that 1942 patent.

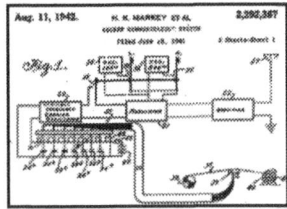

UFA

Universum Film-Aktien Gesellschaft. German motion-picture production company that made artistically outstanding and technically competent films during the silent era. Located in Berlin, its studios were the best equipped and most modern in the world.

Volstead Act

In 1919 Congress passed the National Prohibition Act (also known as the Volstead Act) written by Andrew Volstead, a leading Republican member of the House of Representatives. The act provided for enforcement of the recently ratified Eighteenth Amendment and prohibited the manufacture, transportation and sale of beverages containing more than 0.5 per cent alcohol. The act was signed into law by President Warren Harding in 1922. The main force behind this anti-alcohol legislation was known as the Temperance Movement. "Prohibition" proved to be almost impossible to enforce and was extremely controversial and unpopular with American citizens. Nullification of the Volstead Act occurred with the ratification of the Twenty-first Amendment (which repealed the Eighteenth) in December 1933 and brought an end to "Prohibition."

Von Braun, Wernher (1912-1977)

Was a leading figure in the development of rocket technology. German (later American) engineer who worked on the German V2 rocket projects in 1930-1944. After WWII he emigrated to the United States along with many of his coworkers. He headed the effort to build the giant Saturn V rocket used to launch the Apollo missions to the moon. It is true that, at age 13, he caused a major disruption in Berlin when he fired off a toy wagon loaded with firecrackers. The wagon was "propelled" several blocks and caught fire. Von Braun, however, was collected by his father after he was taken into custody by the local police.

Wells, H. G. (1866-1946)

He was considered one of the founding fathers of modern science fiction (or *scientifiction*). His early works are well-known, especially in the science fiction community, and include *The Time Machine* (1895), *The Island of Dr. Moreau* (1896), and *The Invisible Man* (1897). *The War of the Worlds* (1898) was adapted in 1938 by Orson Welles (no relation) as a radio drama. This famous broadcast caused panic among some listeners who tuned in after the drama had begun and thought the events were "real." In 1933 he published his novel, *The Shape of Things To Come* and later wrote the screenplay for Alexander Korda's film adaptation of global warfare, *Things To Come*.

Zuse, Konrad (1910-1995)

Was a German engineer and computer pioneer. His greatest achievement was the completion of the first functional program-controlled computer, the Z3 computer in 1941. He also designed a high-level programming language, Plankalkül, *circa* 1945. This, however, was a theoretical contribution, since the language was never actually implemented within his lifetime.

ABOUT THE AUTHORS

Brad Linaweaver is a Nebula finalist for the novella version, and Prometheus-award winner for the novel version of *Moon Of Ice*, endorsed by such luminaries as Robert A. Heinlein, Ray Bradbury, Isaac Asimov and William F. Buckley, Jr. His other novels include *Sliders* (based on the television series) and *The Land Beyond Summer*. Collaborative novels are four best-selling *Doom* books with Dafydd ab Hugh, two *Battlestar Galactica* novels with Richard Hatch, and *Anarquía* with J. Kent Hastings. Linaweaver has sold over eighty short stories, including some to *Amazing, Fantastic, Galaxy*, and a hell of a lot of anthologies. He has written over three hundred articles, as well as various scripts and original stories that have been produced as audio dramas and low-budget movies. He is especially proud of having appeared in *National Review* with a piece on George Orwell. He has written for genre movie magazines such as *Cult Movies, Filmfax, Femme Fatales*, and Forrest J Ackerman's *Spacemen* and *Famous Monsters of Filmland*. Brad shares a second Prometheus award with Ed Kramer for co-editing *Free Space*, a major libertarian science fiction anthology from TOR books. Linaweaver also takes great pride that his writing was praised by former president Ronald Reagan.

J. Kent Hastings wrote "The Information Underground Railroad" which appeared in *The Agorist Quarterly* #1, articles for *New Libertarian Magazine*, a regular column on the subjects of spread-spectrum radio, encryption, and untraceable digital cash, called "Techtics," for *Tactics of the Movement of the Libertarian Left*, the novelette "Revolution Is My Hobby" (as yet unpublished), and the short story "The Blue Light," about solar system colonists escaping from a global dungeon state on Earth, for the *Prometheus* newsletter.

SENSE OF WONDER PRESS 2004

ACKERMANTHOLOGY
Compiled by Forrest J Ackerman
Introduction by John Landis
6x9, 308 pages
Trade Paper   0-918736-25-0 $19.95
Trade Cloth   0-918736-59-5 $34.95

CLAIMED, by Francis Stevens
Selected by Forrest J Ackerman
"One of the strangest and most compelling science fantasy novels you will ever read." —H.P. Lovecraft
6x9, 363 pages, Illustrated
Trade Paper   0-918736-37-4 $15.95
Trade Cloth   0-918736-57-9 $27.95

DR. ACULA'S THRILLING TALES OF THE UNCANNY
Compiled by Forrest J Ackerman
Trade Paper   0-918736-30-7 $19.95
Trade Cloth   0-918736-61-7 $34.95

Expanded Science Fiction Worlds of
FORREST J ACKERMAN & FRIENDS PLUS
By Forrest J Ackerman with 7 new collaborations
6x9, 205 pages, Illustrated
Trade Paper   0-918736-26-9 $17.95
Trade Cloth   0-918736-58-7 $28.95

FAMOUS FORRY FOTOS
Kodakerman Memories by Forrest J Ackerman
6x9, 117 pages, Photos
Trade Paper   0-918736-32-3 $14.95
Trade Cloth   0-918736-56-0 $34.95

LON OF 1000 FACES!
by Forrest J Ackerman
8.5x11, 300 pages, Illustrations, 1000+ Photos
Trade Paper   0-918736-39-0 $29.95
Trade Cloth   0-918736-53-6 $54.95

THE MAGIC BALL FROM MARS and STARBOY
By Carl L. Biemiller, Introduction by Anne Hardin
6x9, 302 pages, Illustrated, Ages 7-12
Trade Paper   0-918736-09-9 $19.95
Trade Cloth   0-918736-10-2 $38.95

MARTIANTHOLOGY
Compiled by Forrest J Ackerman
Edited by Anne Hardin
6x9, 266 pages, Illustrated
Trade Paper   0-918736-45-5 $19.95
Trade Cloth   0-918736-46-3 $34.95

METROPOLIS
Novel by Thea von Harbou with "Stillustrations" from
Fritz Lang's film by the same title.
8.5x11, 262 pages, Illustrated
Trade Paper   0-918736-35-8 $23.95
Trade Cloth   0-918736-54-4 $45.95
Ltd. Edition   0-918736-34-X $60.00

RAINBOW FANTASIA
35 Spectrumatic Tales of Wonder
Selected by Forrest J Ackerman
Introduction by Anne Hardin
6x9, 562 pages, Illustrated
Trade Paper   0-918736-36-6 $29.95
Trade Cloth   0-918736-60-9 $44.95

WOMANTHOLOGY
Compiled & edited by
Forrest J Ackerman and Pam Keesey
6x9, 363 pages, Illustrated
Trade Paper   0-918736-33-1 $21.95
Trade Cloth   0-918736-50-1 $35.95

Complete story/author lists for all titles at:

http:\\www.senseofwonderpress.com

Order through major bookstores or through our secure web site.

www.ingramcontent.com/pod-product-compliance
Lightning Source LLC
Chambersburg PA
CBHW032031240626
47154CB00003B/862